Young
Pitt

Young Pitt

a novel

by

A. M. MAUGHAN

THE JOHN DAY COMPANY

New York

Library of Congress Cataloging in Publication Data

Maughan, A M
    Young Pitt.
    Bibliography: p.
    1. Pitt, William, 1759–1806—Fiction. 2. Great Britain—History—George
III, 1760–1820—Fiction.
I. Title.
PZ4.M449Y03   [PR6063.A8657]   823'.9'14   74–9363
ISBN 0–381–98276–9

1 2 3 4 5 6 7 8 9 10

First United States Publication 1975

Printed in the United States of America

TO

MY MOTHER

Contents

1767

The Fathers

"Alack, sirs, he is mad." SHAKESPEARE.

I

THE CARRIAGE—the Pitt crest very proud and burnished on the doors—carried Hester Pitt, Lady Chatham, down the Kentish lanes. Before her marriage she had been a Grenville, and she had her House's aloofness and strong will, the fierce Grenville veracity, their proud and high reserve. Her five children were clustered about her—Lady Hester, who was twelve; Lord John, who was eleven; Lady Harriet at ten; William, who was eight; and the baby James, just five, in sky-blue satin pantaloons and white socks, sitting on his nurse's knees. All the children were scrubbed and well-combed and bedecked in their best party breeches and sashes, their buckled shoes polished to a mirrored gloss. Lady Chatham regarded them somewhat wonderingly, still astonished that she—who had not married until she was thirty-three—had borne this large brood.

Presently the baby, James, enquired hopefully of his nurse, "Cakes for tea, likely, Mrs. Pam?"

"Why, surely, my poppet," the nurse said fondly, "and peaches and jellies as well, maybe."

"I wish we were not going to the Foxes for tea," the second girl, Harriet, broke out on a note of rebellion. "Why have we to go when papa and Mr. Fox hate each other?"

"You do not take your parliamentary enmity home with you," her mother answered. "You endeavour to leave it at Westminster."

Presently she spoke to the nurse, Mrs. Sparry, in a low voice, using the children's nickname for her, "Oh, Mrs. Pam, they must in truth shine today, and what if Lord John eats with his mouth open or the baby is sick or William suffers one of his shy fits and won't say a word?"

"Now, now, my lady," the nurse assured her. "They are five lovely children. They'll occasion you nothing but pride, I'm sure."

The lodge of Kingsgate, the Fox estate, came into view above the hedgerows, covered—this fine summer of 1767— with bees and blossom. Lady Chatham gave her troop a last hasty survey like a harassed colonel jerking to rights a regiment about to be inspected. She spoke on a half-nagging note, quite foreign to her, "Harriet, don't rub your shoe on your clean stocking. William, hold your head up, as we are always telling you."

The second boy raised his head as she had bidden him. Of all her children he was the most like her, with the clear grey Grenville eyes, the chestnut hair and the painful shrinking from strange company. "Have we to stay long?" he asked.

"Oh, come, William," his mother answered. "I know you do not like parties but you must learn to bear with them."

The carriage stopped and the Pitt children were bundled out. Inside the house Lady Caroline Fox came forward to greet her guests, crying, "My dear Lady Hester, uncommon gracious of you to come. And these are the children—how like Chatham the eldest boy is, and how like you the middle one."

"Your servant, Lady Hester," Henry Fox said, bowing over her hand.

Behind him the hallway of his fine house rose in gilt swags and clover-painted ceilings. Kingsgate was even more gracious than the Pitts' own residence of Hayes Place, seventy miles away. But while Henry Fox and Chatham both loved power and had both married aristocratic wives, Henry Fox equally loved the salt of wealth and Chatham disdained a political fortune. It deepened their dark dislike. Chatham saw Henry Fox as a jobber, and Fox saw his enemy as a self-righteous player to the gallery, full of poses and histrionics.

There were other parents and children present, the Lennoxes, the Spencers and the Cavendishes, all families that were allied by birth or inclination to Henry Fox and therefore unwarm towards the Pitts. The Pitts sat down to tea encircled by their rivals. Lady Chatham and Lady Caroline strove to be neighbourly and altogether English and not to contaminate the children with the fathers' dislike. But it was all hard effort and in face of it Lady Chatham became overconstrained and Lady Caroline over-enthusing. When, after a while, she asked how Lord Chatham was, she spoke in almost tender fashion.

"Still confined to his bed," Lady Chatham replied.

"Still? After so many weeks? Lady Sarah and I will call on our way to town next week and bring him some cherries from the garden."

"You are very kind," Lady Chatham said hastily. "But the physicians are positive he must not have visitors."

"Are they so strict? Why then, what precisely is his malady?"

Lady Chatham answered painfully, "They tell us it is a recurrent fever—some disorder of the blood."

The Pitt children had never heard their proud mother lie before, so blatantly and despairingly. They looked at her astonished. As if to correct all the youngest, James, remarked, in a small, child's voice, inaudible save to those on either side of him, "Doctor says papa is poorly in his brain."

Mrs. Sparry seized the cake from his plate and stuffed it into his mouth. "Eat your cake, James. See, there is a sugar plum in this piece."

The baby fell silent, chewing placidly. Lady Chatham turned quickly to ask after the two elder Fox boys.

"Charles is home from Eton this weekend," Lady Caroline said with much pride. "He is in the Sixth now and quite the leading boy in the school, they tell us. He altogether excels the rest both with his studies and his games. Where is he, my love?"

"Out shooting in the landskip, as I think," her husband answered. "What do you say, Lady Hester—would John and William like to join him?"

Lady Chatham looked at her sons. Lord John—the eldest of the three Pitt boys—was content to remain where he was, not greatly caring for exertion on a hot afternoon. But William saw escape from the party and jumped up. Henry Fox called his gamekeeper. The man touched his battered tricorn and led the boy down the terrace, his whippet scampering at their heels.

They crossed the deep ditch of the ha-ha into Kingsgate's handsome landscape. The tall grass was unmown here, blanched brown at the roots by the bite of the sun, the harvestmen spiders swaying on the blades. A big Eton senior lay in its grassy softness, a fine sporting gun resting alongside him and a silver pencil and commonplace book in his hands. As he heard the footsteps he turned his head, saying carelessly, "God with us, Harris, two puppies at your heels today? Who's this?"

"Master William Pitt, Mr. Charles, if you please," the gamekeeper answered.

"Oh, Chatham's boy," Charles Fox said. "Well sit down, but pray keep quiet. I am making notes for my Latin declamation on Monday." Keeping his eyes on his writing, he asked, "How old are you?"

"I was eight in May."

"Then you'll not have acquired Latin yet?"

"I've acquired some."

"Have you so, William?" Fox remarked, raising a brow at him. "And what classical gentlemen have you studied— Pliny, Polybius, Cicero, Virgil, Horace?"

"I can't construe Horace yet, though I've learnt some of the Odes. My father is working through the first book of the *Aeneid* with me when he is well enough."

"Well, my faith, Harris," Fox said, laughing. "Eight and he claims he can do work the standard of Fourth Remove. I hope he tells the truth, do you not?"

He had the black Foxite brows and black hair, his body already broadening, but with an ease and charm and a self-possession so absolute that he might well have had thirty years rather than the eighteen that were his. In spite of what he said he managed to draw all offence from his words. His guest sat watching him with a boy's dawning admiration. Fox was well used to conquests. He had won Eton as he had won his own family and with as quick and absolute a rule. But he was not averse to exercising his skill here over Chatham's son. "Well, William," he asked lazily. "And to what are you putting all this prodigious talent when you are grown?"

The boy answered slowly, half-shyly, "I want to serve England in the House of Commons like my father."

"Do you, in truth? Well, perhaps we will meet again. Our fathers do not exactly love one another, but doubtless we of the younger generation are more enlightened."

"I should like to be your friend."

"Thank you, William. At Eton, I fear, we do not usually call the eight-year-olds our friends. We call them our scrubby fags. Nonetheless I shall altogether think of you when I am declaiming Latin from the rostrum on Monday."

"From the rostrum?" William said wonderingly. "With everybody looking at you?"

"Why don't you like it?" Fox asked. "Well, thank God you do not claim to be as precocious in facing an audience as you do in studying the classics."

He grew weary of his notes and picked up the gun. The gamekeeper walked with him, carrying the powder-horn and cartouche-case; the whippet running through the long grass and the boy scrambling alongside were both equally forgotten. Fox brought to his sport the same style and dominance he brought to his conversation. The keeper was soon swinging a festoon of rabbits from a grimed fist, William Pitt never taking his eyes from the elder boy.

Presently, under the afternoon sun, Fox set down the gun to wipe his forehead. William laid a hand on the hot barrel, caressing its chased and silvered contours.

"Don't touch it," Fox said, glancing at him. "You could no more handle that gun than you could really work through the *Aeneid*. Come, enough of it."

The boy answered doggedly, with a faint inflection of defiance, "I can construe some of Virgil. If they can't in the lower forms at Eton that makes no matter. My father has taught me and I can."

Fox stood regarding him, then drew his commonplace book from his pocket. "Here, William, here's a quotation set down in my notes. It is Virgil and not over-hard. Look at it, confess you can't read it and then we'll clasp hands and make an end of the argument."

William bent his head over the written lines, wrestling with them for a while, then pronouncing the English meaning,

> "*Roman, take heed, imperially rule the world.*
> *These be thy skills—to set the law of peace,*
> *To spare the conquered, and to quell the proud.*"

The gamekeeper broke into laughter, saying, "Well, Mr. Charles, he's proved his point. His father must be a rare clever fellow if he can teach him to read off all that tongue-twisting stuff so young."

There was an abrupt darkening of Fox's careless good-humour. The gamekeeper saw it and sucked in his cheeks. But William was too young to sense the change. He spoke eagerly, worsening matters, "Will you not lend me your gun for but one shot? I have been watching you and I think I can fire it."

"You are somewhat ignorant of the world, are you not?"
Fox answered. "Were you to ask one of the Eton Sixth to
lend you his bat or the captain of one of His Majesty's sail-of-
the-line to lend you his dividers, you would not get them.
You would get six on the backside instead. Still, if you're prepared to match me in straight contest, I'll let you try your
skill." He pulled from his pocket his silk scarf and held it
out to the gamekeeper. "Fasten this up, Harris. Let us see
how well Master William shoots."

"No, no, sir." The man drew back. "He'll likely put his
shoulder out if he tries that gun. And he didn't say he could
shoot as well as you, sir. He but held to it he could speak
some of his Latin lines."

"You do not know this family," Fox replied. "They think
they can do all things from delivering England when not
another man can to out-classing all in shooting and Latin
studies." He turned back to the boy. "Well, William, the
loser stands forfeit. If you win you get the cartouche-case
Harris carries yonder. If you lose, it may be you'll get what
you would most assuredly get were you at Eton or ranking
midshipman in the Royal Navy—I'll consider it. But at least
I pay you a compliment, after a sort, for I am elevating you
out of the nursery."

He said it carelessly, part in earnest, but in friendly and
amused fashion, as if he spoke man to man. The boy looked
at him, content to be used in a manner adultly, his liking
unlessened. "Will you contest on those terms?" Fox asked.

"Yes."

The gamekeeper went unwillingly some fifteen paces
through the trees, fastening up the white scarf and returning. Fox lodged his own shots squarely into the target without effort, then moved off to the right the better to view the
other's attempts.

The gamekeeper took the smoking gun and bit off the
wadding from the bullet. "Well, son," he said. "We've put
our foot in it, you and I, for I oughtn't to have said what I

did and nor should you. It's true that at them big schools the
seniors aim to keep the young ones in their places. But Mr.
Charles would never have taken you up that sharp if you'd
been Master William Smith or Master William Robinson.
There's bad blood between your father and his and we both
ought to have remembered it." He thrust the shot down with
the rammer. "Come now, do your best. A strong, steady
pull—sight down the barrel in the like manner you saw Mr.
Charles do."

The first shot went true, though the recoil felled the firer.
But the full spite and fury of the gun's bite was too much for
its handler. The second ball flew too low and too wide. The
gamekeeper hauled William yet again to his feet, saying
hastily, as Fox came towards them out of the trees. "Let be,
sir. It was well attempted."

"Not quite good enough, was it, William?" Fox asked.

"No. But I did not really think I could shoot better than
you."

Fox smiled. That he had asserted his skill and dominance
here was sufficient for him. "All right, William," he said
lightly. "The forfeit is in abeyance for the time being. Here's
my kerchief. Wipe some of the gunpowder from your face
or your lady mama will be altogether horrified."

They set off for the house, walking together. Fox talked
of Eton, of Oxford where he would go next term, of Paris
and London, the boy listening rapt and eager. The tea party
was languishing when they came to the french windows.
Lady Caroline and Henry Fox jumped up and drew their
son into the room as eagerly and enthusiastically as if he had
been parted from them for a year. Charles scanned his
mother's gown and appearance critically. "Why, mama, that
fichu does not become you at all."

"Take it off, Caro," Henry Fox said. "Charles does not like
it."

She smiled and unpinned her brooch, drawing the fichu at
once from her shoulders.

"How go the Odes, Charles?" Henry Fox asked. "Are they acquired yet?"

"Yes—they are learnt."

"Charles is declaiming before the whole school on Monday," Lady Caroline remarked. To her son she said, "I wish, Charles, you would let us hear some of it now."

"My good mama," he answered on a laugh. "You will bore Lady Chatham from all patience."

"No, indeed," Lady Chatham said. "Pray oblige us, Charles."

He rose with a show of reluctance but he knew his magnetism. He spoke with great ease, never correcting a word, his gestures unrestrained and fluent. His audience was entirely his. His Lennox cousins gazed at him lovingly, and little William Pitt sat intent and admiring, his chin on his fists.

"Excellent, Charles," his father said when he had finished. "But I wish you had given us the twenty-sixth—'For peace prays the mariner—' for I vastly prefer it."

Fox answered lightly, "William here will render it for you."

The boy looked at him aghast. As the eyes of the room turned on him, he pressed himself further back into the chair as if he would have to be prised from it.

"Come, William," Fox said. "You are under forfeit to me. This is the manner of it."

The boy got up, his reluctance deep and genuine. His mother watched him anxiously, for she knew how greatly he hated to be thrust forward under strange eyes and feared he would not be able to acquit himself. He began the words, over-hurriedly at first, then coming to control.

> *"Otium divos rogat in patenti*
> *prensus Aergaeo—"*

He spoke in a clear, natural boy's voice, not by rote, but plainly understanding what he was saying. The Foxite room forgot he was a Pitt and warmed to him.

"Well, Lady Hester," Henry Fox remarked when all was done. "Tell Chatham I think we have both sired well."

The tea party broke up. As the Pitt carriage rattled away down the drive, Lady Caroline said briskly, "Why, what a monstrous relief that is over. Did you hear Lady Hester prevaricating about Chatham's illness? She was positively determined she was not going to disclose its real nature. I own I blushed to hear such bare-faced lying when there were guests at my tea-table."

"They always did slam fast the shutters on themselves," Henry Fox answered. "But a few bones rattled in their closet nonetheless. What of Ann Pitt—she dominated London society for a decade, then vanished in a night, into a private madhouse in Harley Street, some say. Or George Pitt, brought back in a closed carriage from Turin, but the day labourers on his estate say there were shouts and sounds of struggle coming from it. Chatham always boasted himself as to his intellect. It would pay the dog in good coin if, after all his bombast, his mind went the same way as, seemingly, his cousin's and sister's did. But doubtless that is too much for which to hope." He put his arm fondly about his son's shoulders. "Why did you bring the boy forward, Charles— for he hated it."

"It was but a lesson—that it would be wiser not to thrust himself forward, since he has not the temperament for it." He picked up his gun again and began to examine it. "Brodie's of Windsor have a rifle somewhat in advance of this—a breach-loader with walnut stock and damascene overlay."

"Brodie's guns never retail for less than seventy guineas," his mother remarked with an exclamation. "At least wait until your birthday."

He laughed, saying, "Oh, my good mama."

"If you want it, go and order it," Henry Fox said, smiling.

"I will send them a bill of credit by the next cross-post."

After Charles had left them, Lady Caroline looked at her husband. "You indulge him too freely, Henry."

"Why, my love, you know I do not believe in denying him anything."

"I know. But life is not like that. You do not get everything you want the moment you want it. Life is full of pricks and it would not surprise me if our guest this afternoon, young William Pitt, were one of them."

He answered in a voice of much surprise, "What, Chatham's son? That shy little boy? I thought Charles had him entirely at his beck."

"Mark it," she said tartly. "That shy little boy will be a thorn in Charles' flesh for as long as he lives."

II

AFTER SPENDING the night with friends at St. Nicholas at Wade Lady Chatham reached Hayes Place the next evening by six. The children were playing round the carriage in the driveway as she came alone and slowly into the library, pushing her hood from off her chestnut hair. About her on the walls hung the portraits of her husband's line—the poet, Christopher Pitt, whose verses still echoed in men's ears; the other-worldly face of Bishop Pitt, serene above his lawn sleeves; her children's great-grandfather, the one-time Governor of Madras, the doomed Pitt Diamond in his hat. She stood regarding them, stiff and repelled, as if she faced an enemy.

There was a step outside. The boys' tutor, the Reverend Edward Wilson, came in, his face alert and intelligent above his white bands and plain stock. "How went the Kingsgate enterprise, my lady?" he asked.

"I think Lady Caroline and I deserve a ribbon and star,"

Lady Chatham answered, adding in a quiet voice, "How is he?"

"Asking for William."

"Yes—I do not doubt it."

Wilson stirred restively, saying as if he had long wanted to broach the matter, "I think myself William ought to be sent away out of this house for a time. Could he not go to one of his Grenville uncles? Or, failing that, there is an exceedingly goodhearted Cambridgeshire dame I know, who was once housekeeper to me. She would use William like a mother, and the fens in high summer are wonderful fascinating for a boy and of better air than a sickroom." She was silent and he went on, "The other children do not see their father. William does, and he has too quick and retentive a mind for what he sees not to leave imprint there."

Lady Chatham drew a hard breath. "I and William—sometimes I think we are the supporters, as in a coat-of-arms, propping a heraldic splendour that once lit continents but would fall now without our weight behind it." She said, after a space, "I can't deny Chatham the boy—the hope and comfort of his father. I fear what would happen if I did, and so, as you know, does Addington."

"It is marking William, my lady," Wilson said in a steady voice.

"Oh, my good friend, this has been an awful decision—awful for Dr. Addington—a thousand times more awful, God knows, in my case. Don't contrive to make it yet harder for me."

He stood silent, then made her a grave, acknowledging bow. The children came running in from the terrace, James to pull at his mother's skirts. "Mama, this is a nice house. I don't want to leave it."

"Why, my pet? Why should we leave it?"

He said earnestly, "We leave all our houses when papa begins to hate them."

She gathered him up and held him in her arms. A stick

knocked three times slowly and imperiously on the ceiling above. The children at once stopped their play, standing still and somewhat forlornly. Lady Chatham set down the youngest one and turned instantly to the door.

"Will you not send one of the servants, my lady?" Mr. Wilson said. But he knew the suggestion to be in vain. Chatham, in his present sickness, could not bear any about him except his wife and second son.

She shook her head and went out. Wilson looked at the children, then put an arm about William's shoulders, saying with determined cheerfulness, "Come—your father will want to see you. Make yourself respectable after the journey."

Upstairs there were jugs of hot water set in the dressing room with towels and fresh linen. William was slow to begin setting himself to rights. Wilson, watching him, saw his plain unwillingness to go to his father. He said gently, "Your father would not hurt you."

"I know he would not. But to see him—to sit and watch him when he is—" Almost it seemed to his tutor he was going to use the word 'mad', but he left it unsaid.

"These things occur," Wilson answered with a sigh. "Some call them acts of God. For my part I call it an act of the devil. But there are many in far worse case than your father. Dr. Addington is exceedingly hopeful this spasm will pass. Meanwhile there's naught for your mother and you to do save to shut your teeth and hold on."

Lady Chatham joined them. Brought to the door of his father's bedroom, William went in. The sickroom was shuttered against the daylight, a single shaded candle standing in a corner far from the bed with its drawn-back curtains. A hand from the bed grasped the head of an ebony cane, the great diamond on the forefinger blazing balefully in the dimness. The gouty foot rested huge and distended in its swathed bandages; and above it, shapeless as a hulk in the dark room, loomed the figure of William Pitt, first Earl of Chatham, second son of an obscure Cornish squire, one-time Prime

Minister of England, still Lord Privy Seal, the carver of empires and designer of victories—the Great Commoner.

The sick man shifted a little. The candlelight fell on his profile—the great, beaked, scornful nose, the eyes with their purple glints of anger, the pursed mouth. Yet the face had a torment as if the man behind it groped for an aptitude he had lost and sought for despairingly. The thin candlelight lit the noisome ravages of skin disease on his hands, the stained bandages protecting his wrists under the bedrobe. It was as if England herself lay in the bed, still trailing wisps of old power and puissance but stricken, gasping and doomed.

"William," Chatham said. "My son—my comfort. Come—are you afraid?"

"No—for I know I am well with you."

"Good." The voice had no more than a hollow ghostlike mock of its old imperious sonances. "The port is yonder on the escritoire. Do not pour any for me. The doctors tell me strong cordials excite the mind—the mind that is not now there. Once it could formulate battle orders without effort. Now it cannot apply in concentration long enough to read two lines together in a news-sheet."

The boy was already a veteran drinker, plied with port by the doctors since he had been five to tide him over the precarious, delicate years of his childhood. Chatham liked to have him drink beside him, since it gave his much-loved son the semblance of being already grown, ready for wine and high politics and the talk of statesmen. But the truth was that, in the dark room, with the ruin of all that had been Chatham in the bed, the son had a need of it much beyond what the dazed and sick man could comprehend.

"So you have been to Kingsgate," Chatham asked. "Did you meet Charles Fox?"

"Yes—a big, dark boy. He shoots wonderful true. I like him very well." He added hastily, "But I will not stand his friend if you do not want me to."

Chatham laughed in cracked fashion. "I do not name your

enemies, William. They will come upon you fast enough. But Charles Fox is a second son of a second son—as you are. It would be strange if the fates were to weave on their loom a like pattern to what has gone before—Pitt against Fox." His thoughts had gone back to the past. "Seventeen-fifty-nine—the year of Hawke among the shoals of Quiberon Bay, the year of Wolfe on the Heights of Abraham, of Clive's first victories in India, of Minden—and of your birth. Three continents and three oceans fell to our overlordship that year. We called it *annus mirabilis*—our year of miracles. All my path was victory then, and in this too, that you continued to draw breath when every doctor told us you would never survive your first year of life." He groped for his son's hand and gripped it. "Only in that are there still the sweets of victory—all the rest lies sapped by the folly of fools. Your elder brother will inherit the title and estates—but you, you are William Pitt, second son of great Chatham, himself a second son, and yours is the legacy of nations." His fingers—roughened and wet with the suppurations of his disease—tightened on his son's clenched ones with the energy of despair. "Time has us by the forelock, you and I, William. Already in America the slow match smoulders close to the powder keg. If my labour of Empire, my labour for my land's greatness, my victories are to be preserved, I am persuaded it can only be by you. And I would have you tell me that you will not fail me."

"I want to go the same path as you but I find it ill now when people look at me. What when I have to get up and make speeches and have all London stare at me in the streets?"

"That is child's talk," Chatham broke out with a burst of anger. "A child's babbling. Good God, have I yet not taught you enough?" He seized his stick and jabbed with it at the bedcurtains as if he groped for air and were slashing with a sword at an enveloping shroud. "You all oppress me. God knows but this house oppresses me. I must be out of it—out

—before it overwhelms me with melancholy. And the five of you that I have sired—I cannot bear you about me. I would have you all, with your fripperies and noise and immaturity, a hundred miles away."

His anger ebbed. He went on, on a half groan, "It is not your father who speaks, William—for he loves you. It is but his disease. Do you remember your Milton, boy?

> *"Which way I fly is hell; myself am hell,*
> *And in the lowest deep a lower deep*
> *Still threatening to devour me opens wide,*
> *To which the hell I suffer seems a heaven.*

"No man knows what sickness is until he bears it in the mind. My mind crawls—with delusions, with violence, with black suffocating melancholies and as black elations—and my body crawls in sympathy. Addington tells me he can do nothing for this skin irruption until the stress of my melancholies abate. I lie here as befouled as if I had the pox. But that was not the manner of our failing. It is our minds that fail, as my mind has failed me—in an hour when I and all my countrymen have most need of it."

His voice trailed off into whispered murmurings, now and then to be caught by the ear, fierce with the beat of hope against despair. "For this is England—not to be done with though the cynics hold her so—not to be done with though the rats gnaw and fools govern—not to be done with if there is yet a Pitt."

He raised himself suddenly on the pillows and spoke in all his old strength, clearly and ringingly as if he faced his assembled peers. "My lords, it is not America you will bring to ruin, it is ourselves. Everywhere there is ruin piling up about us. My lords, I know I can save England and not another man can—England—America—ruin."

The diamond on his finger winked in the candlelight. He gripped his stick and brought it down ferociously on the tray on the escritoire, so that glasses and decanter slivered, and the port splashed upon the wall like gouts of blood. He shouted to some unseen enemy standing passive beside the bedhead, "No, do not light the candles. No—no—I'll have no man see me thus."

The fierce cries died down to racked groans. William wrenched the door open and shouted. There were Mr. Wilson's footfalls and the swirl of Lady Chatham's skirts on the stairs. She flung herself across her husband, palms, breasts and lips pressed close to his, whispering, "Oh my husband, there is nothing that cannot be righted. Be calm, my love; be patient."

"The laudanum, my lady," Mr. Wilson said, and snatched the little bottle from the mantelshelf. She held the measured draught to Chatham's lips. He turned away his head, muttering, "No more of these vile sedatives. It is they that help to people my mind with black fancies."

"A little," she said. "A sip."

His hand crept up and stroked her chestnut hair. "My sweet Hester, I bear hardly down upon you. I bear hardly on the boy. Yet God answers this one prayer—you are both strong. And it is not forever."

"You will be cured, my husband—soon—soon."

Mr. Wilson had brought the boy out. When Lady Chatham followed he was still in the corridor. She put her arm about him, feeling him tremble a little under the embrace. "Oh my dear little son," she whispered. "I do not know which is the worse—to be a Pitt or to love a Pitt." She dragged back her calm. "But it will pass. He has a great career to pick up, and he has you, William, and in you are all his hopes."

The stick knocked again, timorously, and she turned and went slowly back into the bedroom. William went down to the study alongside the library. His books lay here—the *Aeneid*, the arithmetic primer, the algebra—and he sorted them out, opening the Latin and taking up a quill. Outside beyond the french windows the other children were at play on the velvet grass under the trees, his sister, Harriet, persistently calling for him. He cast them one longing glance but did not look again.

Mr. Wilson had followed him in. He reached over, firmly closing the book and drawing it away. "Enough of work for the present, William. Go and join the others. Your sister is calling for you." Still there was hesitancy and he went on, "Come, you had rather go out. What is the purpose of all this study?"

"Sir, I have got to be Minister of England."

"Got to be, William?" Mr. Wilson asked, raising his brows. "I don't doubt you will rise very far, but that is a very great height, and why the compulsion—why is it so earnestly required of you to become Prime Minister?"

He was answered after a silence and in a low voice, "Because if I do not, I will send my father mad."

BOOK I

1780–1783

The Dwindled Island

"As to this country it is sunk, never to rise again. We have dwindled into an insignificant little island. We have neither wisdom nor virtue left." HORACE WALPOLE.

I

HENRY DUNDAS'S carriage turned into Chancery Lane. Dundas was a big man, handsome, high-complexioned and bold, with strong unfancying Scottish nerves to play him few tricks, but he did not greatly like the sight of the silent and sultry city—the deserted shops, with their splintered shutters, their draggled blue bunting, their scrawled rain-washed notices, 'This is a Protestant shop'.

The young coachman turned, muttering in a frightened Lowland voice, " 'Tis no night to be abroad."

"Drive on, Robbie."

The coach passed the Inns of Court, with their green squares of grass and unstirring trees. No lights showed in the windows of the lawyers' chambers. All seemed empty of folk. But suddenly, from among the sprawling lanes behind Fleet Street, a voice gave the "View Halloa", not with full lungs, but very softly, so that this—the cry for the sighted fox, the call of the hunter for the quarry—sounded like a hissing on the summer night.

The carriage was flung to a halt, the door jerked open. A voice spoke from the dark, "A Protestant, are you? Where's your blue cockade?"

"I dinna know what you talk of," Dundas answered.

"Do you not, now?" the man said. "Well, I hope you be a

freeborn honest Protestant Englishman as we are, but your tongue ain't got a true ring. We'll see what your guts are made of."

He bent forward and spat in Dundas's face. Dundas roared out in his broadest Scots, "Why, ye skulking, murderous dee'il, I'll brae ye."

"A Scotsman, my lads," the other said in delight. "A dirty Scotsman."

The horses, sensing the pending violence and terrified by it, swerved away in a clattering of hoofs and harness. The coachman leapt from his box and began to run, and Dundas, with the carriage between him and his accosters, ran too, into the maze of the Inns of Court—the little alleys feeding the frowning buildings above them like tendril roots, set about with stairs and passages, little square courts, dark shuttered windows and bolted doors. He was quickly parted from the coachman, the echoing pursuit close upon him. But there were other footfalls nearer. A hand seized his arm. A voice said, "Quick, sir—with me."

Ahead under an archway a light sprang up. A porter stood on the threshold of a side entrance with a lantern, flanked by two other dim figures, the porter calling, "Sharp now, sirs, sharp."

Dundas and his companion bundled in. The door was slammed, the porter saying as he rammed fast the bolts, "All's well, sir. This is the Stone Building, Lincoln's Inn. They can't get at you here—at least that's our hope."

He raised the lantern. In its light in the narrow passageway Dundas saw the face of his befriender and those of the other two young men flanking the porter—all haphazardly armed with either army firelock, duelling pistol or stick; all, together with the porter himself, of a grey cast of countenance, as if here in London there had been little chance of sleep in recent nights.

"Why, my utmost thanks for that," Dundas said, struggling to regain his breath.

His rescuer asked, panting also, "You've suffered no hurt, Mr. Dundas?"

"You ken my name?"

"I've been seated in the Strangers' Gallery many times when you have spoken in the House."

"And I know your name likewise, as I think," Dundas said. "For I was in the Lords twa years ago when your father took his last fatal seizure there. I ha'e a strong picture o' it in my mind, recalling how you braced yoursel' to take his weight as he fell. 'Tis Mr. Pitt, is it no'?"

A brief, stiff bow answered him. The porter lowered his lantern, saying in practical fashion, as if the last few nights had inured him to treason and violence, "Now you fetch the gentlemen up to your chambers, Mr. Pitt. And mind you, sir, when you get there don't let a light show or there'll be worse done than just a few smashed panes."

Three flights of steep stairs led up to Pitt's lawyer's chambers, crouched under the eaves and ill-furnished, the floor carpets worn and the coal scuttle scantily filled. Dundas reckoned the rent here would be no more than nine guineas a year. He saw the proud Pitts, since Chatham's death brought to poverty, with this second son scrabbling a livelihood of twenty-shilling briefs and thin lawyer's fees. It put him in mind of himself as a young lawyer in Fleshmarket Close in Edinburgh with only one guinea in his pocket that had gone on buying a lawyer's gown.

The other two young men—not lawyers, since they wore no white bands, but both of an age with Pitt—had likewise toiled up the stairs. Pitt brought them forward, presenting one as Mr. William Wilberforce and the other as Mr. Edward Eliot.

"You ran much risk, sir," Wilberforce said. "A Scotsman on Black Wednesday showing himself in the streets of London."

He was small of stature, somewhat hunched about the shoulders, but with a smile of singular sweetness. At his side,

Edward Eliot had a pleasant easy grace.

"I've been biding in the north in Edinburgh three weeks," Dundas answered. "I was warned at Hackney toll the city was no' a place this night for any of the Roman Catholic persuasion. But I thought a Lowland Scot who sits to worship in a bare kirk at Melville could maybe pass wi'out having his flesh eaten."

"They are eating the flesh of any now," Eliot said. "Americans, Frenchmen, Scotsmen, Jews. We were but visiting our friend here but we did not dare risk the streets again when we saw what the night would be."

Dundas glanced at Pitt. "You were abroad?"

"I was coming from my watch."

Eliot saw Dundas's puzzlement and went on, "They do watch and watch about with the regulars. The regulars make the expected jokes that all here are retained for the defence and that they had rather be shot in the breast by a rioter who is aiming at them than in the back by a Lincoln's Inn volunteer who is not—but with so many of the troops in America the truth is they are glad to have them."

"You mean the Inns o' Court are forming volunteer associations?" Dundas asked. "God wi' us, they've only done so in the past when invasion threatened. The disorders canna be as serious as that?"

"Sir," Wilberforce said. "You have indeed been in Edinburgh three weeks."

Dundas was given now for the first time the tally of London's week of riot. He heard with astonishment that all four Inns of Court—Lincoln's Inn, Gray's Inn, Inner and Middle Temple—where many of the lawyers had their lodgings and, as a body, had pressed for some easing of the penal laws against the Catholics, were threatened with burning. Thomas Langdale's distilleries and warehouses in Holborn were reported already burnt, since the mob knew him for a Roman Catholic; Lord Mansfield's priceless library in Bloomsbury Square sacked also. For four dawns there had been dead from

both sides in the streets, often not given burial but thrown
by the rioters at daybreak into the Thames.

The city was sometimes given to violence but this was
much beyond anything that had ever gone before. It seemed
to Dundas that rumour and lack of sleep had wildly exag-
gerated a few scattered disorders. He kept his scepticism to
himself. Pitt had least to say of all. Dundas glanced at him,
seeing him tall, with the grey-eyed Grenville aspect and much
else pertaining to the Grenvilles besides. There were deep
reserves here and deep defences. Dundas had no love for the
Grenville chill and aloofness. He did not greatly warm to
this silent young man, thinking him stiff and unapproachable
like the rest of his mother's family.

Pitt had turned to the side table to pour wine, saying as
he handed the glass to Dundas, "I can but warn you it's bad
and cheap."

"Your wine will improve as the briefs come in and you
rise in your chosen profession."

"But the law is not his chosen profession," Edward Eliot
remarked with a smile. "You'll see him on the floor of the
House presently, Mr. Dundas, instead of in the Gallery where
at the moment he spends a vast deal of his spare time."

"So he's an avid observer o' our debates? Well then, Mr.
Pitt, what's your judgment on us? Whom among us do you
hold to ha'e the most ability?"

"Why, Charles Fox. He stands head and shoulders above
any other, if you will excuse it that I give my opinion
bluntly."

It was said with a boy's eagerness, the reserve for an instant
altogether lifted like something tossed away. Dundas laughed,
saying, "No man pretends himsel' to be the equal o' Fox
in debate." He raised his glass. "To your first day on the
floor o' the House. May the King's peace be back by then to
the streets o' London."

"To a peaceful London and to your own good health."

The wine was tossed back. Wilberforce and Eliot were

sampling theirs in moderate fashion. But Dundas saw with much astonishment that Chatham's son, at barely twenty-one, was almost as hard a drinker as himself.

On a sudden an ominous prickly tang wafted in upon them. There was no mistaking the rankness of this smell. It convinced Dundas instantly all was as much amiss as he had been told.

"My faith," he said. "That's the reek o' the city burning. Can we no' see what's being done?"

All four were moved by the same impulse. Pitt—knowing the building—led them from the room, up a rickety ladder and out through a skylight window to where the chimney pots of Lincoln's Inn clustered in the night. The acrid taint of burning and gunpowder lay over the city, the sky with a glow to it; the sound reaching them, now and then, of a thin crackling, sometimes hard by, sometimes distant. Almost it might have been Guy Fawkes' night with crackling fireworks and blazing bonfires. But it was more baleful than that. From the roof-top they looked down on a London bathed in the brilliance of her own burning, the fires orange-red about her, the smoke drifting upwards to spread a haze across the moon. To the west lay the Strand, Admiralty House, little Downing Street, bowered about by its summer parklands, and the long tree-girt Mall, with Buckingham House, blackly silhouetted at the end, all studded with fires like the caverns of hell. Intermittently musket fire from the beleaguered militia and the pistols of the rioters crackled along the torn streets.

"Oh God wi' us," Dundas said in a husky voice. "Who's behind it—who led the mob to this?"

"Your countryman, sir," Eliot answered. "Though he has forgotten by now he is a Scot and so have they—Lord George Gordon."

"That madman! We knew him to be lunatic every time he opened his mouth in the House. We should ha'e set him under restraint—chained him to the bedfoot like any other deranged fellow."

At his side Pitt made a small movement. It had no meaning for Dundas standing there on the roof-top looking down
upon burning London. But in after years it was to prick and
probe into his memory like a bodkin.

There was nothing now but to go down, Dundas in wild
anxiety for his young family. The building was wide awake
and in much bustle, the servants slamming doors, the porters
clustered about their lanterns in the doorway of Lincoln's Inn
Hall, the senior benchers standing bleak-faced in groups.
Outside, beside the fountain and under the trees, were pricks
of light glinting on red regimentals and white pipeclay. A
young officer hurried by, with his sergeant, both wearing the
lemon facings of the Northumberland militia, and both with
weary, sweaty, soot-streaked faces. Dundas caught the officer's
arm. The other tried impatiently to shake off his grip but
Dundas tightened it. "Gi'e me but a moment. My poor wee
coachman's abroad somewhere on this hell-born night and my
wife and family are left at home wi' scant protection. I must
find a means o' getting back to them."

The officer turned and peered at him. "Mr. Dundas, is it
not—the member of Parliament? Your coachman's well
enough, sir. He took refuge in an ironmonger's shop in Broad
Street. They hid him in the cellar. As to your wife, where is
she?"

"In Wimbledon."

"At least it is seven miles out," the officer said. "They may
not have extended their devil's dance that far." He gave a
weary rub at his military wig, sending it awry. "Black Wednesday, in truth! The prisons broke open—the distilleries
burnt down—Downing Street cut off—the Bank under most
furious assault—the rioters vowing they will loose both the
lions from the Tower and the lunatics from Bedlam on to the
populace. And the King the only man among them, the only
man among mid-wife magistrates and old women cabinet
ministers. If we are not too late and the city is saved from
being guttered it will be the King who has saved her."

"We can let the gentleman have a horse and a couple of men, doubtless, sir?" the sergeant suggested.

The officer nodded. "Wait a few minutes, Mr. Dundas. We'll get you through, if we can." He swung round, calling to the young lawyers clustering about him, "Come, sirs, I want you all, whether you are volunteers or no, whether you are civilian gentlemen or no. Cordon off the buildings from Chancery Lane to Lincoln's Inn Fields. And for God's sake shoot if they try to storm you with their brands. The Riot Act's read now. There'll be no hanging afterwards."

Dundas and his little escort mounted into their saddles. The cordon formed about the outlet into Chancery Lane— half civilian and half military—prepared to open to let them through. Dundas saw in it the three young men in whose company he had passed the last hour, their coats thrown hurriedly on, their makeshift weapons in their hands. There was much smoke about now. To the shout of "London's burning", whose like had not been heard for a hundred years —since Pudding Lane and the fury of the flames devouring Old St. Paul's—Dundas rode down Chancery Lane and turned towards the city's south-western limits.

II

DUNDAS REACHED his villa fronting Wimbledon Common at half past four in the morning. The Scottish servants were up, clustered together, apprehensively watching the smoke above London. But Dundas's wife, Elizabeth Rannie, lay in the fourposter, her lace bed-cap with its pretty fringe framing her face. She looked at her husband without welcome and listened indifferently to his tale of the night's rough happenings.

"The rioters have left the village alone," she said, in answer to his questions. "There are no Papists here in Wimbledon and they have not yet smelt us out as a household of Scottish

churls." She added, "You left me without sufficient for my
purse when you went north. I have had to scatter bills of
credit all round me like leaves in an autumn gale."

"God wi' us, you're the most extravagant o' women."

"It is my dowry that I spend, is it not, sir?" she said acidly.
"I came to you an heiress even if I did not bring you political
connections."

The youngest girl, sleeping in a child's pink-draped bed
at the end of the room, murmured and stirred. All the three
girls had plain, engaging Scottish faces, with scatters of
freckles seemingly blown from off the Pentland Hills where
Dundas had been brought up. He dearly loved his daughters
and he went to the child. Elizabeth watched from the bed.
Seeing her face still beautiful in spite of its hard lines, Dundas
felt again faintly the pulse of his old love for her.

He came to his wife in the bed. But their marriage was a
sourish thing to them now and he woke no passion in her
this June dawn. He said with resentment, "You knew more
o' love on our wedding night."

"I was but fifteen on our wedding night," she answered. "I
may have had an instinct for love but had I known aught of
life I would not have consented to being bound to any man
so young."

By morning, 8th June, 1780, a tenth of London was
reduced to ashy rubble. But some of the city's old resilience
had at last awakened. The Bank—three times furiously
stormed during the night—still held behind her tired cordon
of Guards and volunteers. The Inns of Court stood unburnt,
their weary defenders lolling over their arms. All Thursday
and Friday reinforcements of militia limped in, footsore
from fierce forced marches that had brought them from the
Scottish border or the hills of Cumberland. With their coming, order crept back to the streets of the city. By the week-
end Lord George Gordon lay under arrest and the foreign
nuns, housed again in their windowless convents, were dig-
ging up from beneath hedges and under the roots of trees

the holy relics they had buried before their flight.

Few public men had come out of the week of fury with credit. In Downing Street Lord North had watched the pitchy faggots thrown against the walls of Number 10 with unchanging calm. But the Prime Minister, weary, slack and amiable, had left it to others to grip the riots by the throat— to the King, who had defended his city like a tiger; to John Wilkes, the Lord Mayor, and Holroyd, commanding the Northumberland militia's outnumbered stand in the streets. Yet North was still popular. September's General Election swept him back triumphantly to Downing Street. Two of the young men Dundas had first met during the Black Wednesday of the riots came into Parliament on this tide—Edward Eliot, brought in for St. Germans in Cornwall, and William Wilberforce (Dundas's neighbour now across Wimbledon Common) returned for Hull where his family's banking business was established. Pitt continued to work on his lawyer's briefs. But Dundas did not think it would be long before he too was seen in the lobbies of Westminster.

On a November night, late back from the Commons, Dundas went up to his wife's bedroom. Almost it was as if she had tried to make a bower of love here—her hair freshly dressed and pretty under its lace cap, her sprigged muslin dressing-gown brand new, the sheets pressed in heather so that they smelt as sweet and fragrant as a Scottish moor. But for all this she lay feigning sleep. He said, not heeding her steady breathing, "Bess, I ha'e to talk wi' you. I voted against Government tonight."

She opened her eyes and answered in a weary voice, "I thought you reckoned North a capable Minister?"

"Aye, capable enough in peace, in the guid times. But he's no' the man if it grows black—as it did during the Gordon Riots, as it might do also in America."

"Will it go ill for us there? I thought we fought but a rabble in arms."

"It was Burgoyne said that, and he sails back a paroled

prisoner. For my part I think North canna stay this rough course. I am getting out from his ranks—gi'ing my vote to Fox." She lay silent and he said sharply, "It is a very great decision. Are ye no' even interested?"

"I grow bored beyond bearing with this pursuit of the winning side. I am out of breath and out of patience with it."

"It has to be the winning side wi' such as you for a wife."

"No, do not blame me," Elizabeth said. "You were determined on London—determined for a place, whatever government held at Westminster. I was content at Melville, with the little houses of Lasswade, where the Esk flowed instead of the Thames and where you did not neglect me day and night for your career." She added, "So you are going to quit North who set your foot on the ladder?"

Dundas answered, using the old endearment he had not used since they had been young, hot lovers at Melville in the early years of their marriage, "Sweet, it's the hard way o' politics."

She turned on her side away from him, as if she were in tears.

"Aye, aye," she said. "Maybe it is the hard way of everything."

Within two days Wimbledon had much to gossip over. Elizabeth Rannie had quit Dundas, walking out from under his roof to the arms of her lover—an army captain, as hardbitten and adventuring as herself, it was said, though she had gone to him penniless. Dundas had come back to his children, to his still house and disordered bedroom to find no sight or sound of her. All around there was much wagging of tongues. The little village of Wimbledon, from the great mansions of the Spencers and the Rockinghams to the pretty villas fringing the Common and the window boxes of Walnut Tree Cottages, could do nothing but hang over garden gates and hedges endlessly speculating whether Dundas would apply to the Justices and whether they would see his errant wife brought forcibly back to him, in a closed carriage, with the officers of the Watch escorting her.

III

IN HIS lifetime Chatham had planned the careers of all his three sons. Even in the nursery their nicknames had pointed them to their professions. James had been to his parents, 'our little tar'; John, 'Redcoat Jack'; William, 'the Counsellor'. The eldest and the youngest had both been settled, the one in the army and the other in the navy, while their father lived. But whereas the King's forces plucked officers straight from their school books, Parliament was harder, and the second son, on whose shoulders Chatham had piled his broken hopes, still struggled fiercely towards this goal, as though driven by his father's spirit.

With two sons serving, the one war Chatham dreaded had come about. He who had much loved America, her endless forests, her great shining lakes and storming waterways, her stockades and homesteads, plantations and orchards, had pleaded that none of his sons should bear arms against the Americans, though he had longed for them to do battle with France and Spain and others of his land's converging enemies. This dying wish England honoured. John, Captain Lord Chatham, had been posted distant from the main theatre of the war, to Gibraltar. James Pitt—at nineteen, lieutenant in command of His Majesty's sloop, *Hornet*, attached to Sir George Collier's squadron—cruised in waters other than those that washed American's coast. It was a hard thing to be a Pitt in this war, for they watched their countrymen endure death or wounds for them, the cause—as they held— sick, and the enemy honourable.

In December Pitt, with Wilberforce and Eliot accompanying him once more as his guests, walked back to Lincoln's

Inn. Inside the Stone Building Richard Pepper Arden was standing at the door of his chambers. Arden was Pitt's fellow lawyer and, in the House of Commons, the parliamentary colleague of Wilberforce and Eliot. An accident had broken his nose in boyhood. Its somewhat pugilistic aspect contrasted cheerfully with the sobriety of his lawyer's white bands. He greeted Pitt with the enthusiastic announcement, "A visitor awaiting you, Billy—naval officer's gold braid. Since your servant's out I bade him make free of your chambers, and all but lashed him to the chair as if it were his own main mast. What could be better than to have a brief flourished at you?"

"Nothing, unless it were a packet of letters from my brother. My faith, it would be the best of gifts if we could have James with us at Hayes for Christmas. It might well be that. There's been rumours enough that Sir George Collier's squadron is due home for victualling and refitting."

The warmth had leapt into Pitt's face and he turned to the stairs as if their steep flights were of no account whatever. Dundas would not have recognised him now—here among his friends and in eager expectancy of news from his brother —as the same aloof and silent young man of the Black Wednesday of the Gordon Riots. Wilberforce and Eliot following at his heels could barely keep pace up the flights.

The visitor, standing with his captain's gold-braided cocked hat under his arm, turned from the window to accord them an unelaborate seaman's bow. He discerned instantly which of the three was Pitt by some likeness to his brother, and directed towards him a grave scanning glance. "Mr. Pitt? May I present myself—Captain Sewell, back with despatches from Sir George Collier's West Indian station."

"Why, by that I think you will know my brother," Pitt said eagerly. "I am happy to make your acquaintance, sir."

Sewell's face, beaten by the winds and the weather, set into even sterner lines. "I fear making my acquaintance will occasion you no happiness at all." He added, in curt fashion as if in reproach of himself for not sooner making the suggestion. "Perhaps we should speak alone."

But it was over-late for privacy. As Wilberforce and Eliot, knowing now what the news was to be, drew back towards the door, Pitt said in a voice from ·which the control had momentarily gone, "I can guess your mission. But how—I thought—we all thought—there had been no engagement."

"It was fever, sir," Sewell answered quietly. "He died in his cabin." Even in this short space he had assessed the young man with whom he spoke. He most carefully and courteously turned away to take a canvas-wrapped parcel from his pocket, spreading the contents on the table. The sad relics lay there—a silver watch engraved 'James Pitt', jewelled shoe buckles, two or three guineas, a silver pencil. "His chest and other effects are stowed in *Greyhound*, due into Spithead later this month," he said. "All was done for him that could be. He was buried at sea in very decent Christian fashion, nor' by nor'-west of Barbados, before his ship's company. It sounds a cold and lonely resting place to a landsman. But a sailor feels otherwise, and I would not mind lying so myself when my time comes."

He drew his cocked hat from under his arm and pounded it with a single blow into some manner of shape. Pitt stood contending fiercely with his grief. But he managed to force out the courtesies, saying, "Sir, you've toiled up those stairs and done your office as decently as was possible. Will you at least take a meal with me?"

"I thank you, no," Sewell answered. "Doubtless it will be small comfort to you and your mother but I have other wretched offices of the same nature. I shall be at Number 22 Conduit Street for the next sennight if you care to call on me there."

Eliot and Wilberforce brought him down. At the bottom of the flights Sewell paused as if their steepness had told on him, remarking with a backward glance up to the dark landings, "I've not quit such heights since I came down from the topsail rigging as a midshipman. Damn—I did not break it over-delicately, I think, and these blows are the devil."

"He has had his share of such," Eliot said. "His father suffered a seizure in the House of Lords, as I daresay you know, and but six months ago his eldest sister, Lady Hester, died also."

"Three bereavements in less than three years then. As a family they are not fortunate. Still, they owned the Grand Concern for a time."

"The Grand Concern? That was the old Governor's name for his Pitt Diamond, was it not—now in the possession of the Court of France? I know nothing of its origin."

"I do," Sewell said. "The Dodds—who bought Governor Pitt's old house, Swallowfield in Berkshire, a generation ago —gave me the history of the stone—an Indian diamond, they said, stolen from the Parteal mines on the banks of the Kisna by an escaping slave of Aurangzeb, the Great Mogul. Possibly there's much fiction woven into the chronicle. The slave is said to have gashed the calf of his leg to conceal the diamond in the flesh, then eluded the Mogul's guards and made his way to an English merchantman lying at Madras. Her master cut his throat for greed of what he carried, though remorse drove him to drink and self-hanging afterwards. The master sold the diamond to Ramchund the Hindu for a thousand pounds, and Ramchund sold it to Governor Pitt for forty-eight thousand pagodas." He rubbed his cheek thoughtfully, his breath hanging about the winter air. "The Governor both gave and obtained a fair price since the diamond might have broke in the cutting. Nor did he know there was blood on it. But the Dodds say the wraith of the Great Mogul's slave still cries along the Queen Anne's gallery at Swallowfield and the sound dies away on the dawn breeze."

Wilberforce smiled, saying, "Sir, do you believe it?"

"No, I do not believe the Swallowfield ghost tale," Sewell said with a faint answering smile. "But considering their ends—the Great Mogul's empire rent to pieces by the

Indian princes in the space of five years—the Parteal slave
—the British shipmaster—I would not touch that diamond,
even if King Louis offered it to me as a gift and Queen
Marie Antoinette added a kiss from her pretty mouth as a
further persuasion."

They looked at him in silence and he added with perfect
good-humour, "Indeed, gentlemen, I know precisely what
you are thinking—that sailors are superstitious dogs. So we
are. But though the diamond brought great gifts—the Parteal
slave gained his freedom, the British shipmaster the better
vessel he desired—it exacted from them all a huge price at
the finish."

"There's one you've left from your tally," Eliot said.
"Ramchund the Hindu."

"He disappeared back into the bazaars of Madras," Sewell
answered. "The Dodds don't know what became of him
but—" He broke off and laughed. "Why, doubtless he lived
to a prosperous and comfortable old age with his grand-
children about his knees. As will the line of the House of Pitt
—as will the line of the House of Bourbon. And all this will
be shown as the old wives' nonsense it is."

He tipped his hat to them and went out.

Pepper Arden, coming from his chambers, heard the ill
news with a shocked incredulity. "Not poor young James?
They're scarce done mourning Hester yet. Should I go up to
him?"

"Not now," Wilberforce said. "Leave him alone for a
space."

IV

Pitt set off the same evening to break the news to his mother
at Hayes—not with his own servant, Ralph, too old for such
faring, but with Wilberforce's young and vigorous Yorkshire

groom. With frost on the roads it was near midnight when they reached Hayes Place. Mrs. Sparry—still at Hayes, though her charges were now grown—came down with candles and a cloak about her nightgown. She gave a cry, saying, "William—at such an hour? God save us, not more bad news?"

"Oh, Mrs. Pam, it is James this time."

Lady Chatham had come down to the stairfoot in her dressing-robe, Harriet just behind. She who had had so many recent blows was brought very low by this, sitting on the stairs silently weeping, her face in her hands. William and Harriet had never seen their mother's proud Grenville head bowed in such desperate grief. They came to her. She clasped them both, whispering, "Oh, my dear children, guard yourselves, for I doubt I can bear much more."

She was persuaded back to her bed at length. Pitt and Harriet sat on together beside the dying fire. Harriet was twenty-three now, grown dark-haired, pretty and learned, for Chatham had set his two daughters under the same tutors as his sons. She and her younger brother were still as close as they had been as children. But the news of this night overwhelmed them and they sat quite silent, one at each side of the hearth.

Mrs. Sparry joined them. She sat for a while, quietly dabbing her eyes, then broke out, "I can't help but remember him the day we went over to Mr. Fox's to tea. Sweet he was in his new ruffles. And now he's gone, and so soon upon Hester."

Hester's death indeed had been even sadder, for she had married very young, and her three tiny daughters, left in the charge of their indifferent father at Chevening, had a need now for their mother that they did not yet understand.

The Pitts struggled through yet another week made sharp by the pangs of bereavement, though heartened a little by a package of letters from John in Gibraltar—greatly heartened too in that Sir James Lowther, with an election pending in his pocket borough of Appleby, had come forward offering to bring in Chatham's second son for the seat.

No man greatly loved Lowther, the most powerful of the borough patrons—'Lowther-of-the-Cat-o'-Nine-Tails', with nine seats at his disposal. But even he, the most dictatorial of all, was not too exacting. He required of the young men he brought into Parliament that they were as hot against the American war as he was himself. But otherwise they went their own ways and could shout their heads off about parliamentary reform and the abolition of every pocket borough in the franchise without the blink of an eyelid from him.

Three days before he was due to take his seat in the Commons Pitt rode down to Hayes again. His mother was setting lavender between the sheets of the great bed in what the Pitts called their 'best bedroom'. Here Chatham had died and here he had lain during the black months of his mental collapse. None of the household save these two—the only two Chatham could bear near him—had crossed the threshold then. The room's old oppressions and old sad tokens were about them—the view from the window stretching beyond the winter woods of Hayes to the roofs of the houses which had been built as Chatham lay sick, breaking his prospect of heath and tree, and which so offended against the solitude his reeling mind craved that he had threatened to burn down their new-risen walls with his own hands; the serving hatch hewn in the wall by the bedhead where, in his worst hours, one or other of them had had to place his food; the volume of Homer on the bureau from which the son had been required to read endlessly to ease his father's hard dying.

Lady Chatham rarely mentioned Chatham's breakdown; William not at all. It seemed to his mother he was no more able to speak of his father's sickness than he could have brought himself to speak of some youthful horror of fire or shipwreck. She seated herself by the window, enquiring of London. Her son answered her cheerfully. "All's very well there. Edward Eliot asks after Harriet a hundred times a week. As to myself I was presented to Charles Fox in Westminster Hall the other evening. He even recalled our meeting at Kingsgate when he was still at Eton."

"He had much charm and self-possession then."

"He has even more now. My faith, I wish I had somewhat of his knack—how he can come into a great gathering of strangers and enemies and be as little upon the defensive as if he were by his own hearth."

"You learnt many lessons in this room," Lady Chatham answered. "But not that one."

She brought herself to speak of the past suddenly and with vehemence. "This room has wrought much on us both. The Grenvilles were as proud as Lucifer—as you well know, my son, for this same blood works in you. I thought nothing could ever humble it. But madness can humble anything— even the Grenville pride. I have been near on my knees to my brothers for him. He sold Hayes in his sickness, then all but broke his heart to get it back, and I pleaded endlessly with Thomas Walpole until he cancelled the sale. I begged money for his debts. I was never done stooping, yet I would have stooped even more to see him restored and in health again."

"I know how much you bore," he said in a low voice.

"And you, William. Addington and I threw you to your father's madness too. You were then but seven. All that your father did to you he did to you in love. But what boyhood was it that brought you from this sickroom to your books and back to this sickroom again."

"It makes no matter now. It's over—altogether done with."

She said quietly, "It would please me more if you did not so determinedly jerk down your sleeves and hide the marks of it. It would please me more if—sometimes—you would speak of it."

V

DUNDAS'S WRECKED marriage occasioned eager gossip up and down the corridors of Westminster—the more since his case was the twin to that of Sir Richard Worseley two weeks earlier. Worseley too had quit Government for Opposition. The weary Prime Minister had remarked that all his cuckolds were deserting him. It was a remark that pleased many, but not the two to whom it referred.

January found Dundas back at Westminster. It was a grey, vile, unpromising time for him now—Elizabeth Rannie soon to be declared dead to her husband in the eyes of the law, but in fact in Captain Fauconer's arms and bed; his children bewildered over their mother's going; his own bed cold at Wimbledon, so that he sought other beds in quest of angry proof to himself that whereas his wife had thrown him off other women could well bear with him.

To avoid the popular entrance through Westminster Hall Dundas turned down the narrow medieval alleyway that lay along the outer wall of the Painted Chamber. He expected to find all deserted here. But William Pulteney, one of the country gentlemen, came and joined him. Pulteney wore his customary thin and threadbare coat, seemingly not feeling the bite of the wind from the river. Dundas answered his greeting dourly, then apologised. "My petition for divorce is heard this week. And I'm poor company, thinking o' my girls rendered motherless and he and she who made them so due to be wed in the month."

Pulteney was silent. Dundas went on, "I once defended an adulterous wife in the Edinburgh Court o' Session. She was a bonny and tearful lass and I fought her useless battle for her to the end. I didna think then I would one day be as her husband—save in this, that she would ha'e gone back to him had he been willing, whereas my wife would no' come back to me for a thousand guineas."

"You could compel her back, Dundas," Pulteney said in a quiet voice.

"Aye, I could. But 'tisna to my taste. And if I did, what sort o' a hell would it be to us after?"

Pulteney gave a brief, acquiescing nod. He was stern-faced, with strong, forbidding brows and a silent aspect. He had no look of seeming to invite confidences. But he received many. 'Pulteney knows all our secrets' was a phrase often heard in the lobbies and corridors.

But a more unwelcome meeting was upon Dundas now. Two men were coming from the direction of the Cotton Garden—the Third Secretary of State, Lord George Germain, and, by his side, with the gleam of his Garter ribbon and the flash of his star pricking through the wintry dimness, the Prime Minister himself, Lord North, 'Old Boreas', stout, with rheumy blue eyes and lips puffed in the January sharpness. For a moment there was a hesitancy—North with desertion to forgive, and Dundas the much-repeated appellation, 'cuckold'. But North at least was not a man of rancour. He spoke, giving a brief, near-sighted bow, "Why then it is you, Dundas—and Pulteney? Upon my word, this, my namesake, the north wind from the river, cuts like ice."

"It will be warmer inside, my lord," Pulteney said.

"Too warm, doubtless, when you gentlemen of the Opposition come to your feet," North answered placidly.

Here in the precincts of Westminster he was always unruffled. But the face he showed in the House was not the face he showed in Downing Street where, without sleep, he would sometimes break into uncontrolled weeping, complaining he had no friend in England, and where, with Lady North given to swoonings and agues, all seemed close to nervous collapse.

"I hear we have a new boy tonight," he went on, turning towards the little side door that nestled between the Painted Chamber and the Royal Gallery. "Chatham's son—so his lineage is high. I wonder if, like his father, he will set the Thames alight."

"What First Minister's son ever amounted to anything?" Germain remarked in a sour voice. "Walpole sired a nonentity, as did Bute."

"And my poor boy broke down in his maiden speech, as you tactfully omit to mention, Germain," North said, with a cheerful grace. He felt for his quizzing-glass to discern the few steps up into the building. "Even Chatham's fires burnt low at the finish. And indeed I have often pondered on what the illness was that so sapped him—gout, or some distemper of the blood perhaps, or even a seizure."

"Pulteney knows, I'll warrant," Germain said. "Pulteney knows all our secrets—even those of the Pitts."

Pulteney in fact knew what few at Westminster did, that Chatham's great mind had reeled into madness for a time. But he answered, with a faint humane smile lifting the sternness from his face, "I never talk of sickness. I should be a chronic invalid in a month if I did."

They walked down the Long Gallery, passed the Clerk's room and into the lobby of the House of Commons. A group stood about the fire here, the deaf man's voice of Sir John Honeywood ringing out most penetratingly from their midst.

"What about these goings-on at Wimbledon, eh? It used to be a respectable neighbourhood. That new boy, Wilberforce, the banker's son from Hull, has a house there. This is a new mode, is it not—these wives walking out and having to be put away?"

There was a hasty shifting among his listeners at sight of Dundas. Sir John roared remorselessly on, " 'Tis all right, Loveden, he can't hear me. 'Pon my soul, singular it should happen twice in a session. Still, as I said to the housekeeper but ten minutes ago, if I see one green swan on the Thames I shall see another before the week's out, depend upon it."

Dundas sought none but his own company now. North and Germain had gone on, and Pulteney, seeing how it was with him, gave him a grim, understanding nod and left him. Dundas stood watching the steady influx of members going past him into the debating chamber. Henry Creuger came by, the Commons' one American, who sat for Bristol. The House always gave him courtesy and a fair hearing. But it was nonetheless a hard situation for him here among the ranks of his countrymen's enemies, knowing that either his own men were dying or theirs were. He went in, set-faced, the doorkeepers touching their hats to him as he passed.

Presently Pitt came in with his two sponsors. He and Dundas gave each other no more than a formal greeting. As at Lincoln's Inn Dundas thought this young man coldly self-contained. But Jessel, the deputy doorkeeper, came off his stool with a wide, somewhat broken-toothed grin, asking, "Mr. Pitt? I remember you, sir, as a babe, being carried up the stairs to the Gallery to hear your father's last speech before he went into the Lords. Very young you was. We all said, 'He won't sit quiet—we'll have to have him out.' But sit quiet you did."

"I remember a little of it myself, Jessel," Pitt said with much more warmth than he had used towards Dundas.

"So you've got my name, sir," Jessel answered. "Why, then here's Mr. Fox and the Speaker will be sharp behind."

There was a burst of laughter from the vestibule. A group of the great men of the Opposition came up from it—Sheridan, Burke, Coke, Lord John Cavendish—and at their head, commanding them, Fox himself. He was very stout now, far beyond what his thirty-two years warranted. But his ease and assurance and man-of-the-world charm had come to their full growth. The marks of success were strong upon him; the marks of contradiction too, so that he appeared half dandy, half sloven, his hair straggling rough shorn under its purple hair powder, but his scarlet-heeled shoes the height of fashion, his jewels magnificent, his waistcoat glimmering in its scarlet and gold threads. Though he styled himself pridefully 'the man of the people', he took an equal and passionate pride in the bastard blood of the royal Stuarts that flowed in his veins, his way lying among the great ducal houses, with their Palladian porticos, their Gobelin taestries and acres of landscape gardens dotted with lakes and beech avenues and fallow deer; their routs and faro tables and willing servants. The pattern of his childhood still held. He who had always got what he wanted still did so. Few men denied him. The many women he desired for his bed did not seem to deny him either. Leading the Opposition in the Commons, he looked ultimately as sure of Downing Street as if the house stood with its doors already wide to receive him.

He called to Pitt across the lobby, "Welcome and well met, William. Time presses now. But Lord Rockingham is receiving at his house at Wimbledon tomorrow and he desires you to be there. Eight o'clock. Can I rely on it?"

"Yes. My thanks to him, sir, and to you."

Dundas watched sourly, thinking that Chatham would not have been so easily commanded. Fox went on into the chamber. His followers rose to him as dotingly as his parents had once done at Kingsgate, asking him if he were going to speak, if he would come up to the eating-house afterwards, whether he would later grace their tables for faro. And he, the rising and dazzling star in the darkening political skies, took it all carelessly as a royal due.

The Speaker's procession was coming slowly down upon them now—the attendant first with his white gloves and black rosette; the Serjeant-at-Arms following bearing the Mace; the Speaker himself, the skirts of his robes carried by his train-bearer, who balanced in his other hand the hilt of his sword sheathed in white leather; the Chaplain in the rear. The doorkeepers and messengers in the lobbies and corridors set up the cry, "Hats off, Strangers," and those of the public who stood there at once pulled off their hats as though to the King himself. The Speaker paced gravely on, his face shadowed by his great grey wig. As he came through the double doors the House rose to him.

Dundas slipped in on the heels of the procession. With prayers done and the Speaker in the chair, Pitt and his two sponsors came from the Bar of the House, making their three ceremonial bows. The House turned a hard stare towards Chatham's son. Even the Chaplain had a long scrutiny for him as he handed him the Bible. A few could remember forty-six years back Chatham standing here for this same purpose. They heard for the second time the words, "I, William Pitt, swear by Almighty God that I will be faithful and bear true allegiance to His Majesty, King George, his heirs and successors according to law, so help me God."

"Well, Dundas," George Sutton said, as the new member took his place a long way back behind the bulk of Fox's shoulders and the slant of Burke's untidy wig. "Is it going to begin again in this generation?"

"Why, man, they're both on the same side."

Sutton gave him a wry look. "So were Chatham and Henry Fox—at the first."

VI

CLIMBING FROM his carriage the next night in Lord Rockingham's driveway Fox came face to face with Pitt and was at once greeted, "I am very glad to meet with you again, sir."

For a space Fox regarded the son of his father's old enemy in the light of the candle lanterns. But the pleasure in the words was genuine. All was as it had been in the summer woods of Kingsgate fourteen years ago—the older man with his assurance, his vast knowledge of the world, of men and of women, that he had acquired almost from the schoolroom, still commanding the younger; the younger waiting on him with the same eagerness and admiration.

"Sir?" Fox said goodhumouredly. "It was 'Charles' at Kingsgate, and the Opposition Front Bench is not so far above you now as was the Eton Sixth then, I do assure you." He glanced about him. "I do not see your carriage."

"I don't rise to a carriage, Charles. Wilberforce gives me hospitality for the night."

"Ah, yes, I recall. He is southside the Common now, but five minutes from Scotch Harry, westside. And what of that domestic business there? For my, part I think the wife deserves a ribbon and star for enduring Dundas the nineteen years she did."

"At least Dundas did not drag her back by the locks. Many men would have done so in preference to hearing themselves called cuckold."

"He keeps her dowry," Fox said with a touch of impatience. "And he is not quite forty and personable in appearance though in nothing else. If he gets his freedom, there will be another wife and another dowry and more avid seeking for the winning side." His face had darkened. "Presently the dog will scent the odour of success about me and come running at my heels. When he does it will give me vast pleasure to kick him back where he came from."

They were admitted to the house. The rooms were already packed, the menservants very splendid in their blue and silver Rockingham livery, the joint arms of the Watsons and Wentworths worked in glittering threads on a medieval dorser slung from the stairhead. Fox's entrance brought a brilliant crowd about him instantly. The Duchess of Devonshire came to cling to his arm, crying in her high and pretty voice, "La, Charles, there was such a rustling in the scrub when we drove past the curling ponds. Only conceive what a scare I had. I thought it were Jerry Abershaw, and my diamonds would be snatched off my neck in a thrice."

With her plumes towering above her head and the famous beauty that had toppled London she had much attention. But there were many glances also being directed towards an exceedingly pretty girl, with a little lacy beribboned cap perched high on her blanched curls, composedly drinking iced cordial. She was not the daughter of the house, for the Rockinghams had no children. But the arriving guests greeted her almost as if she were, courting her as 'dear Miss Weddell', and 'Susan, child'. A crowd of admirers was urging her towards the supper room. She turned at length, half stumbling upon the three steps down to it and leaving behind a shoe, seemingly too big for her. Its great diamond buckle blazed whitely against the colours of Lord Rockingham's carpet.

There was an immediate jostling of male guests to reach it. A young buck got his hand to it first, remarking with a fashionable extravagance, "Permit me to drink a toast from this trophy—to the divine eyes of Miss Weddell."

"Oh come, sir, give it to me," Miss Weddell said, though she was clearly pleased.

Lady Rockingham, standing with a woman guest, remarked, midway between exasperation and affection, "Do you see Susan wearing my shoes again? She thinks the buckles draw attention upon her."

"Why, God bless us, Lady Rockingham," her companion answered. "That exceedingly pretty miss would have a beau in every corner were she in kersey stockings and wooden pattens. She'll marry a duke, I vow, and bowl about in the handsomest carriage in London."

"Indeed," Lady Rockingham said with a sigh. "A duke would not commend himself to her at all unless the heads turned when he came into the room. Sometimes I think we did the Weddells an ill favour when my half-sister married into them and gave them a taste for being where the candles burn brightest."

The faro had begun. Fox held the centre table, the Duchess of Portland behind one shoulder, the Duchess of Devonshire at the other. Pitt stood looking on. The tables lured him with almost as strong a sirens' enticement as they did Fox. But no man here was staking less than a hundred guineas, and that was half a year's income for him. Some of his desire to throw caution to the winds and to plunge deeply in edged into his face. Fox, glancing up at that moment, saw it, and so, from across the room, did Susan Weddell. She waved back her doting court—to its plain annoyance—and crossed over, saying in a low voice and with a brief introductory bow, "Sir, unless you are a very rich man—and indeed for all I know you may be—I would counsel you not to play. You can lose three thousand guineas a night here—this being the house of the richest man in England, and these London's most notable gamesters."

"Thank you, ma'am," Pitt said. "That were a friendly warning."

"Indeed, sir, it were meant to be. I would not have you walk out of my Uncle Charles Rockingham's house a ruined man." She gave him a second smiling bow and allowed herself to be sucked back into the vortex of her admirers once more.

By four in the morning the bulk of Rockingham's guests had left. Men shrank now from those two politically outmoded words, 'Whig' and 'Tory'. But the great aristocratic Whig houses that had thrown out the Stuarts and saved—as they held—the land for the Protestant succession were still a power in politics, their broad green acres and Adam houses dominating shires and hundreds as the fiefs of the barons had once done. It was the lordly Whig élite—the Devonshires, the Portlands, the Rockinghams themselves, the Spencers, the Carlisles, the Cavendishes—that lingered about Rockingham's gaming tables.

Their talk had turned to politics. "Your new boy, Charles," Rockingham remarked presently. "Chatham's son. Is he any good?"

"He has not opened his mouth in public yet—not even to address a few convivial freemen in a Kentish hostelry."

"God help him when he gets to his feet in the Commons if he is as untried as that," the Duke of Portland said dryly. "Still, he seems a self-contained young man. He may survive it."

Fox laughed. "He may in truth survive it, but he will not love the experience any more than he loved declaiming Latin at my mother's tea-table when he was a boy. Your Grace mistakes the mask of self-possession for its reality."

"Well, Charles," the Duchess of Devonshire said, taking his arm, "at least in this generation it seems the Pitts have learnt their place."

"Sweet," he answered smiling, "it is only when the Pitts learn their place that they become bearable."

VII

PITT—WITH a bull's-eye lantern, supplied by Rockingham House for the purpose—made his way back towards Wilberforce's villa, lying midway between High Street and the Crooked Billet. Another lantern blinked under the dark trees on the fringe of the Common. Pitt came face to face with Dundas, wrapped in his capes and pacing aimlessly in the black shadow. "You!" Dundas said shortly. "I had forgot it were the night o' Lord Rockingham's revels. For my part I couldna sleep—I came out for a breath o' air."

His empty bed had been an ill place to him this night. Pitt, in a like case, would have loathed the condescension of pity. His restricted boyhood at Hayes served him poorly in finding the right urbane comment here. He fell awkwardly silent.

The grate of wheels on the frosty road came in time to aid him. A post-chaise, with a military outrider, loomed up, driving smartly down Wimbledon Parkside towards the village, its candle lanterns flickering bravely, its yellow paintwork bespattered with all the wintry mud that layered the roads from Portsmouth to London. The occupant—a Major in British Army scarlet—saw their lanterns and leant from the window, calling, "Gentlemen, have we come off the London road?"

"Aye, you ha'e," Dundas answered. "You should ha'e taken the left-hand fork at Tibbett's Corner."

"I began to suspect as much when I saw the houses," the Major said. "Damn! Dark and ice and frost are no helpful pathfinders."

His black despatch box lay beside him on the carriage seat. He kept his hand on it with an air so habitual he might almost have lived with it thus for the whole of his three-thousand-mile journey. "What's the intelligence from America?" Dundas asked.

"All is for Lord North's ears first," the officer answered goodhumouredly.

"Och, man we are both members o' Parliament, and discreet, I trust. Can ye no' tell us, in general terms, whether the news is good or bad?"

"Well, sir," the officer said with a faint smile. "In general terms there's no news of either description—nothing when I left New York save winter quarters and an unholy quiet. But Cornwallis is assembling his baggage train in Charleston. He'll march when the roads are fit for it. Indeed he may have marched already, since spring comes early in Carolina. And of him we have hopes—we have great hopes."

He touched his cocked hat to them. The chaise was brought about in a wide circle, dwindling off into the night towards Putney Bridge and London. Pitt and Dundas parted. The side door of Lauriston House had been left unbolted against Pitt's return. He shot the bolts behind him and mounted the stairs. But Wilberforce sometimes slept badly and was up writing his journal at the escritoire in his bedroom. He called and as Pitt came in set aside his quill, his small figure outlined by the candle-glow against the wall. He was already a deeply religious man, his influence with Pitt very great, though sometimes chafed at. But whereas in public and among strangers, it was Pitt who preserved a wary gravity, and Wilberforce, who, with his singing and mimicry, was considered a godsend by London hostesses, in their own circle or alone together, they were apt to change roles. They did so now, Wilberforce regarding the other with a sudden seriousness over the pages of his journal; Pitt, light-hearted after Rockingham's revels and eager to talk of them. "The mode's monstrous expensive among the nobility, Will— stakes as high as the Monument. Charles was breaking about even when I left. I hope for the remainder of the night the cards fall well for him."

"I wish he would forswear the tables since it would seem he will come to Downing Street one day," Wilberforce answered. "It has its ill side—setting at the head of the Treasury a half-ruined gamester who threw away forty thousand pounds of his father's fortune on the cards while his father yet lived, and who wins or loses four thousand guineas in a night at Brooks's."

"He is still the one man who can save us from this morass of unjust war and bad debts North has steered us into. I know how your mind runs, you old Yorkshire sobriety. You require virtue in Downing Street."

"Men have strange ideas of virtue. They should look at the root of the word."

"I can give you the root—*vir*, Latin, a man. *Wer*, Old High German, a man. Virtue, that which makes the whole man. The four cardinal virtues, the four things on which the personality swings. But in Charles's case, his talents are so huge the rest can be winked at. It does not matter."

"Perhaps it does not matter in the fat years," Wilberforce said. "But I think there are times when, if the old Christian verities are not at least acknowledged, it will go exceedingly ill for us."

Pitt looked at him. "What times?"

"In the despairing hour, I suppose. When you can scarce discern the lights on new Westminster Bridge."

The dawn was creeping in upon them. Pitt turned and drew aside the curtain, revealing the grey-lit Common and the lights still blazing in Dundas's windows.

"Dundas sleeps as ill as yourself, Will."

"His divorce went through this afternoon. He is a free man now."

"I think he finds it a cold, hard liberty," Pitt said.

VIII

MISS WEDDELL and Wilberforce were known to each other —both of Yorkshire, both apt on occasion to frequent the salons of Hull and the pump room of Scarborough. Though Susan referred to Rockingham as her 'Uncle Charles Rockingham', her relationship with the vastly wealthy family was more tenuous. Lady Rockingham's half-sister had married William Weddell, occasioning some gossip through the Three Ridings since, a generation back, the Weddells had served behind the leech jars in Joseph Tomlinson's dingy apothecary's shop in York. The childless Rockinghams had taken a great fancy to this pretty, quick-tongued and fatherless girl; and, on her side, Susan could not escape quickly enough from the quiet village of Skelton and pleasant sleepy Ripon, into the high living of fashionable London.

Wilberforce, coming into the Palace of Westminster by the way of the King's staircase, all but walked past her standing in the Arcade to the House of Lords. "Well, Mr. W. W.," she said somewhat haughtily as he checked in time, "I thought you were entirely going to ignore me."

"Forgive me, ma'am," Wilberforce answered goodhumouredly. "You know my poor sight. Everyone is but a blur to me until I am within a few paces of them."

She gave him a pardoning nod, remarking, "I met your friend, Mr. Pitt, last night—though I did not know then he were Mr. Pitt."

"He has told me, ma'am. He said you had the eyes of the room, his own included."

"Indeed I hope I had," she said calmly. "It's true the Duchess of Devonshire was there. But she is quite old—twenty-eight or twenty-nine. As to the men, if the Duke of Devonshire and the Duke of Portland went as mere Mr. Jones and Mr. Robinson into the pump room at Scarborough Spa no one would regard them twice—and my poor Uncle Charles Rockingham, for all he could buy the Palace of Westminster six times over, does not stand out in a crowd."

Her words were almost at once borne out. The peers were coming in in quick succession under the stone porch that gave on to the Lords' vestibule. There were visitors also, clutching written orders of admission. One—especially knowledgeable—was indicating each peer by name. "Yonder's Sandwich—Jemmy Twitcher himself—the First Lord, shambling along with his head hanging. The one following is Thurlow, the Lord Chancellor, and he came up from little and the dram shops of Holborn. This now is Lord Shelburne. Damned if I can see Lord Rockingham though, and he leads Opposition."

"Why bless you, sir, he's but ten yards from you," one of the attendants said.

"Oh my faith, so he is," the onlooker remarked in a surprised voice.

Susan gave a doleful shake of her head, then turned from the subject to ask, "When does Mr. Pitt make his maiden speech?"

"He has not decided yet, ma'am."

"When he does will you give me a written order of admission, then I need not apply for a ticket to the Serjeant-at-Arms' office? I am accustomed to the decencies of life. I much prefer the House of Lords and tea in one of their handsome committee rooms. But for this single occasion I am altogether prepared to toil up all those stairs in the Commons to that draughty ventilator room that your housekeeper has neglected to dust for a hundred years or more."

"For my part I think you will find it well worth the toil."

"I think so. But many are assured Mr. Pitt will fail. All the sons of great men do, they say. The ghosts of their fathers down them, and you, in the Commons, are a savaging lot when you are disappointed." She smiled. "But you and I, with our sound Yorkshire judgment, Mr. W. W., have the knack sometimes of singling out where to place our wagers."

IX

But Miss Weddell had no time to obtain her order of admission. Dundas, coming in with Pulteney three weeks later, found the lobby deserted and asked Jessel, the deputy doorkeeper, what had drawn every single soul into the chamber.

"Mr. Pitt's up, sir," Jessel answered. "He weren't expecting it neither but the House called on him, and went on creating terrible until the Speaker he says, 'Mr. Pitt', so he had the floor whether he wanted it or no."

"Why, I thank my stars that never happened to me," Dundas said.

"That's what Colonel Barré says," Jessel said. " 'God damn my eyes, Jessel,' he says, 'but a maiden speech is bad enough when you've wrote it all down the night before with a wet kerchief about your brow and memorising every word. I don't know what'll happen now,' he says, 'but it'll be diverting and I'm going in to see.' But the truth is they're that hot to see if Mr. Pitt is anything like his old dad they won't wait."

Dundas and Pulteney went on through the empty lobby. Beyond the double doors Pitt would be speaking, or might already have come to a mute stop. The little debating chamber, only sixty feet by twenty-eight, was so small and intimidating, with its sea of faces and its lowering galleries, no more than nine feet above a man's head, that to speak here for the first time had a nightmarish quality as of mounting the gallows and addressing a hot-breathing crowd only

inches away. Army men who had had balls lodged in cheek-
bone or shoulder, naval officers who had kept station on some
heaving quarter-deck during the rakings of Quiberon Bay,
without stirring an epaulette, had sometimes been rendered
altogether wordless by it, subsiding helplessly on to the
benches while the House glowered or mocked. Even men
trained to the law had sometimes broken down. Some found
the ordeal so great they did not speak again for the rest of
their parliamentary lives.

"Well, all's been made o'er-smooth for him until now,"
Dundas remarked. "It's but justice if the fact that he's his
father's son deals ill wi' him for once."

"The silver spoon, Dundas?" Pulteney said with a faint
smile.

"Aye, the silver spoon."

They went in. The silent feel of the House, its voiceless
mood that they were both adept at reading beat upon them
instantly—rapt and intent, the Gallery quite still, even the
doorkeepers on their stools listening absorbedly. Pitt, speaking from the Opposition benches was commanding all. West-
cote, earlier in the debate, had called the struggle with
America 'a holy war', and was being roundly answered.

"For my part I am persuaded it is an accursed war. It was
conceived in injustice; it was nurtured in folly; its footsteps
are marked with blood. To this country it has brought nothing but a series of severe defeats or ineffective victories over
our brethren in America—men making glorious exertions
for their liberty on whom we attempt to force unconditional
submission. There must be few in England who can refrain
from grieving for the loss of so much British blood spilt in
this cause; or from weeping on whichever side victory might
be declared."

"A chip of the old block here, Dundas," Sutton muttered
as Dundas seated himself alongside him. "Or, as I judge
Burke to have remarked twice already, the old block itself.
A speaking-voice like Garrick's into the bargain."

"Aye, no' only his father, but fortune too, seems to ha'e made a special pet o' him."

The House never excused failure. But it was unstintingly generous towards success. With the debate ended and the tide of members washing back into the lobby again, Pitt was surrounded at once.

"They tell me you spoke excellent well, my boy," Sir John Honeywood roared with a congratulatory dig of his ear trumpet into Pitt's ribs. "Didn't hear a word myself. You mumbled. All you young men mumble nowadays. You've fairly driven me to buying this damned ear trumpet, and it don't help much. Still they tell me you spoke very fine."

The Ministers had begun to come out. They knew now that this new young man would prove a rod in pickle for them. But after the fashion of their kind they had only congratulations for him. Even Germain went by with a curt, "Well done"; and Sir Grey Cooper paused to say, "Excellent. Your father would have approved."

"Felicitations, Mr. Pitt," North said, following at the heels of his colleagues. "That was entirely the best maiden speech I ever heard in my life."

It was acknowledged by a stiff bow. Dundas marked, not for the first time, Pitt's resentment for the premier whose American war had brought Chatham to so hard a deathbed. He thought it a young man's grudge—ungenerous and fierce. Then Fox's bulk loomed up through the double doors, his hand falling on Pitt's shoulder and this gesture was received much more eagerly.

A thin, dry, cracked chuckle broke in upon the lobby. Old General Grant—the House's oldest member—stood, rocked by his laughter, his faded army scarlet catching the firelight at his back, his white stockings lying in folds about his thin shanks. "Yes, yes," he said gleefully as the eyes turned upon him. "You stand there, clapping each other on the back, wringing each other's hands. But you'll fight, you two, as your fathers did before you, and I'll live to see it."

Fox's hand slid abruptly from Pitt's shoulder. Pitt remarked with a genuine astonishment, "Why, General, you must expect to live to be as old as Methuselah."

"Good God, the boy thinks it will never happen," Grant said with another quiver of laughter. "I'll tell you this, Mr. Pitt—in the old French wars, even if there were not a coney stirring the whole distance between Ticonderoga and Fort Duquesne, if the battle were pending I could always smell the powder. And, mark it, the smell of powder hangs strong about you both, even though you can't discern it for yourselves."

His broken chuckle echoed again while Lord Chatham's son and Lord Holland's looked upon one another with an awkward scepticism.

Fox drew Pitt aside down the corridor—black-panelled and set with two wall mirrors—that led past the Clerk of the Commons' room. They were alone here. But ahead North's cumbersome figure was turning into the Long Gallery, the blue gleam of his Garter ribbon athwart his shoulder.

Fox cast a glance after it. "That man," he said. "That calamitous man—that monstrous disaster in a blue ribbon. My faith, William, sometimes I am plagued with bad dreams that he will make me miss my destiny—that I shall fail to turn him from office and into the Tower where he belongs."

Pitt smiled and answered, "It would surprise me if any man made you miss your destiny, Charles."

"He would pay for it if he did." The wall mirror caught their likenesses. Fox glanced at it, remarking, "I have changed since Kingsgate. There are at least seven stones more to me."

"You've not changed greatly."

"And you, I think, not at all." He bent his black brows on Pitt rakingly and acutely. "Your calm, assured maiden speech that has so hugely impressed the House this night—

come, is it not to be admitted it was not in fact so effortless an exercise as it seemed?"

"Not to any other man. But to you—yes, it's admitted."

"All has been too enclosed about you, William. Your quiet Kentish Hayes—your cloisters of Cambridge. You should have gone to Eton as I did. After two terms there no man has breath left for shyness."

"My faith," Pitt said in disgust. "They don't discern that in me, do they?"

"Only myself and your friends, Wilberforce and Eliot," Fox answered with a laugh. "Not the other five hundred and fifty-five. Your friends know you well and I observed you at Kingsgate before you had quite learnt how to put on your Grenville armour."

He nodded and went back. Wilberforce, who had been waiting just inside the lobby, joined Pitt and they walked together down towards the Long Gallery. It was over these flags that the Plantagenet and Norman Kings of England had walked from their kingly apartments to their royal chapel of St. Stephen's. Here was the womb of the building—the Palace of Westminster sprawling above and about them, its hidden chapels, crypts and cloisters proclaiming it had once been holy ground, its ancient grey melting in daylight here and there into honey-coloured Tudor sandstone or rose-red Georgian brick, its medieval corbels scowling or grinning or puckering their stony brows towards the sky, its summertime grounds tumbling untidily into the Thames in green willow and green lichen or breaking into the tended formality of the Speaker's Garden. In the Painted Chamber, just ahead, Chatham's body had lain in state. All things seemed to have directed his son's steps towards this building, its demands and activities. But no man found a maiden speech other than a rough baptism. Pitt drew a deep breath. "My stars, I am glad to be through that."

"If I did not know you I would have said you never turned a hair."

"But you do know me," Pitt answered with a faint grin. "And you know I turned several."

Wilberforce drew his small black-bound journal from his pocket, groping for his reading-glass and turning the leaves as they walked. "I wrote a prediction concerning you the night of Lord Rockingham's rout. Would you hear it? It's but a sentence—'I doubt not I shall live to see Pitt the first man in the land one day.'"

"That was a vote of over-much confidence, was it not?" Pitt said in a slow voice.

"Did you not think the same once?"

"Yes, perhaps I did, as a boy, with the walls of Hayes about me and before I knew the odds. But there's Fox—eleven years my senior and most brilliant, bearing all the lineaments of leadership. He has only to get to his feet and we are all under the wand of the magician."

"I hope for you there will not be a day of disenchantment."

"You old morality, is it at all likely that there will be?"

The Commons' Library, with its great shelves, candles and thick carpeting, opened in front of them. Save for the librarian, in his high stock, only North was there, bent over an open volume on the table. He did not turn at their approach and, as they roamed round the books, the high shelves and bright bindings hid him from them.

There was a striding step on the flags outside. Lord George Germain came in, all the great acres of Knole, its silver furniture and forest-covered deer parks in his commanding Sackville step. But the Third Secretary's hauteur only masked the strain that lay upon him. He swept to North's side, and again the tall shelves came between the two Ministers and the two back-benchers.

"My lord, the Atlantic despatches are in."

There was a crisp snap and stir of papers. North's voice broke out, sharp with strain, "Cowpens? Hannah's Cowpens?

Is that the name of the township? God with us, Germain, eight hundred casualties—"

"The figure includes wounded and prisoners. As to the latter, Cornwallis is in pursuit. He will get them back."

"But that the Americans should so successfully bayonet charge our regulars—in faith, Germain, it is in the dark hours, pacing the Downing Street floors, that I begin to feel we shall be beat at the finish. And I long to be out of it. It is with me as Cowper writes in this new long poem of his here—

> *Oh, for a lodge in some vast wilderness,*
> *Where rumour of oppression and deceit,*
> *Of unsuccessful or successful war,*
> *Might never reach me more. My ear is pained,*
> *My soul is sick, with every day's report,*
> *Of wrong and outrage with which earth is filled."*

There was a silence. North said at length with a shaken laugh, "Come, do not regard me with such owl-like gravity. You are used to my spasmodic tremblings, and the country does not see them."

"It is to be hoped the country does not feel them either, my lord," Germain's voice replied tartly.

Pitt and Wilberforce, entrapped behind the high shelves, stood regarding each other with discomfort. "Let us be out of this, Will," Pitt muttered, and thrust the book he was holding back among its fellows.

They came round to reach the door. But Germain had quick ears and swung about with an exclamation of wrath. "Oh God save us, the greatest pestilences on this earth are Americans, reporters and Opposition back-benchers."

"Oh come, Lord George," North said. "We chose to speak together in a public room."

His composure had come back to him. It seemed that while the Americans had already brought him to his knees, the Opposition in no circumstances could, and that there were two Norths—the one altogether unnerved by his agonised and doubtful war, the other winning all his nightly battles in the Commons, never losing his vast skill in the debating chamber or his unruffled aspect outside it. Seeing him calm now under the candlelight, his countenance puffed from sleeplessness, a little unwilling admiration crept into Pitt's face.

North noted it. "Yes, yes, Mr. Pitt," he said in gentle fashion. "You young gentlemen opposite have a simple physic remedy if I should find the burdens of office too toil-some—resignation. But there is an addiction to power. You will not believe that now, I fear, though you well may do so in twenty years' time. A man clings to it as he might cling to the memory of a childhood in which he was never happy, or to a nervous disability that plagues him but which he feels is part of himself." He turned back to Germain. "Come then, point out Hannah's Cowpens to me. Upon my soul, these names get even odder."

Pitt and Wilberforce went out into the dim corridor. Pitt was silent for a long space but he broke out at length, "What a war it is, Will—the American dead lying hard by their hearths and homesteads in defence of their nationhood; the British dead lying by Burgoyne's redoubts, far from theirs, in defence of their King and their country's honour; thinking at White Plains, 'God help poor America, is this the end of her?', thinking at Saratoga 'God help poor England, is this the end of her?' I like my causes better ordered. I like most heartily to desire victory for one side or the other." The triumph of his maiden speech had ebbed. He added bitterly, "Perhaps it is as well my father did not live to see the worst of it."

X

HARD UPON the British defeat at Hannah's Cowpens came
tonic news for English ears. Cornwallis, overmatched at
Guildford Court House by three to one, and Lord Rawdon,
also opposing a greater strength at Hobkirk's Hill, had both
come to victory. It was as if the British Army fought its battles
again under the ancient auspices of the saints, of Crispin and
Crispinian, standing outnumbered and against the odds, its
old gilt and scarlet and pipeclayed splendour returned to it.
Englishmen let their minds dwell once more on the old pattern of their conflicts—the last battle they had come to assure
themselves they always won. Relief pervaded London like
the spring sunshine.

On the morning of the news of Hobkirk's Hill, William
Pulteney made his way across Old Palace Yard. About him
all was high triumph—the news-vendors calling, "More good
news for England," and the bookstalls and sellers of Westminster toffee doing a trade buoyed up by the cheer and
bustle of victory. Pulteney's grim countenance was unchanged, his coat, as usual, somewhat threadbare. The House
considered Pulteney's cheap stuff coats a strange quirk, for he
was married to the heiress of the great Bath estates. But
Pulteney had small love for spending his wife's fortune on
himself, and while he plied his wife and daughter with
gowns and gifts and carriages, his own habits were as Spartan
as when—before his marriage—he had been a poor man.

There was a touch on his arm. His brother, Governor
Johnstone (Pulteney, at his marriage, had changed his name
by deed poll to enable his much-loved wife to keep her
estates and her wealth), had come up behind him. "Well
then," Pulteney said, turning. "Have we time to go up to
Bellamy's for soup or a coffee before the House sits, Governor?"

Even to his family Johnstone was still 'Governor', though

his governorship was a hollow thing now, his one-time province—Florida—long since alight with the smoke and fires of rebellion.

The pleasant eating-house, with its Queen Anne wheel-back chairs and wide windows, overlooked the scene in Old Palace Yard they had just left. At a table near the door were five young men who called themselves 'the Old Firm', but whom Germain dubbed 'the Cambridge cubs'—Pitt, Wilberforce, Eliot, Pepper Arden and the Devonian, Dudley Ryder. Bellamy, in his spotless apron, was standing by them, saying, "I have had to put my coffee up, gentlemen. It is five pence now."

"You run the most expensive eating-house in London, Bellamy, as I suppose you know," Pepper Arden said.

"And I serve you the best fare, sir," Bellamy answered solidly. "You go across to Mr. Waghorn's where they serve the Lords, and you won't get veal chops like mine, I'll warrant."

He came across to where Pulteney and Johnstone had seated themselves by the wide window. The previous customers had left a litter of used cups and the day's *Advertiser* on the table. Bellamy set the cover to rights, gathering up the news-sheet with a grunt. "Four brothel keepers advertising in the columns today," he said. "All for country girls, though they wrap it up pretty circumspect. I own I abominate it—those young girls, with their red cheeks, coming up to London where they'll be eaten rotten by gin and the pox in a year or so, because this is where they think life is and there's plenty of ladies of fashion to do the like. They'll be foreigners to read this, and Americans. They must think us randy as alley cats."

"The latter do at least," Johnstone answered. When Bellamy moved away he spoke to his brother, his mind now on his return to America, three years ago, as one of the peace commissioners for the fruitless talks of 1777. "Many Americans came to my table in Philadelphia at that time. They all thought us a dissolute people. I would say, 'Nonsense, nonsense, no Englishman thinks of an American except he conceives him in a racoon-skin jacket, with a Bible in his back pocket that he can't read, and no American thinks of an Englishman save he conceives him as a fop with scent behind the ears and his hand down the front of a woman's bodice; and both are wrong—the one image is as false as the other.' But then I sailed back among our own people—weary of all their greatness—and I began to think that if we were not yet as the Americans conceived us, in a decade we would become so."

Pulteney sat with a carven stillness.

"You'll think the Americans have made a moral man of me, brother," Johnstone went on with a half sigh. "They had room for the task, God knows. But I do not love it when I see half London staggering from bed to bed, diseased and poxed, lecherous and cynical. Nor do I love it when I see sinecures dangled and grabbed. It is too near to what the man in Philadelphia conceives happens, and he has the Quaker blood of Penn in his veins and cannot tolerate that he should be governed by a legislative body full of those—as he thinks—ready to buy any man and bed any woman."

"And yet it seems to me both nations have much to give the world," Pulteney said quietly. "The Americans, resourceful and independent, building their settlements on the edge of wilderness; and the King in his robes enthroned above his peers, under some blackened rafters that Saxon masons hewed out of English oak eight centuries ago. Both traditions tug at my coat, Governor. I should be sorry if their intermingling is to end in the drifting smoke of some abandoned British redoubt."

"'If the cats should be chased into holes by the mouse'—so the Army sings to its marching tune, *World Turned Upside Down*. You think the British cat will be chased into the hole by what, hitherto, we have regarded as the American mouse, brother?"

"I think it may be."

"I, too," Johnstone said. "For Cornwallis's victory means nothing. He will march on in the heat of high summer through the Yellowed Jack pines of Virginia, his army full of wounds and sickness—the red clay earth—the red coats of his men—the forty-pound packs on their backs—the mosquitoes to swarm and plague and harry them—and something other to harry them too, the American militiamen, relentless, dogged and determined. And unless he can reach the sea, with the black and yellow hulls of the King's ships riding upon it, I have small hope for him."

Across the room, the five young men, seated about their own table, were talking of the same matter. "I begin to think Cornwallis is getting too far from his base," Eliot remarked. "But doubtless he can always fall back to the coast. The Navy will be there to take him off."

"He will be in an ill case if it is not the British Navy," Pitt said.

"Why God bless us, Billy," Pepper Arden said. "It always is the British Navy."

After the splendour of the British stand at Guildford it was easy to believe once more that the King's ships rode paramount. But behind Cornwallis, and with an equal splendour, the Americans picked themselves up from the earth to hunt, to harry and pursue. The summer crept into a mute autumn. As silence blanketed all Cornwallis's movements and no frigate beat in upon the Atlantic tides with word of him, a dark thread of anxiety began to spin its way through the golden optimism of the summer months.

XI

THE BRIGHT October that the Americans named an Indian summer and the British, St. Luke's Little Summer, had turned to November of 1781 when Dundas climbed from his carriage outside Number 10. He was to have been present this night at the Norths' customary Sunday supper party—it being still on the premier's conscience that he had publicly used the word 'cuckold'. But there were wisps of fog steaming from the river and curling about the Downing Street chimney pots. Dundas had come to offer his excuses that he might press on home to Wimbledon.

Lady North greeted him. With her figure mis-shapen from overmuch childbearing, she was a plain, un-beautiful woman. But she had the same amiable grace as her husband. She would not have Dundas go before he had exchanged a few words with North, and brought him to the dressing room where North stood in breeches and waistcoat. The long summer recess had not refreshed the Prime Minister. Deep weals of sleeplessness marked his face.

"I fear the fog is going to rob us of Mr. Dundas's company tonight, Frederick," Lady North said.

"I thought it well might do, Dundas," North said. "None but a fool would want to journey over Wimbledon Common in fog after fall of dark. Wait until I am clad and I will come down with you." He turned to a selection of his coats laid out on the settle. "I think I will wear the plum-coloured velvet, my love."

"As you will, my dear," Lady North answered.

North hesitated, then picked up a brown brocade. His own vacillation struck him. The agitation that his enemies never saw but which so often chilled his friends swept upon him. He broke out almost on a groan, "God knows, my will is paralysed. I can scarce stiffen it long enough to decide the coat I will wear. If I make a decision on America I change it a hundred times pacing the floors at night. Nor do I know whether my quailing spirit has failed the land, or the land's quailing spirit has failed me." He drew a hand across his eyes. "Where is Cornwallis, Dundas—Virginia, Maryland, New Jersey? And why so prolonged a silence?"

"Och, my lord," Dundas said. "French frigates in the Atlantic, Dutchmen in home waters, American riflemen in the New England trees—there are a thousand causes for lack o' intelligence. You're no' beat yet."

But he doubted his own words. North, sleepless, weary, agitated, was a beaten man, whatever might be the case of the country he led.

Even in the short space the fog had thickened. They went down together into the handsome hall where the firelight played across the black and white marble of the floor. As Dundas turned to take his leave, Lady North bent her head, listening intently. A carriage had turned into the street and was coming up through the fog with a blind and urgent haste. Above the slither of the wheels and the stuttering hoofbeats Dundas heard the angry Scottish oaths of his own coachman and the Cockney shouting of another.

A hand crashed the knocker like a discharge of musketry against the eardrum. The porter, already at the door to let Dundas out, opened up immediately, and the fog steamed in towards them, creeping across the chequered floor. Lord George Germain stood on the threshold, the fog in his nostrils. They heard his snarl to the porter, "His lordship— at once—at once."

The porter stood aside. Germain marched in. He seized North's arm, drawing him for privacy through the nearest available doorway into the waiting room. The door shut on them. Lady North was trembling, half in tears from shock and apprehension. But she made a brave falsehood of it, saying, "These London fogs—they sting my eyes so."

Dundas found himself outside in the street. There was much confusion here, his own and Germain's carriages attempting to turn, but, in the fog and the narrow confines of the little cul-de-sac, both with their traces tangled and their coachmen cursing each other. Dundas waited on the step. Within the space of five minutes the door opened again and Germain came out. He saw the confusion, exclaiming in fury, "Get your fellow to rein to one side, Dundas. I am to the King."

"Aye, and what ill news do you bring him, my lord? Is the hunt up and Cornwallis running?"

"Running?" Germain said in what was close to a snarl. "It has gone beyond that. Viewed, checked, cornered and brought to the kill?"

"What?"

"Oh, he's surrendered, Dundas. What other do you expect from any witless British general caught a hundred miles from his base and the Americans about his ears? He signed the articles of capitulation at Yorktown on the nineteenth of October."

The fog caught at his throat and he coughed. Dundas said slowly, "The Americans ha'e fought like giants to contain Cornwallis. But the main British army's yet unscathed. It's no' the end."

"Boreas thinks that it is," Germain said. " 'Oh God, it is all over'—that was how he greeted the news inside yonder. You would have thought I had presented a pistol to his breast and discharged the shot. He flung wide his arms. I saw men fall in the same manner at Minden when a ball took them in the chest." The words brought much back to him and he stood silent, gazing out beyond the fog to old woundings and past battles. "It is twenty-two years since Minden," he went on. "I held back the cavalry that day and I was court-martialled and cashiered for it, as you know. I was not a coward, Dundas. I was an arrogant, stiff-backed Englishman. I would not stoop to take my orders from a Hessian in a green coat, even though he were a prince of the blood. But we will have to learn to stoop. We will have to stand bareheaded in the rain to beg our trade. Our greatness is done. This is the end of it."

Behind them Number 10 stood shuttered and silent. Dundas spoke at length. "I still say that in the days o' our

health we would ha'e brushed one such reverse as this like a
fly from our coat and kept on."

"Yes, doubtless," Germain answered in a bleak and bitter
voice. "But these are not the days of our health."

XII

ON THE Monday evening, with no news-vendors crying yet of
Cornwallis's surrender, Pitt and Pepper Arden set out
through the still-lingering fog to Offley's Coffee House.
Pepper's talk had turned to his fiancée, Ann Wilbraham. It
often did these days, and Pitt was hearing yet again of Ann's
grace and beauty, Ann's starry eyes, the divinity of Ann's
figure. Few walked abroad in Henrietta Street this dank
night. But Offley's—which was much patronised by parlia-
mentarians, not only for the excellence of its mutton chops
and Burton ale, but also because Offley had served his
apprenticeship under Bellamy in the eating-house of the
Commons—had a little scatter of clients at its polished tables
and under its bright candles. Offley admitted ladies with their
escorts to his front parlour. Pulteney and Governor Johnstone
were seated there with Mrs. Johnstone.

Hurrying footsteps followed Pitt and Arden into the
vestibule. A young man came in after them out of the fog, his
hand nervously groping for the hilt of his sword. He made
them a quick, breathless bow, saying, "Messieurs, will you
assist me? Permit me to give my name—the Sire de Rocque.
I am French and my accent proclaims me as such. I would
place myself under your protection this night."

Despite the war, Frenchmen and Americans—if they were
circumspect—could walk freely in the streets of London, as
Englishmen could likewise walk in the streets of Paris. Pitt
and Arden saw small need for their protection. But that de
Rocque spoke in earnest was plain. They offered him coffee,

pledging themselves afterwards to escort him to his destination.

De Rocque accepted with an obvious relief. They cast off their greatcoats, Pulteney beckoning them over. In the warmth and with the smell of fresh-ground coffee all about, de Rocque lost his unease and began to speak of his travels which were taking him on what the English would have called a Grand Tour about Europe.

"So you are seeing London, sir?" Pulteney asked with a smile.

"Ah, *monsieur*, no, for your abomination of a London fog hides all," de Rocque said cheerfully. "*Voilà*, there was I this evening outside the Theatre Royal in Drury Lane with the performance cancelled and my way to make back to my lodgings in the Long Acre. It is not, I think, far, but whether I went towards it or away from it I could not tell."

Pulteney and Johnstone exchanged a sudden alert, alarmed look of mutual grimness.

"The performance cancelled?" Mrs. Johnstone repeated innocently. "Why, pray, that is most unusual. Is one of the principal players sick?"

De Rocque sat toying with his cup. "You do not know?" he said at length in a still voice. "No, doubtless, you do not, since it is but a half-hour since it began to be made public. Forgive me that I break it to you. Your General, Milord Cornwallis, has capitulated to the Americans and my own countrymen on the Chesapeake river."

The talk died away along the length of the room gradually, as the tide might ebb out, sighing over the sands. One of Offley's customers pushed back his chair, saying angrily, "You're a liar, sir—a scurvy French liar."

"Sir," de Rocque said, flushing and laying his hand on his sword.

Pitt and Pepper Arden got up and came between, realising at last that they had best take seriously the charge to protect de Rocque this night. Mrs. Johnstone, seeing both the

Frenchman and the Englishman seemingly about to draw, called out in a high, nervous voice, "Oh, pray, stop them, someone, for heaven's sake."

"None of that in here, sirs," Offley remarked, turning sharply. "You are frightening the ladies."

"It's a damned lie," the Englishman said, though he allowed himself eventually to be persuaded back to his table. "Damned Frogs—they'd have us entirely beat and all thirteen colonies lost every day of the week."

Persuaded on all hands to finish his coffee, de Rocque gulped it down. But he was anxious now to get back to the Long Acre before the murk and enmity of the night closed yet more thickly about him. He looked appealingly at Pitt and Arden. They too swallowed their coffee and rose, de Rocque at once getting up and turning to the vestibule. "Allow me, *messieurs*," he said. "I will fetch all three great-coats."

While he was gone the little knot of English folk drew together about the fire as if finding a thin solace in one another's proximity.

"Is it true, do you suppose?" Pepper Arden muttered.

"Damn it all, can you not smell that it is?" Johnstone growled. "There's the reek of defeat over the whole city."

"And what was your part?" the Englishman who had accosted de Rocque said furiously across the room. "I know you all for Opposition men—the aiders and abettors of treason—the comforters of the King's enemies. Good God, if it is true, I hope you rest satisfied."

"It has an uncommon strange feel for satisfaction, sir," Pulteney answered grimly.

De Rocque returned with the coats. Pitt and Arden brought him out into the street. They flanked him as they walked, but all was as deserted as if they were traversing moorland. The taste of the fog crept upon them, brackish, bitter and sour. "I am sorry for this night's news," de Rocque said presently. "No—that is to lie. France has endured much at your hands. But, *messieurs*, what of it? You have lost one small British army of six thousand men in surrender, true. But you have still thirty-two thousand effectives left out there under arms to your colours. It will take more than a Yorktown to make England quit the.field."

But, despite his words, some of the dejection of the city, its sullen and shuttered state was borne upon him. He asked in a puzzled voice, "Is it always thus quiet—so few lights?"

"We don't light our windows when we are beat, sir," Pepper Arden answered a little tartly.

"But you are not beat yet," de Rocque said in surprise. "*Mon Dieu*, have I not just said it?"

They had come to Covent Garden—once the Convent Garden because the nuns of Westminster had sold their fruit and flowers and herbs here. Customarily at this hour, it was a bustling spot, the stalls up to cater for the patrons of the Opera House. But no stall was left on the great central gravelled square of the Market—not a single rosy Kentish apple on offer, not a London woman selling her bowls of hot broth or porridge from the steps of the sundial, not one of the little braziers on which she heated her wares twinkling to light some life back into the cold shocked city. In the reek of fog and defeat there were only three other living beings in the great square—a young buck trying to persuade two hackney chairmen to take him to Great Swallow Street, the chairmen refusing, one saying sullenly, "I've no heart for carrying any tonight, sir, and that's flat."

De Rocque had fallen silent now. As they reached the Long Acre and the door of his lodgings he glanced back at the sad street and darkened windows. "So you are beat," he said on an intake of breath. "*Mon Dieu*, you are beat. It is over for you."

He thanked them and passed inside. Pitt and Pepper Arden were left to the groping journey back to Lincoln's Inn. Ahead of them a faint blur of light blinked and wandered. The Watch's hoarse voice came to their ears out of the fog,

"Eleven o'clock on a November night, and all's well."

"Does he say so?" Pepper Arden said. "He can't know what has come upon us on the Chesapeake."

XIII

ALL THAT winter the floods of disaster came sweeping in. Englishmen had always had a fierce and insular belief in themselves. From their long and lordly past they drew great reserves, believing themselves, in courage and endurance, at least the equal of any other nation. But they knew now that the untrained men of Breed's Hill and the hungry men of Valley Forge had stood longer to their guns. Not only was America slipping from the grasp of England, something other was going—a self-respect, a pride, a puissance, an intangible and precious thing.

North still struggled on in Downing Street. His once huge majorities in the Commons were dwindling. By 20th March, 1782, the country gentlemen and independents had quit him. The House crowded in to debate, Fox with the flush of victory upon him. Outside it was snowing and the flakes hissing against the great panes were the only things of softness and stealth against all the blaze and battle inside. None doubted now it was North's last night as Minister.

"We've got him," Pitt exulted to Wilberforce on the Opposition back benches. To these—the young and the callous—North's ten years of office were a lifetime, and they had small pity for one whose toil had ended in so huge a disaster.

North rose in his place. He knew that if he allowed the motion for his dismissal to be put it would be carried. For a little space he became again the skilled, decisive North of his early Ministry, fighting the Opposition for the floor of the House with a strength and determination all thought

America had crushed from him. He won, and tossed his resignation into the laps of his enemies.

They heard it with a wild acclaim. The debate, which all thought would last the night, was over in a few moments. The House came shouldering out into the lobby. Many late-comers, delayed by the snow, were still arriving, Henry Creuger among them, with the snow on his capes and on his boots. At the sight of the crowded lobby and the deserted chamber beyond he checked. The set strain which had lain on his face through the years of White Plains, Valley Forge, Guildford and Hobkirk's Hill eased like the lifting of a weight.

"'Tis all right, Creuger," Sir John Honeywood roared at him. "You've done it. You've won, you know."

"Felicitations, Creuger," Sutton said with a wry and bitter smile. "This is the end of the road from Concord."

"Thanks be to God for it, Amen," Creuger said in a still voice, and his American 'Ay-men', echoing where the 'Ah-mens' of England customarily rang, fell like the benediction of the snow against the ancient chapel windows of St. Stephen's.

The lobby was now a-seethe with peers and doorkeepers, public and reporters, even the vestibule and the stairs leading up to the greatcoat room jammed. "Come, gentlemen," came doorkeeper Pearson's stentorian bellow, "let the Minister pass."

"Ex-Minister," said North's placid voice.

He came through the press. His capes were swinging free so that the blaze of his star and the blue gleam of his Garter ribbon blinked on his breast under the candles. Yet he had no need of Orders this night. Calm, equable and smiling, he came on. The crowd cleaved to let him pass. Pitt and Fox were directly in his path by the vestibule steps. Both had harried him all their brief parliamentary lives. But they fell back out of his way, giving ground to him as before the splendour of an eastern potentate.

North went towards the door leading out into Old Palace Yard. At his heels were the two men most closely connected with him in the conduct of the war—his First Lord of the Admiralty, Sandwich, with his shambling, shuffling gait, and Germain following, with his striding Sackville hauteur. All three had the greyness of exhaustion on them but they kept face. Germain's glance fell upon Creuger standing just inside the vestibule. Of all England Germain had fought America the most implacably. He, who was still under sentence of cowardice, still, after twenty-two years, marked by the verdict of Minden that he could 'never again serve King and country in a military capacity', had fought this war as Third Secretary tooth and nail, as if to blot out the stigmas of the past. But even Germain acknowledged now the end had come. He made Creuger a brief, bitter bow and went past him into the dark and snow.

North turned on the threshold. His own carriage stood on the snowy cobbles of Old Palace Yard. But almost everyone else, believing the debate would last the night, had dismissed carriages and coachmen. North's glance went to his stranded enemies. He said with a hint of his old gentle humour, "You see, gentlemen, what it is to be in the secret."

He followed Germain and Sandwich out. Yet, as he went, it was as if many ghosts rose from the dark alleyways of Old Palace Yard—red-coated wraiths of Burgoyne's army and Cornwallis's—tramping after him through the swirl of the snow to lay down their arms and battle honours; and if the wind whipped back any snatch of music it was the fife and triumphant drums of *Yankee Doodle*.

XIV

"WELL, GOVERNOR," Pulteney said to his brother, Governor Johnstone, in the dark of Old Palace Yard. "Who's to be Boreas's successor?"

The wind and snow whipped about them. But the
Pulteney-Johnstones, disdaining the blizzard, had merely
wrapped their greatcoats about them and plunged out into
it. Behind them they left the Palace of Westminster as rowdy
as the hustings on the last day of polling—Pitt and Wilberforce and the younger ones celebrating the downfall of North
by singing songs mounted on the eating-house tables; Bellamy
serving them, but not at all pleased by the uproar, saying as
he moved from one to another, "I tell you plain, gentlemen,
I don't hold with this."

Fox's celebrations were as raucous. None doubted he
would continue his night at the gaming tables, among the
toasts and plaudits of his friends, and end it between soft
sheets and warm breasts.

"Boreas's successor?" Johnstone shouted back against the
wind. "No mystery there. It will be Rockingham—a nonentity—a man whom if I see him on Tuesday I have clean
forgot what he looks like by Wednesday."

He stepped for a moment into the shelter of a side door.
Above, the din and triumph of the eating-house thundered
out, making Westminster kin to a Thames-side tavern. Johnstone cast an angry upward snarl towards it. "God damn my
hide, it's a pretty exhibition is it not? These doting fathers
—they should have given their good offices earlier. Henry
Fox should have brought his wife to bed of a second son ten
years before he did and Chatham should have performed
the same service on Hester Grenville twenty years before he
came to do it. Then perhaps we might have had two with a
semblance of statesmanship in them at this hour instead of a
couple of spoilt and exhibitionist young cubs whose heads I
could clout."

"You are hard on them," his brother remarked. "They
both knew something of tyranny when they were boys."

"Tyranny!" Johnstone said on a growl. He broke into one
of his strange bastard half-British, half-New England oaths.
"Hell and tarnation, each was the apple of his father's eye."

"That is what I mean," Pulteney said. "That is where it lay—Fox, given all he wanted the instant he required it, brought to confuse the desire with the right. And what if he is denied the thing he desires above all others—the thing to which he believes he has a most just and unalienable right? What then, brother, what then?"

Johnstone was silent.

"As to Pitt," Pulteney went on. "What greater tyranny is there than the tyranny which says, 'Do this, or I, whom you love, will go mad.' That is what he grew up under, and it is a prison. It has the nearest aspect to lying in chains in a dungeon that I know. And I wonder, in truth, what compulsions Chatham has planted in him and how ruthlessly he will follow them."

"Well then, their fathers have marked them. But this is no hour for pity. Our country is dying on her feet, brother, and Rockingham is not the man for her deliverance."

"One, at least, of your spoilt and exhibitionist young cubs will be in cabinet at Rockingham's back," Pulteney said. "Fox."

He was proven right. In six days all fell out as predicted—Susan Weddell's Uncle Charles Rockingham stood Prime Minister of England; his First Secretary, Lord Shelburne; his Second, Charles James Fox.

XV

LATE ON a Saturday evening in April there was a pounding of knuckles at the door of Pitt's Lincoln's Inn chambers. Ralph Holmes, the old servant, put his head out of his own room, half-dressed, muttering, "Now, sir, now, who's this at this hour?"

Pitt also was in his shirtsleeves. He took a single candle and

made his way through the parlour to unbolt the outer door.
On the landing two figures stood, one with a lantern, the
other in handsome army scarlet, the gold of his colonel's
epaulettes square at his shoulders. The light roamed upon
the face of Pitt's elder brother. Four years had brought
John Chatham even closer in likeness to his father. Almost it
might have been the Great Commoner's face before high
politics and madness had ravaged it. The younger brother
saw it with a most poignant stab. He said on an intake of
breath, "John!"

"My faith, William, those stairs!" his brother remarked,
struggling for breath. "Did you not receive word from me
from Gibraltar that we were re-embarking?"

"Not a line—nought from you since January."

"Well then, I have made the passage home more successfully than did my letter."

He entered the room, followed by his own servant. Ralph
Holmes came hastening out of his bedroom, his waistcoat
on awry and half buttoned. Pitt rekindled the candles. As
the light sprang up Ralph seized John's hand, exclaiming,
"Why, Lord John, Lord John, you are your father's very
image."

There was much welcoming warmth now between all four,
though the two Pitts held it sternly by the throat in case the
emotion and the suddenness of the reunion overwhelmed
them. John's servant, Richard Lovell, had also been with the
family a long time. "Richard," Pitt said, taking his hand. "I'm
glad beyond measure to see you back."

"Glad be I to be back, Mr. William," the servant answered
in his rich Somerset accent. "Terrible strange place, Gibraltar. England be that green and that quiet after her."

The attic rooms, with their small hearths, were ill-
equipped for preparing even a light meal; nor were the
Portugal Street cookshops open at this hour. Pitt and Ralph
turned to the task of borrowing up and down the stairs and
about the scattered courts of Lincoln's Inn. Presently a cold

fowl, veal chops, a half cheese, a pie, butter and biscuits lay about the parlour table, half to be borne off to the servant's room for Richard Lovell, the other half left to John Chatham.

The elder brother ate, with a plain showing that at this moment he had little desire to talk. He pushed away his plate at length, saying, with a weary yawn, "William, I'm devilish fagged."

"The bed's ready for you in the next room, though you'll find it uncommon cramped and narrow."

"Better than a troop carrier, I'll warrant—flung against the bulkheads a dozen times a night, the Navy calling us damned lobsters and regarding it as sport." He yawned again. "I take it 'tis too narrow for the pair of us. What of you?"

"The chair will serve."

Once inside the bedroom the elder brother dragged off his scarlet coat and officer's bright polished gorget from about his throat then sat groaningly to wrestle with his boots. The younger stooped to assist him, straightening at length with the boots in his hand. John gave him a sharp, scanning glance. "You stand about six foot now, William. You've become taller than I."

"Does it make much matter?"

"None at all. I always were over-topped by my younger brother."

He had never before shown resentment for the other's attainments and gifts, lazily relieved he was not the son who had had to exert himself under the prick of Chatham's ambition. But he was stained, as all the British Army were, by disappointment and defeat. Yorktown touched them even here in the shadow of Lincoln's Inn, even after victory at Gibraltar. Nor was it only Yorktown. Four years and three bereavements lay between this present meeting and their last. It made their reunion hard and awkward.

All but one candle was snuffed. As they settled for the night, Pitt said, "Well, thank God you are safe and home."

Now in the dark they could speak a little of their loss. "But what of the three who are not safe and home?" John asked. "What of Hester?"

"She never regained her strength after the third babe. As to James, they did what they could—the flagship sent her own surgeon. But few men recover from the black vomit."

"And father?"

"He went five days after you sailed. In truth, you expected he would."

"Yes, I expected it. He commanded me to sail. I had better things to do, he said, than to weep over an old dying man. But he kept you. He had to have your voice in his ears at his dying. He had to assure himself there was still an England for the governing and still a Pitt to govern her."

The younger brother made an inarticulate mutter, shifting on his makeshift bed and propped cushions. John said in a curt voice, "He always was set for you to rule England, though whether it were but a sick man's fancy I have no means of knowing." He reached up and snuffed out the last candle by the bedhead. "Well, I have come into my inheritance, William—John, second Earl of Chatham, commissioned Lieutenant-Colonel in the soundly beat British Army, my estates a wondrous mess of debts and decay. If you ever come into yours it is likely to be in an even worse shape."

With extra horses procured from the livery stable in Holborn the two Pitts and Richard Lovell set out the next morning for Hayes. About them all the Sunday bells of the city were pealing. These at least were as proud as ever and they rang their lusty and incomparable clarions—the deep-toned, the measured and the gay—so that a Londoner could pick each one out of the air and name the church it spoke for.

"What of the other belles of London?" John asked. "For my part I always thought Tommy Townshend's daughter, Mary, took pride of place among them."

"You have not seen our new Yorkshire acquisition—Susan

Weddell, a connection of Rockingham. She's as fresh and pretty as if she had but stepped from one of Gainsborough's canvases."

There was a stiffening in his brother's face. No mention had been made of Mary Townshend in John's letters home. But plainly something had flowered here during the years under Gibraltar's frowning outcrop. Pitt made a clumsy retraction. "Though that is not to say that Mary Townshend is not equally so."

"God with us, must you try to humour me? I may have inherited the title. but not the affliction, I hope."

The servant, Richard Lovell, riding a few paces in the rear, let fall the Army valise from his saddle hook with a dusty thud into the roadway. He dismounted to retrieve it, saying in his Somerset accent, "Sorry be I for that, Lord John. Ride on. I'll catch thee up."

Both could remember his same soft voice saying over the butter churns in the dairy of Burton Pynsent, "His lordship no better then? Sorry be I for that, Lord John—sorry be I for that, Mr. William."

They rode on dutifully, as if they had still been boys. "Forgive that, William," John muttered at length. "You and mother had an exceedingly ill time of it."

"It doesn't signify."

Presently the houses of Hayes were about them, the church spilling out its congregation into the morning sunshine. Their mother stood with Harriet and Mrs. Sparry at the lychgate in conversation with old John Till, the rector. As her eldest son dismounted she ran to him and flung an arm about his shoulders. Against the black binding of the prayer book her knuckles showed white. But when she raised her face from his shielding epaulettes, it was calm again and tearless.

After the village had pressed about to offer greeting, they went on into the house. Harriet's old dog, Muff—blind now in one eye—was sprawled in front of the hearth in the library. She picked him up, stroking his silken neck and fondling him. "This is a right royal day, Muff," she said. "Everyone who loves me, safe under this one roof again."

"Everyone who loves you?" her younger brother remarked. "Ned Eliot would all but lose an eye too to have you use him as you are using Muff at this moment."

She nodded. But her face had taken on a gravity and a shadow and they spoke of it no more.

XVI

As IF to add to the land's ills, influenza swept her all that damp cold spring and early summer. The war still drifted, the new Prime Minister drifting with it. Sometimes there was the sense of having a grey ghost in Downing Street.

With July the fickle climate changed, leaping at one bound into high summer. Wilberforce and his two customary week-end guests, Pitt and Eliot, attempted an afternoon's fishing in Wimbledon Park Lake. But the great lake—cradled in willow and watermint—offered no sport. Only the cleaving brilliant blue of the kingfisher and the equal azure blue of the devil's-needle-dragonfly, trembling on the reeds, broke its glassy calm.

The fishermen gave up at length and turned back, taking the village right-of-way through the trees of Rockingham's mansion. Ahead there was a brush of skirts across the pine needles. Lady Rockingham's voice broke upon them. "Yes, yes, it is that hateful house—cold and draughty even in such sweltering weather as this. For my part I wish we had never gone back."

She was pacing with her half-sister, Mrs. Weddell— Susan's other aunt—and Susan herself, in billowing summer skirts and straw hat. The two older women passed with brief bows. But Susan lingered to impart the day's news. "Did you know my Uncle Charles Rockingham has influenza?

The Italians would say it were all due to the influence of the stars. But in my uncle's case damp Downing Street and the strain of the war are much more likely." They expressed hopes for Rockingham's quick recovery and she added, "They are bringing him out here this afternoon. The physicians tell us the country air may well restore him."

She followed the two older women, the three young men continuing on their way. A few moments later a carriage turned in at the lodge and jolted past them to halt at the portico. Susan, Mrs. Weddell and Lady Rockingham all ran over to it; the servants gathered round; a chair was brought out. Lowered into it, piled with rugs, grey-complexioned, pallid, sweating, his eyes closed against the sun's brightness, Rockingham was borne up the steps into his house. In the midst of the hot flushed ruddy faces all about him he looked a dead man already.

The three passers-by, their aid not required, watched much appalled. Pitt had gone as white as if he too were ailing. Throughout the rest of the day Wilberforce found him a silent guest, brooding on what news might come out of Rockingham House. But the country air seemingly did all that was expected of it. By Sunday afternoon Rockingham was reported much mended.

Wilberforce, on Monday, brought his guests out to an early breakfast on the lawn, all three in boots and spurs in readiness for their journey back to London. The scene was very fair. Before them lay the Common, its ponds and trees young when Elizabeth Tudor had hunted stag among them; on the one hand the pretty village melting into the summer woods in thatch and brown and red tile; on the other the gentle blur of the Surrey hills; the Queen Anne houses, their gardens deep in roses, the waxy blooms of their water-lilies turned now to ivory or pale pink, curved crescentwise about the broad bay of grass. Pitt's preoccupation with this sunlit scene seemed great. "That's a deep reverie, Billy," Eliot remarked presently.

Pitt stirred and said, "I was thinking that one day doubtless I'll look back at being sat with you both at breakfast on the lawn at Wimbledon, among the green peapods and the strawberries, and say it was my happiest hour."

"You'll know many moments of triumph before you are done," Wilberforce said with a sharp glance at him.

Pitt answered with a faint smile, "But triumph is something different."

On a sudden the bell of St. Mary's, Wimbledon broke the summer stillness in slow and measured peal. Before the meaning fully broke upon them Wilberforce's groom came round the corner of the house, leading the three horses.

"So he's gone then—his lordship," he said, with a jerk of the head towards the church steeple. "Hatchment's out above t'door at Rockingham House yonder." He saw their astonished shock and added in his earthy Yorkshire vowels, as if wholly to explain Rockingham's fate, "He were t'Minister. It's a killing job, my masters."

XVII

ROCKINGHAM WAS succeeded by his First Secretary, the Earl of Shelburne, a man of brilliant intellect, but devious and difficult, disliked and distrusted. For all they stood the same ground politically, Fox could not abide him. He served under him three weeks, then quarrelled and quit the cabinet. Many hoped it was a temporary rift—not least Shelburne himself. Beset by mounting troubles, he would have given much to win Fox back once more.

London was subdued this summer of defeat. But on the last Wednesday in July—it being the occasion of Mary Townshend's coming of age—the Townshends drove with their daughter to Ranelagh Pleasure Gardens, taking with them as guests the two Pitts and their sister. John Chatham was openly laying suit to Mary Townshend now. But it seemed a halting, hesitant courtship, not pressed forward over-rapidly by the suitor, nor perhaps hotly encouraged by the parents.

At the interval, after Mrs. Farrell had sung of her 'Yellow-Haired Laddie', and Gregario Patria had set aside his flute, Mary Townshend and Harriet Pitt left the Townshends' table to walk. Ranelagh admitted all who proffered the half-crown entrance fee. About the great centre piece of the Rotunda, with its festoons of flowers, painted masks, fiddles and flutes, was circling a strolling mass of dukes and marquises, chandlers, grocers, housekeepers, professional whips and pugilists. At one of the tables Susan was seated with her aunt, Mrs. Weddell. Their presence was surprising to some since Rockingham had been dead no more than a month. But, as usual, Miss Weddell had a flock of young men about her. She waved to Mary, then unexpectedly abandoned her clustering followers, coming up to ask, "What occasions your visit here tonight, Miss Townshend?"

"My coming of age," Mary answered simply.

"My faith, I wish it were mine. Think—you can wed any man in the kingdom now and your parents won't be able to do a jot about it."

"Yes, I can, can't I?" Mary said, with a faint flushed glance towards John Chatham still seated at the Townshends' table in his colonel's scarlet.

She presented Harriet. The three girls walked on together, passed the wall tables with their painted harlequinade back-cloths of shy Columbines and their swinging lamps. From one of them a woman's voice remarked penetratingly, "Is not that Mary Townshend, the new Secretary of State's daughter?"

"Oh, I can't endure being pointed at," Mary muttered. She was a reserved, gentle-voiced girl, not too robust. "You two continue without me."

She fled back to the anonymity of her parents' table.

"Well, Miss Townshend is altogether contrary to me," Susan said, advancing again. "I like the looks."

Harriet smiled. "You don't lack them at all, Miss Weddell."

"But what when I am forty and grown fat? If they look upon me at all then it will be because I have secured a notable husband." She frowned down upon the dark mourning ring on her finger. "Lord Rockingham was a kind protector to me. It is not that I don't mourn him. But I mind exceedingly in case I finish as some dull apothecary's wife, as my grandmother did, weighing out scruples and minims with a jar of slimy leeches beside me, and not a head to turn when I and my dull husband go into the pump room at Scarborough."

Harriet's name was spoken. Edward Eliot came eagerly down the gallery stairs, his three younger brothers with him.

"You here, Mr. Eliot?" Harriet said.

"As you see—burdened with my brothers, though."

The four young men bowed to Susan but their attention was set upon the tall, graceful Pitt girl. Edward Eliot especially could not take his eyes from her. Susan, noting it, said in a voice of growing boredom, "Well, Lady Harriet, I will leave you to your admirers."

She turned to rejoin hers. The matting caught at her heel. As at Rockingham House the overlarge shoe with its brilliant buckle was dragged from her foot, this time to lie close to Pitt. He had it in his hand before the rest of her waiting court could seize upon it.

"Demme, ma'am," remarked the young buck who had dogged Miss Weddell about Rockingham House and was now dogging her about Ranelagh, drawing his handkerchief across his lips. "There'll be no offers this time to toast your divine eyes from that trophy—members of Parliament being most deucedly concerned that they don't demean themselves under the public gaze. To own the truth, I've never myself toasted any lady in public. But I would do it now, by God, if yonder gentleman will but bestow the trophy on me."

An interested cluster of Ranelagh patrons, of all degrees and social levels, were now keenly observing them. The buck put out his hand, as assured as the rest that no member of Parliament or any other in the public eye would drink this manner of toast in a London Pleasure Garden. But Susan Weddell's much-admired looks and straight-speaking Yorkshire tongue had done their work on Pitt. A waiter, passing with a tray, proffered a bottle of madeira. Receiving no check, he tipped a minute quantity into the heel of the shoe and went grinningly on. Pitt raised the shoe first towards the lady and then to his lips. "Lord, Mr. Simpkins," one of the onlookers remarked to her husband in a cheerful wheeze of Cockney vowels. "How nice! How romantical!"

Miss Weddell's face lit with an evident delight. But there was little delight elsewhere. John Chatham had risen to his feet at the Townshends' table with a brow of thunder. At a little distance Tommy Townshend, strolling about the Rotunda, came striding back. He too looked less than pleased and he broke in upon the group. saying sharply, "Come, 'tis ten o'clock, and the music's done. We'll get back to Albemarle Street and drink Mary's health there."

The Pitts, joined now by the Eliots, were borne back to Albemarle Street in the Townshend carriage. The ladies gathered about Mary, admiring her birthday gifts, the young men serving the golden peachy punch, fragrant in its great bowl. Edward Eliot came at once to stand behind Harriet's chair.

"It was a good Ranelagh tonight, was it not?" she said, turning her head. "Signor Patria's fingering of the flute is dazzling to me."

"I did not notice."

She laughed. "Did not notice? Mr. Eliot, where were you looking?"

He said steadily, "At you."

"Well, indeed, there's no law against it," she answered in a quiet voice. "But perhaps it is a little profitless."

Pitt and Tommy Townshend had been absent from the gathering about the punch bowl. As they came back into the room John Eliot—the second of the Eliots—glanced round to remark to Townshend, "We're remiss, sir. We should have felicitated you on your appointment as the new Secretary of State."

"Don't leave William from your felicitations," Townshend said goodhumouredly. "We have just been discussing the matter, with myself as Lord Shelburne's emissary. William here will kiss hands tomorrow as the new Chancellor of the Exchequer, so use him courteously or he will clap a tax on your hair ribbons or pocket watches as soon as regard you."

"Oh, my dear brother," Harriet exclaimed in much delight, squeezing her brother's arm as if she could scarcely bear to let it go. Edward Eliot's face had lightened with an equal pleasure. Only the elder brother stood silent.

The guests at length were borne off to their various lodgings, Harriet by means of the Townshends' carriage to her friend, Lady Williams. Mary remained by the hearth, her head bowed over the punch bowl with its golden dregs.

"I saw you promenading with Miss Weddell, Mary," Mrs. Townshend said presently. "With all her beaux she does not bother much about her own sex as a rule. What had she to say?"

'Only that now I may please myself as to whom I wed."

Her mother and father exchanged a glance above her bent head. "I hope you know what you are doing, miss," Townshend said.

She answered with uncharacteristic vehemence, "Yes, I do. John has told me—he has been altogether honest. It will be all right."

She went quickly from the room. "It always will be all right when one is but twenty-one," Townshend remarked bleakly.

"Perhaps there is no cause for concern, my love," Mrs. Townshend said. "The Pitt children seem well enough to me—though with one in his colonel's regimentals and the other about to become a Minister of the Crown, it seems ridiculous to call them children now."

"It was a juvenile exhibition at Ranelagh tonight, none-theless," Townshend said in a grim voice. He rubbed his long lugubrious chin that the cartoonists allowed their pencils to dwell on pleasurably. "Shelburne is taking the devil's own risk appointing a boy of twenty-three to the Exchequer. My lord's had doubts enough over this appointment. He'll have more, mark it, when he hears of the Ranelagh nonsense this evening. But there are advantages. We want peace with America and William will be wholehearted as to that. And we want Fox back in the cabinet and William will be wholehearted as to that too. Damn me if I know why Fox ever went, save these confounded personalities began to creep in."

"I own I like to think of William moving into Number 11," Mrs. Townshend remarked. "The place is full of roses just now."

"It is not, you know," Townshend said lugubriously.

The hackney bore both Pitts through a midnight London. They mounted the steep stairs at Lincoln's Inn in silence, as they had sat in the hackney in silence, John with so lowering a brow his brother might have been arraigned for treason rather than appointed to cabinet.

Inside with the bolts shot behind them they regarded each other. Pitt said at length, "When I drank the toast I thought I were still a private member."

"And if you had been—or even now as temporary Chancellor of the Exchequer in what all consider is Shelburne's temporary Government—why, with your lack of coal and candles, your truckle bed, your one servant, I scarce think you could support the daughter of a tallow merchant in any degree of comfort as your wife. As to a girl accustomed to Rockingham's staterooms but with none of the entailed Rockingham wealth to supply a dowry for her—you could not support her little finger." He asked shortly, "Does she attract you?"

"She attracts half the men in London. Yes, she attracts me."

"But not overmuch. Nor do you attract her overmuch. She has placed her wager on you—in the same fashion as the rest of her circle stake at faro—that you'll have the heads turning one day." He tossed his greatcoat angrily upon the nearest chair. "Chancellor of the Exchequer or not, you're still an impoverished second son, landless, and like to spend a deal more time unpaid on the back benches. If you intend marriage now, it had best be with a marvellous rich wife. As to the other—an illicit relationship with some dairymaid, begetting bastards as Fox has done, two certainly, four as they tattle it in the coffee houses—that was not my way, nor yours, I think, nor, by large, the way of our House. Fox, too, has the means to support mistresses and bastards. You have not."

"I know that. I can wait." He added, with a small break in his reserve. "You are right. I should have left her public toasts to her lisping fop."

"It were a damned fool action—witless enough for a private member, trebly so for a Minister of the Crown. But, my faith, you do these things—you go along steadily and with judgment for a time, then you do something that is utter rash. Impetuous Mr. William, that was what our nurse called you when we were children." He took up a candle and turned towards the bedroom, saying over his shoulder, "One day you are going to make a laughing-stock of us all."

XVIII

The next day Pepper Arden, meeting Pitt on the stairs, pressed his hat athwart his heart and made as though to drop on one knee, remarking, "Good morning, your grace, my lord and sir."

"You become more of a prize idiot every day, Pepper," the new Chancellor of the Exchequer answered with ingratitude and passed on.

Ministerially the Chancellorship of the Exchequer was a somewhat lowly position, not carrying with it full cabinet rank. Pitt could not attend cabinet meetings unless expressly ordered to do so by Shelburne. But the Chancellor's official house, Number 11, Downing Street, was almost as fine as Number 10 next door, its roses sprawling over the wall to mingle with Shelburne's in much fragrance and colour.

Shelburne was a difficult man to serve; a still more difficult man to love. He, who had known so little affection as a boy, was never free now from the need of attempting to awaken it. He complimented men overmuch to their faces, then, when the answering warmth did not come, rent them as soon as they quit his presence. His cabinet found him feline, fawning upon them one moment, clawing them the next. But they could not but approve the strange vein of public courage in him that had set him adamantly on peace with America.

As Townshend had surmised, Shelburne heard the tale of Miss Weddell's shoe and was not elated thereby. He referred to it the next afternoon walking with Townshend down the Long Gallery. "In a London pleasure garden—with half Battersea and the whole of Hackney Wick gaping at him? It was scarce ministerial conduct. Perhaps I—or you—should inform him so."

"I hardly think it is necessary," Townshend replied uncomfortably. "He did not know then of his appointment and in any case it was uncharacteristic of him."

"It was, in truth," Shelburne said, with his acid smile. "For my part I always thought the boy was conceived in an Arctic snowstorm, unlike his father who was so great a play-actor he must certainly have been conceived in a property basket backstage at Drury Lane. Still, you have hopes of him, Townshend, and, of all men's, yours is the discernment I most value."

This, as Townshend suspected, was not how Shelburne spoke of him in private and his long face lengthened yet further. They had come into the lobby of the House of Commons. Ahead Sir John Honeywood's voice thundered out upon them. "Devilish odd Shelburne and Fox falling out. Sutton here says Fox hit Shelburne in the eye. Going a trifle far, is it not? I expect Shelburne will call him out."

"Heaven witness for me, I never did," Sutton groaned. "I said Fox and Shelburne both let fly." He roared into Sir John's ear trumpet, "I said they let fly."

"Well, it don't matter which eye, I suppose," Honeywood roared back. "I should think Shelburne is regretting by now poor Rockingham snuffed it."

Two spots of angry colour had appeared on Shelburne's high and handsome cheekbones. "Our deaf and witless knight yonder is correct in that," he said. "Rockingham has bequeathed me a veritable Pandora's box of troubles. And our Achilles—Charles James Fox—sulks in his tent at Wimbledon."

XIX

BY CHRISTMAS Shelburne's cabinet resembled a ship-of-the-line whose officers fully approved the course their captain was steering but who nevertheless simmered with mutiny in the wardroom. All the men who served under him chafed at him. As the groans of "what have I done to deserve Shelburne?" echoed nightly in the parlours of Albermarle Street, his new Chancellor of the Exchequer dubbed him, in private, 'Chief Kickensick'. Shelburne owed the nickname in part to the visit of the Mohican chiefs to Chatham some sixteen years back. The Pitt children had never before seen such painted finery, such proud feathers and bright beads against the background of the Surrey downs. Shelburne's hard, high cheekbones, with their daubs of angry colour, brought the occasion back to mind.

Fox was in no better case, weary of lack of office, his great talents languishing. He had purchased Rockingham House from the dead man's estate. The mansion was back to its high Whig living again. But his friends marked that he took small pleasure in the routs, the gaming and the company.

"What is it, Charles?" the Duchess of Devonshire asked, seated at cards with him. "Do not tell me any bed in London is denied you?"

"The bed in Downing Street is denied me."

"You will come to it presently. Who is there to stop you?"

"No man," he answered but his voice had the inflection of a groan. "Ultimately, no man, sweet. But time advances and I am thirty-five."

"La, Charles, what age is that? In any case all London believes Shelburne will approach you before Easter."

Shelburne made the expected approach in the February of that year, 1783. For nine months he had had Pitt beside him, urging Fox's claims, and it was Pitt whom he despatched to ride up the long drive where, in the blaze of high summer, Rockingham had been brought to die. The string of race horses was coming in from exercise on the Common, Fox watching from the foot of the terrace. He greeted Pitt, then turned back to the old groom, greatly bowed in leg and shoulder, who was leading in his grey, Seagull. "My friend, Mrs. Crewe, keeps telling me she wants to ride the Gull."

"She will break her neck if she does, sir," the old man answered bluntly. "There's not a woman now in England that could ride that horse, though there was twenty years gone. Your mother, sir, I reckon," he said, turning to Pitt, "for there's a likeness. Does she still ride, sir—Lady Hester Grenville?"

"Not now—not these past ten years."

"Aye, pity—pity," the old man said. "Held the palm, she did, just like your father held it when it came to bringing us the victories."

A faint flick of displeasure crossed Fox's face. He led the way up the terrace and into the great withdrawing room, turning to shut the french windows behind them. "Well, William," he said. "How is my lord and his calamitous peace?"

Pitt's heart sank a little. Once it had been North and his calamitous war. Now it was Shelburne and his calamitous peace. "For my part I trust Lord Shelburne to secure us the best terms possible."

"You are alone, then, if you trust him in any matter. Consider what they dub him in the coffee houses—Malagrida—the Jesuit of Berkeley Square. If he says it is a fine day men look from the window to see how torrentially it rains. If he says it is not the end of the world, they cock their ears for the trump of judgment. Since we speak in confidence, I must own to it, I can't abide the fellow."

"But on public issues he's a brave man. He sticks to his guns and they are your guns too, Charles."

"No, forgive me, William," Fox said after a frowning pause, "but I'll not return to Government so long as the Jesuit continues to head it. I wearied of him in three weeks last time. Cavendish wearied of him in four. Richmond in eight. Grafton in ten. Indeed if you value your own career it may be you should weary of him yourself before he drowns you in the sea of his own unpopularity."

Some image of lonely, assailed Shelburne—struggling to make his defeated peace, craving a loyalty he never believed there—rose to trip Pitt into tactlessness at that moment. He said shortly, "I have not come here to betray Lord Shelburne."

Fox's black brows came together. He saw it was a young man's remark, regretted as soon as voiced. But he could not forgive its Chatham-like hauteur. "Well, then, we have nothing more to say to each other. Your horse is yonder and I am otherwise engaged."

He walked from the room. Pitt stood shaken by his own clumsiness. He took a step after Fox but he knew he could not, for the moment, right matters. There remained only the walk back down the terrace steps and the self-reproaching ride into Wimbledon village.

At Lauriston House Pitt spilled out the woes of the afternoon to Wilberforce. "That I should say such a damned blundering thing. In the House I can find the right expression, as a rule. But in the salons and drawing rooms—my faith—there are times when I put my foot in it to monstrous great effect."

"But that you had not gone there to betray Lord Shelburne was a plain statement of fact, was it not?" Wilberforce remarked mildly.

"Oh, don't be an idiot, Will. It was the choice of phrase—though I meant nothing against Charles's honour, God knows. Still, he has much good nature. He'll not hold it long against me, I daresay." He drew his greatcoat about him. "But he will not come back to Government so long as Shelburne heads it. I have not hardened his attitude there for it was as adamant from the first. And I scarce know how we will get the peace terms through the House if he throws his weight against them."

XX

DUNDAS, INVITED to Shelburne's weekly dinner party at Number 10, was chagrined to find himself asked there half an hour before the other guests, and further chagrined when he was conducted up towards the library and studies—the working womb of the building—rather than taken to one of the withdrawing rooms downstairs. Such marks of favour could only mean Shelburne was going to attempt to win him into the ranks of Government. Dundas had little intention of being won, there being no feel of success here.

He was brought into the great library. Shelburne was standing at the door of the secretary's room talking with Pitt. He broke off as Dundas was announced, saying, "Why, Dundas, you'll bring a breath of good invigorating Scottish air to my dinner-table this afternoon, I don't doubt. Go through to the study, will you. I'll join you in but a moment."

Dundas went past the two men, through the secretary's room and into the Minister's larger study. Behind him he caught one or two snatches of Shelburne's final remarks to Pitt. "Well, if Achilles refuses to quit his tent we can do nothing more about it. I know he loves me about as little as the devil is said to love holy water. I am certain you did all in your power. It astonishes me how early your father's skills and talents have flowered in you."

These courtesies—as often with Shelburne—rang hollowly. Dundas could see the Pitt defences beginning to stick out like spikes on a palisade.

He stood waiting. Shelburne came in presently, shutting the door and setting his back to it. He said with an acid wrath, "I should, in truth, have known better than to entrust that matter to Pitt's diplomacy—or lack of it."

"There are many nights in the House when he does you good service, my lord."

"So I am constantly being told," Shelburne said in a tone that was close to a sneer. "The boy is brilliant, I have no doubt. He must have been managing a department from his mother's womb. But he has not the least idea how to carry the personal approach." He turned to the window to survey his wintry, dun-coloured domain. "He's an icy cub. As you perceive by that remark I repose great confidence in your discretion and an equal confidence in your tacit agreement.

I but voice your own opinion of him, do I not?"

Dundas shifted uncomfortably. "I judge him cold likewise. But there are times when I possess a great fancy to see him wi' the odds against him and the pressures mounting, for I think he would be as his father—a bonny fighter."

"Indeed?" Shelburne remarked with a lift of brow. "Well, he will have plenty of opportunity to show his prowess in that respect when Fox gets his teeth into the peace preliminaries yonder."

His glance went to his desk. A sheaf of documents lay there, pressed down by a vast paper weight, the seals fallen to the lengths of their ribbons and dangling over the desk's edge. Dundas turned his look in the same direction, then back to Shelburne again. "Yes, Dundas," Shelburne said. "From Paris, this morning—the draft of the peace preliminaries." He stood regarding the scarlet ribbons spilling from the desk like trickles of English blood shed to no purpose in this lost war. "And I sit here—the first man ever to sign a beaten peace in this house since it were laid brick on brick —to dole out the rewards and the penalties, and I shall not be loved for it. To the Americans, their independence and a vast slice of our trade. To France, Holland and Spain, their several pounds of flesh. To ourselves, why, the Latin tag is *vae victus*, is it not?"

"Grief to the vanquished. Well, my lord, there's no way for us but to scrabble up again off our hands and knees."

"And you think we will?" Shelburne said thinly. "This is a strange building, Dundas. One can feel the winds and the tides, the pulse and the breathing. And I scarce like what I feel. There is a sickroom smell here, and for my part I do not relish the thought of the future."

XXI

Fox, THE next night, came into Pulteney's box at Covent
Garden Opera House at the end of·the performance. It was
raining hard outside and Pulteney's wife and daughter were
pulling on their cloaks and hoods preparatory to leaving.
"Take the carriage, my love," Pulteney remarked to his wife.
"I will come on foot later."

After the ladies had gone Fox leant upon the balustrade,
looking down into the well of the theatre. "Pulteney," he
said at length. "I desire your opinion. I talked with North
this morning—our fourth meeting within the week. We both
hold the time has come to unite our parties and rid the
land of Shelburne."

Pulteney said in a steady voice, "Between you and North
—a Coalition?"

"As you say—a Coalition."

"I hold it a most revolting compact."

"I take that phrase very ill," Fox answered sharply.

Pulteney gave him a straight look. "What else can I call
it? You have spat blood at North—no less—for ten years—
'that monstrous man, that lump of disease and deformity
in a blue ribbon, that animal full of vice and folly.' You said
publicly in the House that if you ever made terms with him
you would rest satisfied to be called the most infamous of
mankind. I was sat there and heard it."

"God with us, Pulteney, the country's deep in crisis. I
would have thought it were a time to forgo old quarrels."

"You did not argue so when Saratoga and Yorktown were
upon us."

Fox turned, his face dark with anger, and put his hand to
the door of the box. Pulteney called him back with so concerned an urgency all was checked. "Charles, this time wait.
You will injure yourself. You will injure the land. Shelburne
is your man here. He stands the ground you stand on. He

speaks with your voice. Many think that were you to return to cabinet as his First Secretary presently—presently—Downing Street will be yours in full sovereignty. What impediment do you yourself discern in that?"

"No impediment," Fox answered. He came back to Pulteney's chair and set a hand on the back rest. "But I desire it now, Pulteney—not in five years or in six. My powers are coming to their full growth. I have searched my heart and I believe I am in truth most fitted for office at this time. And to be denied it is to roast in hell."

"You were brought up to find any denial a roasting in hell, Charles," Pulteney said with weary grimness. "God help you. If any man should ever come between you and what you want, I do not know whom I should pity the more— you or he."

XXII

LITTLE WIMBLEDON, with Fox residing there and North not too far distant at Bushy, heard the whispers of a Coalition before great London did. Wilberforce, coming into Westminster that evening, sought out Pitt and Eliot beside the lobby fire and gave them the tally of the rumours that were now flying southside and westside the Common. Pitt whipped round upon him and said, "Rubbish! Charles would be hanged at Tyburn before he joined hands with Boreas."

"Your Charles was brought up to get what he desired," Wilberforce answered. " 'Here's the tinder box, Charles, since you would make a bonfire of your father's state papers. Do you desire the most expensive whore in Paris and a night at the gaming tables? Here's five hundred guineas. Since you have a fancy for smashing the Sèvres clock, yonder's the poker.' Now he wants Downing Street. What, in truth, did you suppose would come about?"

"God with us, Will, you talk the most arrant drivel at times."

They had both raised their voices. "Oh, come," Eliot said. He was by far the most peaceable and placable of the three, able, as a rule, to quiet the sudden storms that blew up here. "Why quarrel when all will be self-evident in a day or two? One of you will be proven right."

"The other will have some hard apologising to do," Wilberforce remarked.

"Well, it will not be I," Pitt said, and turned away.

When the House rose, about midnight, Dundas, after a hesitation, came over to Pulteney. They walked together, as by mutual consent, out into the west walk of the cloisters, the square of grass here invisible now in the dark, but smelling this night of rain and the chill of winter.

"Pulteney," Dundas said. "North came to see me at my house in Wimbledon this morning. You ken what's going on, I take it?"

Pulteney said with a brief nod, "Shelburne must be told before this breaks upon him publicly. You have been his dinner guest at Number 10. Will you shoulder the task?"

"Aye, I'll do it." Dundas added dourly, "At this hour, wi' the peace commissioners in Paris trying to secure terms that will no' entirely grind us under, they might well ha'e stood by the Jesuit. Still I'm no' the one to sermonise. I quit all when the wind began to blow in their faces."

"You would be a man of infinite loyalty, Dundas," Pulteney said. "If you could but find a captain."

No man had called Dundas loyal before. He was left to the bite of the wind through the cloisters, the patch of night sky and his own astonishment.

XXIII

THUS AGAIN Dundas made the journey to Number 10,

brought up through the great library with its splendid red carpet and Turkey sofa and chairs, draped in a pale, sweet green, through the secretary's room and into the Minister's larger study. His news imparted, and with Pitt summoned from Number 11 next door and Tommy Townshend from Albermarle Street, he waited in the secretary's room. From the Minister's study came the muted sounds of anxious discussion, the words indistinguishable, until, as it seemed, Shelburne had paced carelessly too near the door. His voice reached Dundas. "The Scotsman wants us to plant a standard in the heather. He would not rally to it himself. He might say, 'go on, my brave boys', in private. He would not say, 'come on, my brave boys', in public."

It was so close to the truth that Dundas hardly resented it. He moved back out of earshot. On the secretary's desk lay the peace preliminaries, its seals affixed, and this—his second sight of the sad document—pricked and roused his Lowland blood. He longed for Shelburne to stand and do battle with the Coalition, not from any prospect of victory, but that there might be no more striking of colours.

Pitt and Townshend came out at length, grave-faced, nodding briefly to Dundas as they passed. He was summoned presently back into the Minister's study. Shelburne stood by the window, his eyes on his dusky garden. Dundas found himself neither looked at nor addressed. He himself broke the silence, asking, "My lord, is it the end o' your tenure here?"

"What other, Dundas, for God's sake?" Shelburne snarled. There were no compliments this night. The tiger's claws were out; its tail lashing. "The man with the haft of the knife protruding from between his shoulder blades does not continue to function as if nought had occurred."

"The King will no' love this Coalition, nor will the country, were she to slough off her sickness and apathy. At least delay. Hold back your resignation three weeks—a sennight. Gi'e the independents and men o' the shires time to gain their breaths."

"To what end, Dundas?" Shelburne said in a bitter voice. "That I might rally men to me—Malagrida—the Jesuit of Berkeley Square?" Below, in the dusk, Pitt was making his way towards the garden gate which linked Number 10 and Number 11. Shelburne's glance was on him, the bitterness sharpening in him. "Most men have affection in their childhoods. I had none. I began to crave it as some men crave strong drink or others crave a woman for their beds. I loaded men with compliments. I bowed or smiled or wrung their hands. But the men did not come. And yonder young Pitt. He scarce knows the meaning of the word 'compliment'. If he ever bowed to win a vote or gain a follower I believe he would go and vomit afterwards. Yet the men came to the father and I am not sure but that they might not come to the son—who, in my estimation, could chill an icicle—were he to stand one day where Chatham stood. And this gift, which I would have valued beyond all others, has been denied me."

He took out his keys, moving sharply to unlock the desk drawer. Dundas said, with urgency, "My lord—"

"No, Dundas," Shelburne answered savagely. "I am done with this battle."

He tossed the Treasury seals on to the desk top. They lay there like the sword surrendered after the lost fight or the coronation ring taken from a King's dead hand.

Tommy Townshend was still pacing about the hall when Dundas came down the stairs. They sent their carriages clattering off into Whitehall, while they themselves walked, turning in the opposite direction through the little postern gate into St. James's Park. The Park was no place to walk in the dark without escort. Townshend's two postillions went ahead, one cradling his pistol, the other with lanthorn and stick.

"If this is politics I have had enough," Townshend said presently. "I am going back to Frognal to grow barley and breed Jersey cattle. Our new masters will want young William though—he's too good to leave out."

Dundas remarked with a degree of envy, "Chatham's son—the silver spoon."

"Oh, yes, yes. A whole succession of public triumphs, but they're a damned bedevilled unfortunate family, nonetheless. The Pitt Diamond—it looks very fine and glistening but there's a flaw in it." He added, "You know his elder brother is betrothed to my girl, Mary. If they indeed go through with this match, I can but hope there's no children."

"Bairns are a great cost to the pocket, to be sure," Dundas said in a puzzled voice. "But their fortunes may recover."

Townshend fell instantly silent. On their right the lighted pile of Buckingham House blazed out upon them into the night. Dundas drew a long breath. "I would ha'e gi'en much to see Shelburne make a fight o' it."

"Oh, my dear Dundas," Townshend said. "The days are gone when anyone in these islands did battle against the odds. Now we reach for the white flag and go blindfold across the lines."

XXIV

THERE WAS no longer any doubt as to collusion—Fox and North together at the opera, together at one another's houses, together when they came down to the Commons. Pitt and Tommy Townshend went grimly in to the Treasury Bench. For these few nights they must still sit there, propping as best they might the dying hulk of Shelburne's Government.

Pitt's grief was all for Fox. But at one in the morning, with the tired and fretful Government benches about him, and himself tired and fretful, it was Sheridan he took it out upon, rising to follow Sheridan and rending the latter's stage connections with a schoolboy's angry burst of spleen. He had never before made a bad speech in the House. But he contrived with this to make up for all. Sheridan was too nimble-witted not to carry the bout. He rose up from the Opposition front bench and remarked with a droll calm, "I will not comment on those personal allusions—their propriety, taste and gentlemanly point must be obvious to the House. However, if I should ever again undertake a dramatic composition let me assure the right honourable gentleman opposite that, encouraged by his remarks and with him in mind, I might be tempted to improve on one of Ben Jonson's best characters—the Angry Boy in *The Alchemist*."

"You merited that cuff, William," Tommy Townshend said wearily as the laughter and the cheers for Sheridan filled the chamber.

The House filed out, Wilberforce walking with Eliot. Pitt was waiting by the lobby fire. The two doorkeepers were still here—Jessel blowing a little last life into the coals with the bellows, and Pearson surlily locking his gin cupboard for the night. Pitt called, "Will."

Since the previous day there had been no speech between them. Wilberforce stopped but did not answer. Pitt went on, "I own to it you were right. The arrant drivel was mine, not yours."

Still Wilberforce's expression did not relax. Pearson and Jessel both had their ears cocked to catch all they could of what was seemingly the certain quarrel. A cast of anxiety came into Eliot's face. Pitt pressed on, making an attempt here he would not have made for any other man. "You said one of us would have some hard apologising to do. Why then, how hard would you make it? Sheridan has already taken me down a whole bushel of pegs in the House, but if you desire to kick the remainder of my pride about the lobby—well do so."

"Oh, you idiot," Wilberforce said, breaking into a smile. "Come and dine with me tomorrow. The Yorkshire pie will be none the worse for having been baked in a Surrey oven."

Shelburne resigned the next day, his cabinet following him in twos and threes. The appalled King learnt what had come about. He would have had any Government but this—any men but these. He tried to press Shelburne to stay and fight, and when Shelburne would not, cast about almost wildly for some man who would. Even his one-time Chancellor of the Exchequer—at twenty-three—was offered the seals and the tenancy of Downing Street, though he refused them as had the rest.

By evening, with the snow brushing idly against the windows of Lauriston House, Wilberforce heard the clatter of the knocker and the voice of his housekeeper, Mrs. Hewlett, greeting Pitt like a mother.

"Come in, and welcome," Wilberforce said, as the door was opened for his visitor.

"Am I so? I began to think I had taxed our friendship over-much in the lobby the other night."

"It is no more but that you sometimes have a sort of southern conceit."

"You mean a Grenville conceit, do you not? Well enough. Keep it in its place." He looked appreciatively at the fire stacked with its logs. "There's a marvellous warmth in your pleasant parlour after the atmosphere at Windsor, growing chillier minute by minute as first one and then another of us refused the seals."

"I would have been glad had the King found a man to challenge the Coalition," Wilberforce said slowly. "I wish, in truth, you had a few more years and a party at your back."

His guest said with a fine Pittite disgust, "No, don't wish the latter upon me—not a party. Always patting its head and keeping it sweet, always feeding it banquets in the Speaker's dining room and tossing it compliments and patronage—a little lapdog thing running after me into the lobby, not because it believes in my measures but because it is my party. My father never loved party. And as for you—if in truth I had a party, you would have none of it if it meant setting aside your convictions."

Mrs. Hewlett bore in the Yorkshire pie, very appetising in its fine brown crust. They ate somewhat silently, their thoughts returning to the day's politics and the land's new masters. "The Coalition will want you," Wilberforce remarked at length, his words almost those of Tommy Townshend to Dundas. "You have too much talent to leave out."

"Am I to go to them thus tamely, Will?" Pitt said.

He was sitting regarding his plate, his upper lip drawn down. Wilberforce knew his mind was on Fox. As he sat silent, Pitt broke out, "Why did he do it? All that zest and energy—all that charm and talent—the magician with the magician's wand." He looked across at Wilberforce. "You were right again, you old morality. You said there would be a day of disenchantment."

XXV

Fox AND North were joint Secretaries of State now, under a quiescent and nominal head, the Duke of Portland. From the country came a weary mutter of anger. But the Coalition had four years of parliamentary life to run and a huge majority in the Commons. It scowled down from the escarpment of the constitution like a baron's castle, palisaded and impregnable.

Pitt quit Number 11 at the end of the week. He would have been in some straits to find accommodation—the cost of rented rooms having soared since the war. But Wilberforce opened the doors of Lauriston House to him. Since it did not seem now he was going to set the Thames on fire, Miss Weddell's wrath with him was great. Coming upon him at the Townshends' she stalked past him without even a nod of recognition to flutter the ribbons on her little lacy cap.

"What on earth have you done to insult the girl so?" Pepper Arden remarked. "Fie, fie on you, William, for not rushing across instantly to join the Coalition."

"And fie, fie on me, and worse, from Pulteney and others for not tearing them tooth and nail."

"Well, no man ever loved a grey neutrality," Arden said, with a curious look at him.

Others too judged his neutrality strange. Silent on the Opposition benches during the Coalition's first session of parliamentary life, he gave no battle. The Betting Book at Brooks's began to grow heavy with wagers that "W. Pitt will accept office with C. Fox and Lord North by the turn of the year".

"I see you still do not love our Coalition, Pulteney," Fox remarked, coming through the lobby on the last day of the summer session.

"I but hope some man will get up and fight you until he drops."

"To drop would be his fate," Fox answered with a laugh. "And in case you pin any hopes in that quarter we do not think young William will stay out long." As Pulteney stood grimly silent, he went on, "Oh, my good Pulteney, he has not said a wrong word to us since Sheridan reduced him to size by calling him the Angry Boy in Jonson's *Alchemist*. And that towering Pitt ambition—what if he stays out? Two rented rooms up three flights at Lincoln's Inn—cold meat from the cook shops because they cannot prepare food on their hearths. Give him a few weeks of mourning for his departed chief, Shelburne, and he will be with us on the Government benches."

"It is not Shelburne he mourns, Charles," Pulteney said. "You were cast as the slayer of dragons, the scourer of the white cliffs. His mourning is for you."

Peace came that summer of 1783, finalised by the new

Government on terms somewhat less advantageous than those Shelburne had almost gained. Pitt's old chambers in the Stone Building at Lincoln's Inn had at last fallen to him again. With the Channel packet plying once more, he, Wilberforce and Eliot crossed in September to France. The old enemy nation, full of the sunshine splendour of Versailles, full of victory and battle honours, her great autumnal forests and ripening vineyards cradling chateaux where the victors of Yorktown danced and dined, seemed to Englishmen blessed by the fates beyond belief. Against the supremacy of France the English visitors felt themselves a paupered people, seeing proud Paris above the sweep of the Seine, buoyant and triumphant; their own capital, with the Thames washing under the willows of Westminster, defeated and debilitated.

Parliament met again in November. The first business before the House was that of the East India Company, now almost bankrupt, its charter near expiry. The East India Bill, drafted by Fox and Burke during the summer recess, had been kept highly secret. But, laid before the House, it broke upon the land now. The buzzing city and the tiny and stunned Opposition learnt what was in store. The Bill swept all the patronage and potential wealth of the company into the hands of the Coalition, giving them—in or out of office —control of its army, territories and assets. With John Company about to become its appendage the Coalition straddled the land like some fierce eastern potentate, tur-baned in cloth of gold and all powerful.

The day after the Bill had been laid before the House the three returned travellers walked down to Westminster stairs. Presently Pulteney joined them, continuing with them, after the first greeting, in total silence. The East India Bill was on most other tongues. Sir John Honeywood's roar came to them through the trees. "What do you think of it, eh, Sutton? They mean to rush it through all its stages before the country gentlemen can get back into town. There'll be no opposition now young Pitt has thrown his hand in. Why God bless my soul, if Boreas had proposed this in his time Fox would have been organising public meetings clean across Westminster."

Westminster stairs had its usual knot of Londoners watching the river traffic. Pulteney and the three younger men mingled with it, those about them unconscious that they now had four of their legislators in their midst. From downstream a wherry rowed by a Thames waterman with a Doggett's badge on his sleeve, and carrying a stout German sightseer in cocked hat and a coat with square salt-cellar pockets, came nosing in to scrape the stone. Pulteney turned his head to regard it, some strange trick of the November sun casting on to his face a look of stern grief, even of mourning.

"Here you are, sir," the Doggett's man said. "Westminster and the Houses of Parliament."

"Is it permitted that I enter?" the German asked. "I am wishing later in the day to hear the discoursing both of your nobles and of your common legislators."

"You can't get into the House of Lords without a written order from a peer, sir. Same applies to the Commons, if you don't want to queue. Still, if you ain't got one, go through the great door to the side there, and ask the attendant in the black breeches and black stockings to let you into the Gallery. Give him two shillings—two shillings," the Doggett's man repeated in the manner of the English explaining their currency, "or he'll say it's full."

"*Danke,*" the German said, scrambling out. He stood surveying the crenellated and corbelled roofs of Westminster —the sun behind them now—and said in his earnest and careful English, "Ach—a most noble building! How sad that it now looks down upon you in your decay."

The small knot of English folk about the stairs watched his retreating figure with a glowering agreement. "Why, Fritzi's right," the Thames waterman said. "And that lot yonder, taking over John Company and making nabobs of themselves. I don't hold with it."

"It don't matter to them a tinker's fart whether you hold with it or no," another onlooker remarked acidly. "I'm a borough man, I've been canvassed—bows—smiles—handshakes. 'Pray, how are you, sir? How is your wife?'—all attention. But once they're in. 'Never mind that you don't approve our Coalition. Never mind that you don't approve our East India Bill. You are of no consequence, sir. You did but vote for us.'"

"Well, there's nothing to rattle round in our pockets now," the Doggett's man said sadly. "And nothing to rattle round in our souls neither, if you take my meaning—no pride—no occasion to say to ourselves any more 'we're a great nation', and that was a fine brave thing to warm your hands against sometimes when the night was cold. I took pleasure in it. I own to it."

Pulteney turned away. Again there was a shadow on his face as if he mourned more than the dying year. Pitt said, half under his breath, "Pulteney."

Pulteney turned on him almost with the curtness of anger. "I know what you would say. Cautiously, from the Opposition benches, you are going to fight them now. And what can it achieve? You will not hurt yourself. You will not hurt them. It is, as I know, as the King knows, as you know in your heart, that there is but one place where any man can stand to aim any blow at all at the Coalition—the Treasury Bench, with the seals of England in his pocket."

He set his back on Pitt and walked on towards the tall towers of Westminster.

XXVI

WITH THE East India Bill passing through its parliamentary stages Dundas was much at the Earl of Hopetoun's house in Cavendish Square. The Hopes of Hopetoun were his neighbours back in West Lothian. Dundas's interest was centred on the Lady Jean Hope, Hopetoun's sister. All the qualifications for a woman taking Elizabeth Rannie's place in Dundas's marriage bed were hers. She was a Scotswoman— and Dundas would not have dreamt of marrying one of any other nation. She bore a title. But it was the brother who dominated the sister, and Dundas's addresses had to go through Hopetoun.

Nothing was said of courtship—Dundas too newly divorced to go a-wooing again in earnest yet. But Hopetoun himself broached the subject, in a general fashion, one December night. "You'll wed again, Dundas?"

"Aye 'tis likely—in two years maybe, when the children ha'e grown used to the thought o' a new mother."

Hopetoun smiled faintly. "You will set your sights high, I think."

"As high as my talents merit."

"Your talents are of no small order. You are what we Scotties call 'auldfarrant'. The winning side would not be a bad present to give any woman at her bridal." With the talk turning to politics he asked Dundas of the progress of the East India Bill through the Commons, remarking, "Public opinion seems hot against it."

"It'll go through well enough, for all that," Dundas said gloomily. "There's nought to stop it."

But there was something to stop it—the King's fierce and possessive love of his realm. George was greeted with catcalls now when he drove out in his carriage, not because he had fought the American War but because he had lost it. He talked bitterly of abdication. But all close to him knew that the few hours of his Coronation when he had stood in Westminster Abbey—a very young man with an abiding sense of duty—had riveted him to England for the rest of his life.

It came to 17th December—a cold clear evening with frost in the throat of the sky. Dundas was again journeying to the Hopes. Distant at the end of the Mall the lights of Buckingham House shone in defiant brilliance. But it was in fact a beleaguered citadel, and no man envied the King his thoughts of his country's future.

Hopetoun had been at the House of Lords. His carriage drew up at his door almost as Dundas's did. He sprang from it, with a flushed face, announcing, "The Bill's thrown out."

"Man, it canna' be. What's been the manner o' the debate?"

"Why, entirely hilarious," Hopetoun said with a grin. "A paper from Buckingham House flashing about, saying in effect, 'If you vote with them you and I are not friends.' They will have George's eyes for it. Still, for the present the Coalition is dismissed."

" 'Tis daft—useless. The King will ha'e to recall them."

"So they think—Fox and North. In a week, they say, and this time as the masters, their feet on his neck and the East India Bill slammed on to the Statute Book in face of public dislike and all else. The King's casting about for a man for the battle. Already he has had Shelburne, Temple, Gower and Camden up yonder to Buckingham House, urging each in turn to take the premiership."

"Aye, and they're all prudent souls. They'll ha'e all refused."

"Why, would you take it on, Dundas?" Hopetoun said. "I would not. It'll be as bloody as the cockpits, believe me. In truth, every time I watch Fox come into the Commons it puts me in mind of the cockpits—the rustle of excitement along the benches, the rustle of the straw in the pen, and in stalks the gamecock, his killer spurs strapped to his scarlet heels. In faith, I pity his challenger." His glance turned south, in the direction of the Mall. "Well, who remains? Who even stayed out of the Coalition? There's young Pitt, I suppose." As Dundas was rendered suddenly silent he went on, "Why, God bless you, Dundas, I meant it as a jest. No one would thrust this mess of defeat and bankruptcy, lost trade, lost allies and lost wars into the lap of a boy of twenty-four."

But the King was prepared even for this. By six the next evening, with the exultant Coalition dining together, George in the yellow drawing room at Buckingham House, and Pitt in the ante-room, were waiting to cross wills; the one hot to find a man for the battle, the other as reluctant as all the others who had waited here to grasp so prickly a nettle as the seals of Great Britain.

In spite of crisis the King was engaged in his customary nightly play with the Princess Sophia in her high chair. She was the fifth-born of George's six daughters—like all the rest in babyhood as fair as a flower, with flaxen soft hair and velvety brown eyes, her ruffles showing the dimples in her elbows.

"Come along, sweetheart," the King said patiently. "London Bridge is falling down, my fair—"

"Lady," the little girl concluded in a triumphant shout, then held out a hand for a reward. "Sweetie, papa."

"Eat it quickly, then," the King said. "Before Nurse Binns comes back."

A stout woman in a mob cap came rustling in, enquiring of the little girl in the high chair, "Has Your Highness been reciting all your nursery rhymes for daddy?"

"Highness feels sick," the little girl remarked in a sad voice.

"Have you been stuffing the child with sweetmeats?" Nurse Binns said fiercely. "I told Your Majesty quite plain she was to have none of those sickly violet comfits." She picked up the baby and bore her out, muttering, "Men."

Though George could sometimes be put upon domestically, he was never less than a King in the Government of England. He turned to the equerry standing quietly by in his soldier's scarlet coat. "What, what, Digby?" the King said, using the staccato expression that came most naturally to him. "We chose the right nursery rhyme, did we not? London Bridge is falling down, and the stocks and the pound sterling with it. Is Mr. Pitt here?"

Pitt was brought in and formally presented. The double doors were shut on them and they were left alone. George was nearing fifty now, stoutish, unhandsome, with protuberant blue eyes bulging in a manner that betrayed his intense anxiety. There was obstinacy and anger in his face, and much courage and kindliness. But they were in no circumstances to observe each other's qualities. Pitt saw the King only as the man who had let Chatham be lowered into his tomb in Westminster Abbey—all that remained of the broken body and the broken mind—without a word of regret or gratitude; who had persisted over-stubbornly against America and blasted Chatham's dream of union between the two nations; George, on his part, seeing the son of the disliked Chatham, taller than himself but equally obstinate, the opposer of the American War and for long the follower of Fox.

"What, what, Mr. Pitt?" the King said at last. "Twice before I have offered you the premiership. And twice you have declined. This time, on my word, I hope you will make the braver choice."

"With respect, sir," Pitt answered. "I have no choice, since I have no majority. My opponents would swallow me up."

"I am quite capable of simple arithmetic, Mr. Pitt," the King rapped back at him. "I know what would happen in the divisions to any man facing the Coalition. I do not deny the battle will be anything less than desperate. But I flattered myself there would be one of you at least prepared to attempt it." He turned his glance to the window, to where, beyond the Mall, rose the dark towers of Westminster. "Even in what some term the bad causes, even against America, many came forward to hazard themselves. But to save the realm from an avaricious and unpopular Government, that gained power by a sleight of hand, to save her from the economic ills and internal sicknesses that will bring about her ruin as surely as invasion or foreign enemies, not one of you gentlemen of Westminster will hazard a finger."

"It would be a useless battle, sir," Pitt said sullenly.

"Yet I am persuaded your father would have attempted it," the King said in a sharp voice. He added more quietly, "I pretend to no great personal attachment to Lord Chatham. But for my part I think he would have dragged himself on his stick or on his hands and knees into Downing Street rather than watch England eaten and pared by the Coalition."

None gave George credit for great grasp of intellect. But often, as by instinct, he found the right persuasions. Pitt regarded him with a young and sullen resentment. It was well enough for the King, secure in Buckingham House or Windsor Castle, while whoever shouldered the battle went nightly to face the stormy music in the Commons, risking, at worst, impeachment, or, almost at best, the ruin of a career. But George's case was in fact as hard as any. He was still fighting—almost the only man who was—and his lonely harassment and despairing care for his realm were touching things.

"If you wish, sir," Pitt said at length reluctantly, "I'll think on it further."

George, with the memory of his two previous refusals, had little hope of him now. He answered curtly, all but turning his back, "Till six tomorrow morning, Mr. Pitt. I shall require your answer by then."

After Pitt had gone the equerry returned to the room. "Well, then, Digby," the King said with a sigh. "When I dismissed the Coalition it was an arbitrary and unconstitutional act, was it not?"

"Doubtless it was, sir," the equerry answered. "But—the monstrous Coalition—the cursed East India Bill—I have never heard them named anywhere but by those titles."

"The monstrous Coalition," the King repeated. "My faith, Digby, you are a soldier and I can say it. I wonder what great crimes I have done to deserve such politicians. They all ran. They all deserted. Bute did. So did Grafton—even North, in this, the worst and blackest hour we have sustained. There's a biblical quotation that puts it all most uncommon apt. *And I sought for a man among them, that should make up the hedge, and stand in the gap before me for the land; but I found none.*" He added, almost as an afterthought, "There was only Chatham. He was a proud, overbearing, dictatorial man——I never liked him. But he did not run."

XXVII

At midnight, Fox, receiving a message that Pitt would be glad of private speech with him, finished the *partie* he was engaged on and left the gaming tables at Brooks's. He had been told Pitt waited in the club's seldom-used back faro room. He turned towards it, the cards still in his hand, making his way first through the little ante-room, with its cushioned chairs and silver wall sconces. Pulteney was alone here, the evening news-sheet open on his knees. He and Fox exchanged a brief greeting before Fox went on through the inner door.

Pitt turned at his entry. They had no greeting for each other but, as by mutual consent, they drew out chairs and seated themselves, one on either side of the great table. The action was marred on Pitt's part by awkwardness, almost a schoolboy's uncertainty. Fox saw him still effectively the master of his countenance but not to an equal extent the master of his movements. He knew this to be the hour of decision and knew too what choice the King had urged on Chatham's son this night.

"Well, William," he said. "The last time we talked you told me you had not come to betray Shelburne."

"It was a clumsy remark. I am sorry, Charles. I blunder sometimes in what I say to other men."

This from this proud and defensive young man was indeed

a concession. Outside the winter night had turned to sleet. It spewed now hollowly against the panes, its sudden gust sounding in the still room like the painful spitting cough of a dying man. Fox spoke softly. "The country has the death rattle in her throat and you would join my talents with yours."

"Charles, on my word, I hold it is the answer. We stand the same ground—we always have—and the sand is all but run out for us in the hourglass now."

Fox regarded him for a moment and then laughed. "This then is your prescription—you and I together, that we might yet rally sick England and have the teeth growing again in the jaws of the lion." He saw again a flash of the old eagerness that he had first seen at Kingsgate and added, "What of my obligation to North?"

"I've rent Boreas much but he would place no obstacle here. He has maintained in the House from the beginning he would release you at need."

"North would certainly release me," Fox answered in a goodhumouredly voice. "He has declared as much many times, both publicly and privately." He added slowly and deliberately, "But I seek no release. I have made some unexpected alliances, I own, but at least they have been with responsible statesmen, not with boys, led by their Kings and fathers into believing themselves the heaven-born deliverers of their country."

The eagerness left Pitt's face instantly. Fox went on on a harder note, "What now, then, William? You have been almost of a mind to take the seals and fight us since last March. But never quite. And I counsel you to heed your native caution again. North and I have a vast following— where is yours? We have an able cabinet—where is yours? Between us we have forty years of parliamentary experience —where is yours?" His careless affability had been replaced almost by menace. "Nor is it only a question of majorities and cabinets. It is a question of what a man is. Do you think you are not savaged in this office—even with the Government benches crowded behind you, even with able men at your side to draw somewhat of the fire? And you—you found it hard enough to get to your feet at Kingsgate, with the room looking at you. What when the world looks at you, and North and I are at your throat?"

Pitt gave him a fierce glance. "Does it not cross your mind I might have acquired a greater schooling since then?"

"Indeed you had plenty of that. You know what we say of you—that you were taught by your old dad at a stool. But, on my honour, Chatham could not even teach you the beginnings. No man learns to be Prime Minister sat in the quiet library at Hayes. He learns it in the hard buffets of the world and of the House, and you, at twenty-four, with your two and a half years in the House and your cloistered years at Cambridge—why, what have you learnt?"

He pushed back his chair. A hard and angry silence lay about the table. At the door Fox turned, saying with an easy, genial, half-exasperated grace—the elder brother moved by some proposed folly in a younger, "William, William, go back to your apprenticeship and leave the governing to grown men like North and myself."

He closed the door behind him. Pulteney was still seated over his news-sheet in the little ante-room. "Well, Pulteney," Fox said, pausing by his chair. "I am persuaded Master Billy yonder is going to snatch at the premiership. If he does, it will afford me as much satisfaction as ever it did watching my opponent play a ruinous card at piquet."

"What have you said to him, Charles?"

"What do you say to any schoolboy?" Fox answered, smiling. "I dare you to it, for you do not dare."

"You can be generous to other men," Pulteney said quietly. "But not to him."

"And you do not ask me why?"

"I know why."

"Yes, since you recall our fathers' battles and their outcome, I warrant you do," Fox said. "And it is not going to happen again." He ran the cards through his fingers, like the crackle of musketry. "My mother said Master Billy would be a thorn in my flesh all my life. But I do not endure thorns. I pluck them out."

XXVIII

PITT SAT on in the half-darkened room. It was very cold now, the coals dimming and flickering, but his anger kept him in warmth. At length the clock on the mantelpiece chimed four, very sweetly and thinly in the winter-gripped room. Pitt rose and went to the escritoire. He wrote to the King, sealed the letter and rang for Brooks for a messenger. George was an early riser. When he came from his bed at six, he would know he had found a man for the battle.

With the messenger gone on, Pitt followed. In the ante-room Pulteney still kept his chair. He asked no question. But the strange alchemy that made all men confide their motives and their minds to him worked again.

"It's done, Pulteney."

"It is not before time."

"Most men will say it is at least twenty years before time." As Pulteney sat silent he went on, "Fox urged me against it but so marvellous dexterously I became hot to do it. He named me an inexperienced boy, and I loathe it, Pulteney—as much as anyone can't abide being characterised by what is undeniable in them. He is still the magician with the magician's wand, spell-binding you into folly or compliance. And if he can do as much to me across a card table in a deserted faro room, how will it be in the House?"

"Does the prospect then dismay you?"

"Yes—North and Burke, Sheridan and Cooper, they do not matter. I can hold them. But Fox—yes, it dismays me."

After a bitter silence he added, "But the battle has to come between us and it had better be now—the same battle as our fathers fought, under the eyes of England and across the two sword-lengths of the Commons' floor."

They sat waiting together while the darkness ebbed. At length came the sound of Brooks's voice turning out the men who had passed the whole night at the gaming tables, followed by his footfalls in the passageway. "Come along, gentlemen," he said, putting his head into the room. "My cleaning women are waiting to set on with the fires. And Mr. Pitt—a note for you, sir, from Buckingham House, just handed in at the door."

He went out again. With the King's seal broken, Pitt looked back at Pulteney, "I am to be at Buckingham House in an hour to kiss hands."

"I wish you well, sir," Pulteney said. He came slowly and stiffly to his feet, his stern glance bent on the other. "You will need all your skill. But skill is not so important at this stage as is courage. They will use you with every fury. But stay there. Clamp your fingers on whatever hold Downing Street offers, and stay there. You must have time to show you are fit to govern, that you are not the arrogant and callow schoolboy they will name you. And for my part I commend to you the advice of Daniel Pulteney, the great Earl of Bath, whose name I took on my marriage. He said that when it blew fierce about the Treasury Bench, there was but one way—to abide the pelting storm."

A hired hackney bore Pitt back to Lincoln's Inn. All was deserted here, only Pepper Arden walking his dog about the fountain. Pitt called to him, "Come up to my rooms, Pepper. I want to talk to you."

"All those stairs on an empty stomach," Arden sighed. "Have at them, then."

The dog, thinking it was sport, bounded before them up the flights. But even he was panting when he got to the top. The shaving water stood heating on the hearth, with the coffee simmering beside it. While Arden poured himself coffee and began to sample the cold meat Pitt seized up jug and razor and went into the bedroom. When he returned he was freshly shaven, carrying his sword and wearing a coat of formal finery.

"Court dress?" Arden remarked with a perplexed look at him over the coffee cup. "At this hour?"

"What's this, sir?" the servant asked, coming in from the doorway of his own room. "All night at Brooks's with Mr. Fox and Mr. Pulteney, and now your sword and your lace. This'll be for waiting on the King, will it not? Are we going back to Number 11 in Downing Street?"

"It will be Number 10 this time, Ralph."

"Oh, God with us," Pepper Arden said in an aghast voice, as the servant seized Pitt's hand in a delighted, congratulatory clasp. "You cannot. You have no majority, no cabinet, no following, no—"

He broke off, pushing away his coffee cup as if it had altogether surfeited him. Pitt had turned to the writing table. For a little while the hasty spluttering of the quill echoed in the quiet room. Then it was laid aside and he drew off his ring. "Take my signet, Ralph, for I want these sealed and delivered. This to my mother at Hayes—this to Mr. Wilberforce—this to Mr. Eliot. Pulteney knows already. For the rest it must be kept secret until the House is told."

"When will that be, sir?"

"Tonight." He glanced round. "Pepper, will you move the writ for Appleby—if you can make yourself heard above the laughter."

"As long as you know it will be that," Arden answered in a bleak voice. "That they will certainly laugh."

"Why, God bless you, I may have been but two and a half years in the House, as they are never done reminding me, but I know it will render them hilarious."

He began to buckle on his sword. The servant lent his

aid, saying in his soft Somersetshire voice, "You're your father's son, Mr. William. You'll see us proud."

"Why, for sure you will." Arden got up, coming across with outstretched hand. "One day I'll sit telling my grand-children that I shared a pair of stairs at Lincoln's Inn with William Pitt the Younger."

Pitt's underlying warmth sprang out. He clapped them both on a shoulder, a hand on each. "Between you, you would put heart into a man going to Tyburn at the cart's tail."

They stood, hearing his footsteps going down the stairs, the litter of shaving gear, of half-drunk coffee, the quills and ink, the signet and discarded coat all about them. "What now, sir?" Ralph asked. "What happens at Buckingham House?"

"He kisses the King's hand," Pepper Arden answered. "The King renders him the Treasury seals—red wax seals, small enough to hang on a watch-chain." He tossed a piece of biscuit to the dog, almost with the gesture of a man seeking to keep a pack of wolves away with a titbit. "And then it's done. Then it will be all hell and foul weather, the devil to pay and not a tithe of pitch hot or ready to pay him with."

BOOK II

1783–1784

The Mincepie Administration

"I suppose young Pitt can do as he likes over the Christmas holidays, but this is a Mincepie Administration, depend upon it." MRS. CREWE.

I

BY FIVE that evening it was not yet known who had accepted the premiership, only that some man had. Fox and North and their followers passed jubilantly through the lobby to crowd the Opposition benches. Behind them the lobby itself and the vestibule seethed in speculation.

"Some man has put his head into the noose then," George Sutton remarked. "One wonders if the King plied him excessively with home-brewed turnip wine before pressing office upon him. It'll be an ill moment for the poor fellow, whoever he is—returning to sobriety to find himself with a sick headache and the seals of England in his pocket."

Governor Johnstone turned a sharp look towards his brother. Pulteney answered with a grim nod. They drew together to the far end of the lobby for private speech. "So he's taken it," Johnstone muttered. "Good, good."

"I say 'good' too. But it will be a most desperate fight."

"Yet my fear was there would be no fight at all," Johnstone answered. "Rouse them—give them a Prime Minister of twenty-four. Even if he goes down, even if he has to stand and watch the spars of his career drifting away from the rocks, if he can but drive one dent into the Coalition's armour he will have done somewhat."

"If it ends in that it will be a hard thing for him."

"It's a hard world, brother," Johnstone said, with all his family's habitual grimness.

They went through the double doors, Johnstone taking his place on the benches. Pulteney continued up the length of the House, going behind the Speaker's chair where stood the narrow doorway, dubbed Solomon's Porch. Here one was still technically in the precincts of the House. Only a partial view of the Commons' panoply was afforded Pulteney—the golden fleurets of the Mace spiked like a medieval crown, the Speaker, half-hidden by the back of his great chair, the green of the Treasury Bench, stretching down upon the right hand. Since Pitt—unseated by taking office—was debarred from the House pending his re-election, no one at all sat here this night. Pulteney could not see the packed and exultant Opposition benches. But their amusement and curiosity, their eagerness to know who had so rashly challenged them, charged the little chamber with the feel of lightning on a sultry day. The Speaker took the Chair, turning his grey-wigged head to call on the member for Aldeborough. The Clerk Assistant coughed, dryly and nervously. But everything else had the stillness that heralded the brewing of a storm. In this quiet came Arden's voice moving a new election for Appleby, in the room of William Pitt, now First Lord of the Treasury and Chancellor of the Exchequer.

A gale of laughter swept in at the heel of the words. John Hatsell, the Clerk, turned his head. Hatsell loved the House —the long tally of its history, its ancient ceremonials. Pulteney saw him flushing furiously, as though he could scarcely bear it that that which had always been a high and historic moment was now taken as a noisy audience might take a hugely comic line at Drury Lane.

The uproarious merriment of the House beat on. Pulteney turned quietly, opening the door of Solomon's Porch and going through into the Speaker's room. Another door here led on to the Speaker's Corridor. Pulteney made his way down it, through the deserted lobby and up the stairs to the eating-house. Pitt was the sole customer here, standing alone by the eating-house hearth. The door into

Bellamy's kitchen stood wide, affording a view of a scrubbed and clean interior—the hams hanging from their hooks above the deal kitchen table, the piles of damask tablecloths, the little table for washing glasses and draining jugs, the great fire with its gridiron and roasting jack. Both the eating-house and the kitchen were huddled close to the eaves of the House of Commons. Any clamour in the chamber reached up here. Plainly the recent clamour had just done so. Broken crockery littered the threshold of the kitchen. Jane, who came in to do the washing-up and whose reddened fore-arms testified as much, was gathering it up, Bellamy beside her, clicking his tongue.

"No use you tut-tutting at me neither, Mr. Bellamy," Jane was saying sharply. "Odd's life, what a yell of laughter! No wonder I dropped the tray."

"Well, well, we can't help it, my girl," Bellamy remarked resignedly. "Put in a chit to the Serjeant-at-Arms' Office. Something must have tickled 'em hugely downstairs."

Pulteney's look went to Pitt who returned it. "Yes, I heard, Pulteney—your pelting storm, the first gust."

Though he did not look as if the laughter of the House had greatly moved him his native awkwardness was at this moment his master. As they turned towards one of the tables his elbow caught a plate on the serving dresser. Bellamy fielded it close to the floor.

"Now, now, Mr. Pitt," he said. "I've had enough of my crocks broke this night." He came over to them, licking his pencil, his serving tablet in his hand. "Now, sirs, what would you like? I have some veal on the spit and a jugged hare, but nothing's ready yet. To tell the truth I expected none of you gentlemen up this quick. What with the best joke of the session—whatever it was—and wanting to know who the new Minister is, I thought you'd all be down in the chamber."

"The best joke of the session and the new Minister are all of a piece, Bellamy," Pitt answered.

Bellamy gave him a searching look. "You, sir? That's scraping the bottom of the barrel, is it not? I mean no offence but I have a son at home who could give you a year or two."

The main door leading from the stairs crashed open and Pearson, the head doorkeeper, came in like a surly thundercloud, not discerning Pitt or Pulteney. "By God, Bellamy," he exclaimed. "You don't know what's going on downstairs. Devil take it if I want to be governed by a whelp who's scarce yet breached."

"That's enough, Mr. Pearson," Bellamy answered sharply.

Pearson looked past him into the room, seeing the other two. He was not abashed. The situation did not exist that could abash Pearson. But he had the grace to half touch his hat and withdraw.

The room began to fill. Every man who came in raked Pitt with a stare, amused, hostile or compassionate. Wilberforce, Eliot, Arden and Dudley Ryder drew round him at once, and Governor Johnstone and George Rose followed. But it was such a thin protective crust about the new Minister it might have been better if they had sat apart and not displayed the poverty of their numbers. Sir John Honeywood entered with an air of bafflement. In the uproar of the chamber nothing had been distinguishable to him and he thrust his ear trumpet close to Barré at his side, remarking thunderously, "Damned incoherent mumblers, the young men these days. I say damned incoherent mumblers. Who was the writ moved for? I did not catch."

"Pitt."

"Over there, sat with Pulteney," Sir John roared. "What about him? I don't think he were present."

Barré roared back, "It's Pitt, *Pitt*."

"God bless my soul," Sir John said. He took his ear trumpet from his ear and shook it as if it had grossly insulted him.

"Why, in faith," Sheridan remarked, seating himself at a table by the window. "If this had been delivered in manuscript to my office at Drury Lane I would have staged it."

"But would it run, Sherry?" Fox asked with a laugh.

"What we consider a reasonably successful run at Drury Lane might not be held so at Westminster. For my part I give it eighteen days." As a gust of amusement went up he called over his shoulder, "Bellamy, where's the service at this end of the room?"

"Be patient, if you please, Mr. Sheridan, sir," Bellamy answered, "I'm serving the Minister."

Sheridan cocked a brow at him. "I hope you can supply the Minister with some fare suiting his age and the season. Mincepies make a vast appeal to the young at this time of year, I am told."

"There's the title for your pantomime, Sherry," John Courteney said. "You should paste up a few playbills upon the doors round Old Palace Yard—'In three very short acts, The Mincepie Administration, or the Schoolboy's Indulgence over the Christmas Holidays.'"

It occasioned another jubilant roar from the room. Pitt sat stonily. But not all were amused. Burke—always passionately earnest about the dignity of Parliament—could not abide this. He snatched off his glasses, saying hotly, "You may laugh. But I hold it is an impertinence to the House."

"It is worse than an impertinence," Conway answered sourly. "It is an indecency. Twenty years ago we knew how to deal with schoolboys who made spectacles of themselves. We strapped their quarters—we bent them across a chair and used a stirrup strap on their backsides until they howled."

"I hold that a quite unwarrantable remark," Pulteney said sharply.

"So do I," Barré growled, "since you make it in his presence."

"He will have worse than that made in his presence," Conway said. "Shakespeare wrote lines on little wanton boys who swim on bladders in seas of glory far beyond their depth." He swung on Pitt. "It surprises me you did not learn that in the library at Hayes."

"I learnt at least that the unforgivable crime is to be a young man."

"Now, now, gentlemen," Bellamy said, coming between. "I'll have no debating here. Besides 'tis Christmas. A little goodwill would not come amiss."

Since it was indeed Christmas—that night the House rising for the Christmas adjournment of 1783—it was an exceedingly expensive time, with the staff of the Palace of Westminster accustomed to receiving their Christmas vails. The guineas were already changing hands here in the eating-house for Bellamy and the kitchen staff, and outside, at the door of her rooms, Mrs. Bennett, the housekeeper, was presenting a plump, smiling, seasonable face. None grudged the staff on the upper corridor their vails—they were hard-working and obliging. But by the time the eating-house, the housekeeper's rooms and the greatcoat room had been worked through most purses were the lighter by ten guineas.

Downstairs in the lobby there were the walkmen, the four messengers and the doorkeepers to satisfy. Pearson, the head doorkeeper, was a deadly extortioner of guineas. If any member failed in this duty at the end of a session Pearson could —and did—make his life a misery, sending him on wild goosechases for non-existent visitors to Gallery, Smoking Room and Speaker's Dining Room. Pepper Arden contended that Charles I had been too late to arrest the five members because he had neglected Pearson's guinea vail and Pearson, in revenge, had sent him down the wrong corridor. While Pearson certainly had not been doorkeeper over a century he had been so thirty-five years. His length of service explained why he was thus submitted to—the virtual dictator of the lobby, surly and sour-tongued.

"Happy Christmas, Pearson," Pepper Arden said, bestowing the required amount. "Don't drain every dram shop between here and Soho Square."

"Well, a man can't listen to what goes on here every night of the week between Hallow'een and Christmas, and stay sober, Mr. Arden," Pearson answered. But he was more benign than usual, having cause to be. Tonight he would go home the richer by over four hundred guineas. "Obliged to you, Mr. Wilberforce. Obliged to you, Mr. Pitt. Season's compliments."

With Pearson left satisfied, Jessel, the deputy door-keeper, had to be sought out. Jessel was the antithesis of Pearson, apt to disappear into vaults and attics to spare the purses of the poorer members. He had taken refuge on this occasion in the chamber itself. As he was approached, he said, "There's no call for that, sir."

"Don't fight me over a guinea, Jessel," Pitt said. "I have battles enough to come in this place when the recess is over."

"I know that, sir," Jessel said in a gentle voice.

He went out. Wilberforce had joined Pitt and they stood together in the darkened House, the benches yawning about them in their draping green baize, the great chandelier lowered now and swaying fractionally at their feet. Already the old half-burnt candles had been removed and the new stood straight and pallid in their sconces, awaiting the new year and the new session. Pitt had not now quite the stony control he had had in the eating-house. "What will be the manner of the battle the candles will beat down upon when they are lit, Will?" He added, with a grim and weary apprehension, "Charles and I were friends once. There's a French saying for it—'If you would have an enemy, choose a friend. He knows where the armour gapes.'"

II

By morning the news had broken upon the land. The newspapers were full of hilarity, all London repeating John Townshend's pithy couplet.

> *A sight to make surrounding nations stare,*
> *A kingdom trusted to a schoolboy's care.*

Sheridan remarked that all the addresses of thanks from the shire towns that had rolled in upon the King in gratitude for his dismissal of the Coalition would now roll out again— the country learning she had a raw boy in place of it. Many were in agreement, the cartoonists depicting the Minister with his cheeks bulging with the famous black Westminster toffee that the vendors sold in little gift boxes outside the Houses of Parliament; or engaged against Fox· in a furious pillow fight; or in long clothes, climbing the steps of Downing Street, a fat, bare-breasted wet nurse peeping fondly at him through the curtains.

Pitt left London the next night to journey the fourteen miles to his home at Hayes. Wilberforce and Eliot went with him, bunched with Ralph in the interior of his elder brother's small carriage. Hayes Place, when they reached it, looked seasonable, with long poles stacked about the doorway, their lanterns hooked upon them and little frosty sprigs of berried holly set on top. From inside came the thin, wheezy scrape of a fiddle and raised Kentish voices of various tunefulness and pitch.

"*God rest you merry, gentlemen, let nothing you dismay.*"

The waits were in the hall; the punchbowl cushioned on the crackling apple logs and pine cones in the hearth and bubbling fragrantly. Lady Chatham, John and Harriet and the few servants were ranged about. Harriet ran to her younger brother, now come to his high and lonely office, and flung her arms about him. The waits made way, regarding Pitt with a local pride in that their tiny village had, in a life-time, supplied two tenants to Downing Street.

"Well, Mr. William," their leader remarked. "Times is

bad. Still as I said in the Bull only last night—comes the hour, comes the man."

A remorseless voice at his elbow corrected him. "You never saw an old head on young shoulders yet, was what you said, Mr. Crabshaw, and, mark it, you said, I shan't see it now."

"Time for one more carol before we press on," Mr. Crabshaw said, breathing gustily. "What would you like, Mr. William, since you're the one to give orders here now."

There was not much tact in this, the elder brother, the bearer of the title, standing by. Pitt turned awkwardly to his brother, "What's your choice, John?"

"For God's sake, why take the trouble to consult me over a carol? In larger matters you don't exert yourself so far."

A shuffle of discomfort went through the waits. The servants stared at the walls. Lady Chatham spoke, asking for *Adeste Fideles*.

"Well, we only know it in English, my lady," Mr. Crabshaw said. "But if that'll serve, here you are."

The little bow-legged fiddler tucked the cloth under the stubble of his chin and began to scrape at the gut. The treble was taken by Mr. Crabshaw's young son, and Wilberforce—who sang finely—gave much necessary assistance, so that the carol finished in a blaze of glory. After the handing round of shortcake, fruitcake and glasses of punch, the waits left, their Christmas boxes tied traditionally in coloured ribbon. The servants gathered round. Their pleasure and congratulations were genuine. Only the elder brother offered no word and no handshake.

Among themselves the undemonstrative Pitts made no great matter of what had so abruptly come upon them. But after the meal as they were coming back to their chairs Pitt paused to speak with his mother. He had not before asked, "What do I do?" about any aspect of his office, as though it had indeed all been learnt here in the library at Hayes. But now Wilberforce caught the mark of inexperience in the question, "What do I do about the servants' vails when I come to Downing Street?"

"It's an expensive house, in truth," Lady Chatham said. "The steward must have ten guineas; the head groom, the head gardener and the cook, seven çach; the porters, four; no one less than a guinea."

The conversation was quietly made. But John overheard it. "Whence comes the money?" he asked his brother curtly. "It will cost you sixty pounds before you even have one foot over the threshold of Number 10."

"I have my official salary."

"Oh, spare us that, in faith. What's the official salary for eighteen days? Thirty-eight pounds, fifteen shillings?"

"John!" Harriet exclaimed wrathfully.

"Oh, my dear John," Lady Chatham said. "For my sake, who bore you both and love you both, stand with your brother in this."

"I'll support him in public, I suppose. In private I reserve the right to tell him I think he has used us very ill." He turned his back to them, a foot on the fender. "It is not the money. It is the ridicule—the Mincepie Administration, to be swept out with dustpan and broom after the holidays, along with all the other useless debris of Christmas—the comic songs they are singing, *The Baby and the Nurse*, he and the King; the news-sheets and their damned cartoons. And he plunges into it all without requesting a word of advice from us."

With Harriet on the point of another angry retort her mother touched her arm, saying quietly, "Children, this is very discomforting for our guests."

After a while, with the evening growing old, Eliot found himself alone with Harriet. Seeing her kneel to tend the fire, with its glow on her skin, he knew himself lost to her. He came beside her before the hearth, both kneeling, the apple log in her hands between them. For a little, in his embrace, her lips seemed warm and answering against his. But after the first responding moment she drew back her head. "Are you not previous, Ned? The kissing bough is not yet lit."

"Oh, my sweet, don't turn all to a boy-and-girl embrace under a kissing bough. It is more serious to me."

She got up, the apple log rolling out of her lap to the hearth rug, and went back from him to the wall. Over her loomed the portrait of her great-grandfather, Governor Pitt, the painted similitude of the great diamond blazing out over the room, brilliant and baleful. Eliot rose too and went towards her. He was about to declare himself, to ask her in outright fashion to become his wife. But she divined his intent and checked it, saying fiercely, "No—be warned."

Her now dead elder sister had married into the rich, powerful and aristocratic Stanhopes. It seemed to Eliot she was telling him that the Pitts, for all their debts and overgrown lawns, their few servants and worn carpets, were yet the natural inheritors of England, and that she intended no less a union for herself.

"Forgive me," he said, with a curt bow. "I see I've unwarrantably thrust myself upon you."

He turned to the door. Behind him she spoke in a breathless voice. "My love."

The endearment brought Eliot about instantly. But she was still standing pressed to the wall under the glowing portrait. "Your parents—" she said. "Your father—does he know?"

"There was no purpose in speaking to him before I knew your mind."

"Then tell him, when you get back to Cornwall, that you desire to make Chatham's daughter your wife."

It was so bewildering a remark Eliot could make nothing of it. "Why? I desire my own choice for a wife, not my father's choice for me."

"Nonetheless, my sweet, tell him. Then later—later, when events do not press so hard—we'll speak of it again. But just now bear with me if you can."

He said after a long silence, "As you wish then."

She moved from the wall, light-hearted and practical again, dusting her skirt where the apple log had shed shreds of its grainy bark. She had never so baffled him. He stood watching her, deeply in love with her, but still as unsure of her as before his lips had met hers.

III

THE NEXT day the guests set out of their own homes, Wilberforce north to spend Christmas in Hull; Eliot, westward to mild Cornwall. At Hayes the Prime Minister's struggle to form a cabinet went on, the posts trotting up to the door, bringing only refusals to serve. Pitt was quickly driven back on his own connections—to his first cousin, Temple, lodged fifty miles away at proud Stowe, and his brother-in-law, Stanhope, whose eccentricities and abilities, mixed in about equal proportions, supplied considerable gossip to every cottage and smallholding between Hayes and Chevening. If these two failed the new Minister he would be in grim straits.

John unbent not at all. There was scarcely even speech between the brothers now. But on the second day of the new year the younger sought the other's company, walking out through the scrub of Hayes Place. A few flakes of snow were falling. They turned to the stile that led on to Hayes Common, halting there by mutual and silent consent. Against the chill half-tones of grey and white, the winter woods and snowy expanse of the Common, the elder brother's scarlet coat and black military cloak were the only bold strokes of colour.

An hour previously had come the express bringing Stanhope's reply, declining, as had nearly all the rest, a cabinet appointment. John remarked on it. "So Stanhope will not come in?"

"He says he will oblige me in any other way in his power. But he'll not serve in cabinet under me."

"He's a sensible man then, and not the eccentric clown I took him for when our poor dead sister decided to wed him." He looked grimly upon his brother. "All rests on Temple now. If you don't gain Temple you as good as have no cabinet."

They stood in silence, the snow brushing upon them. "John," Pitt said at length. "Tomorrow I make the move into Downing Street. I should be glad of one of my own kin by me, at least at the first. Will you come?"

"I had no part in the decision. I want no part in the consequences."

"It is myself I have made the laughing stock, not you."

"I doubt that, on my word."

It ended their brief parley. Pitt turned back to the house. The shabby carriage, with the coachman on top, muffled with wraps and rugs, was grinding through the powdery snow from the stables. Pitt called across to ask who it was who was journeying out.

"'Tis her ladyship, Mr. William," the coachman called back. "Herself and Mrs. Sparry are bound for Stowe."

Lady Chatham was in the hall, cloaked for the journey. Her son knew she had appointed herself to the task of gaining him Temple. "It's a long cold journey for you into Buckinghamshire," he said. "I'll send another express to Temple tonight or see him myself, if time allows."

She answered him, "I was born a Grenville. I am quite the best one for this embassage."

"You have had too much interceding to do at Stowe already."

"Oh, William," Lady Chatham said. "What matters one more occasion?"

Pitt's need of Temple was desperate now. As she had said, his mother—brought up at Stowe—was indeed the best one for the task. He put an arm about her and thanked her. With

Mrs. Sparry she climbed into the carriage, the coachman shaking the reins to take them on their way.

"It is always to Stowe, is it not, Mrs. Pam?" Lady Chatham said, as they jolted out on to Hayes Common. "To Stowe throughout my married life to try to induce my hard proud able brothers to support my husband; and now to Stowe again, to try to induce my hard proud able nephew to support my son. And how will it all end this time?"

IV

STOWE WAS now the domain of the son of Lady Chatham's elder brother, the present Lord Temple. Temple had added great embellishments here. Everywhere were Palladian bridges leaping icy pools; garden temples with fluted Corinthian columns; handsome stone statues of discus-throwers, runners and wrestlers; stone urns filled with winter green; stone stairs climbing loftily to trees and hidden arbours. The wits said that Temple had littered his estate with as much stone as if it had been a stone-hewers' yard in Deptford. But the result was strangely pleasing, as though a corner of ancient Greece had bedded with a little part of England and given birth to a bastard, yet beautiful, landscape, where, in summer, column, arch and plinth were set about in trees and meadow grass, miry pools and moss; and the deep green of Buckinghamshire clung, moist and sweet-smelling, about the stony contours of Athenian symmetry.

"God save us, my lady," Mrs. Sparry said with a gasp, as their carriage turned in past the lodge. "I keep forgetting how grand it is."

Stowe being a good distance from Hayes, it was necessary for the two visitors to stay the night. Temple brought Lady Chatham to the library where they could talk privately. There were many more books than when Lady Chatham had

played here as a girl (though it had been lavish then); many
more splendid pieces of ornamentation. But the shadow of
old tensions was still to be felt. The Nugent-Grenville-
Temples and the Pitts had not loved each other. For all the
Pitts had numbered a bishop and a governor of Madras in
their lineage, the Grenvilles considered them plebian. Men
had watched with sardonic interest the famed Grenville pride
and the Pitt self-will and self-conceit rub sparks from each
other, Chatham and his Grenville brothers-in-law clashing
ncisily, the one calling the other an upstart, the Pitts bestowing on the Grenvilles the nickname they most heartily
detested, 'my lords Gawky'.

Temple handed his visitor wine, the glasses with the
almost warm feel of very old English glass. He did not call
Lady Chatham 'aunt', but simply 'Hester', remarking, "Well,
Hester, I hear you are in fierce straits at Hayes."

"Temple, will you serve?"

Temple smiled with a faint sarcasm. He had expected to
be appealed to for help and it secretly pleased him that the
Pitts should be driven as suppliants to Stowe. "I suspected that was the purpose of your visit. Well, I will do what
I can for William, since he is half Grenville. I suppose he
desires me to have the First Secretary's seals. Tell him all is
well. I will take them."

She thanked him but with a measure of reserve. In the
silence that fell upon them the lights winked beyond the
window on to the splendour of the snowy landscape. Temple
glanced at it, then back at his great room, rich in its fireglow
and gold leaf. "What do you think of Stowe now?" he asked.

"What can I say? It is magnificent."

"I tell my guests it does no more than match our family's
advance these past two hundred years—first country squires,
then Barons Nugent, then Viscounts Cobham, now Earls of
Temple."

"The Grenvilles have come very far."

"But there are yet heights to scale," Temple remarked

dryly. He added, "Tell William I will draft the King's speech for him before I call upon him in Downing Street in two day's time."

She looked at him steadily. "Temple, do not try to sail this ship."

"I possess something in the way of tact, Hester," Temple answered. "The ship, I fear, needs more maturity at the helm. But I promise you, when my hand steadies her, William will not know."

"You Grenville men," she said in a weary voice. "For nigh on thirty years have you worked with the Pitts and yet you never learn."

V

TEMPLE WAS of the stature to carry Governments. If any were able to, he, seemingly, was the man to bear the Mince-pie Administration to at least a decent death. From now on Pitt was most frequently encouraged by the remark, "At least you have Temple."

So, with the little cul-de-sac empty of people, as though the city was weary of this, the latest quirk of government to be visited upon it, the new Prime Minister came to Number 10. Except for its fine brass knocker and foot-scrapers, the house looked nondescript, no more than the house of a prosperous merchant with his brewery at Bayswater or his ships chandlers' office near the Pool. But inside were the great apartments, their double doors causing room to melt into room—the State Dining Room, the State Breakfast Room, the State Drawing Room, the Small Drawing Room, the Cabinet Room—full of their Adam marble and moulded pilasters. The walls had been newly washed down—as was always done between Ministers—and the house was cold. Wilberforce, admitted as the first visitor, thought it compared poorly with the comfort of Wimbledon. But Pitt, when he was brought to him in one of the withdrawing rooms, was surveying the bright paint and the pretty rosewood furniture with pride. "What do you think of my new house, Will?"

"Rather damp."

"It only wants a little summer weather to make it the best residence in London," Pitt said chidingly.

The senior servant of the house, Burfield, came in, bearing a big portable writing-rest. Here in Downing Street he was still known by the old English word, 'steward'—'steward of the household of the First Lord of the Treasury'. He was a man greatly bewigged and vastly stomached, the writing-rest large too, the quill large, the sheet of foolscap on the writing-rest large as well and quite blank. He made Pitt a bow of great dignity, then poised the quill above the foolscap, asking, "How many of your own personal servants would you have me arrange accommodation for, sir?"

"I have one servant—Ralph Holmes. His wife will be with him from time to time."

Burfield looked down at his writing-rest. It was plain he preferred the great peers—Rockingham, Portland and Shelburne—with a list of servants long enough to fill his foolscap from end to end. He dropped the single name from his quill in so tiny a hand it lay lost on the ocean of paper.

When he had gone, Pitt went to the window, looking down upon the cul-de-sac with its pretty private houses angled to a trim square.

"Well, here I am lodged, Will," he said. "And I suppose it has been pretty much folly."

"For my part I am glad to have an honest man in Downing Street."

"You would be, you old Yorkshire sobriety." He stood pondering. "God forgive the arrogance, but I believe, even now, I can govern this country. It is the other things I can't do—the bowing and smiling on the hustings, the great formal dinners with duchesses and diplomats, when what I would have are my friends, and strawberries and green peas on the lawn at Wimbledon."

"When you are weary of the first, the second will always be there awaiting you."

Pitt gave him a look of affection. "How am I to repay it—all your hospitality to me? At least the door of Downing Street will likewise be open to you, whether I am here eighteen days or eighteen years."

Wilberforce smiled, saying, "I wish you the eighteen years."

He joined Pitt at the window. A carriage came sweeping round the corner from Whitehall to halt, the postilion leaping down agilely like a dancing master, and setting down the steps. Temple climbed out and marched up to the door. His commanding blows on the knocker rang through the house.

"Here's your cousin," Wilberforce remarked.

"Yes, as you say—his lordship of Stowe, walking into Downing Street as if he owns it."

Temple indeed walked into Downing Street as if he owned it. But it was his usual mode of entrance and he walked into Windsor Castle and Buckingham House as if he owned them equally. He and Pitt talked alone together in the Cabinet Room, under Van Loo's portrait of Sir Robert Walpole, whose calm alert cynical eyes regarded them as though taking a mocking pleasure in the toilings of his successors. There was fine silver on the side table and two cool marble vases. Temple picked one up and stood examining it.

"Occhio de paone, as I think," he said. "Save for the Duke of Devonshire's pair at Chatsworth these are the only ones of their kind in England. You know the tradition, William, that when a Minister leaves Downing Street he may take with him something of value. When you go, I do beg you take these. They are exquisite."

"Is it not somewhat early to talk of my going yet?"

"True," Temple answered with a thin smile. "They are

giving you eighteen days in the coffee houses. But I must contrive something better for you."

It struck against his younger cousin's pride. But Temple was intent on the vase in his hands and did not notice. He remarked on their future strategy. "For my part I am convinced we ought to dissolve Parliament at once."

"Pulteney thinks—and I am of the same mind—that the better policy is to hold on."

"I do not agree," Temple said bleakly. "You are very talented, William, but you are not yet Fox's equal in debate. Would you have him break you down publicly in the House? It would be a most vile personal experience for you, I do assure you, and quite disastrous for us." He set the vase again in its place and stepped back to survey its contours. "It is not as though I can prop you on the Treasury Bench as I can prop you here."

The Pittite silence that fell on the room drove even Temple to leave the subject. He returned his connoisseur's glance again to the marble on the side table. "My agent in Rome might succeed in procuring me a similar pair to Devonshire's," he said. "I would not have Stowe lagging behind Chatsworth now that Stowe too—" He checked for a moment, then went on with no loss of poise, "I had been about to say, now that Stowe too is to become a ducal seat."

"Is it to become so? I understood the King has said he would create no more dukes save from among his own sons."

"Doubtless you can use sufficiently eloquent persuasions to make him change his mind," Temple said dryly. In the continuing silence, he added, "I feel strongly my services to you entitle me to rise a little higher than mere Earl of Temple. Duke of Buckingham has a better ring. And, indeed, William, I fear I must make it an absolute condition."

"So that is your tally, my lord?" Pitt said. "To serving as Secretary of State in the cabinet of William Pitt—one dukedom."

"You are your father's son at least in bite of tongue,"

Temple remarked with a faint discoloration of anger. "I would not offend me too greatly, if I were you—you, the schoolboy playing at being a Minister. Good God, what would you do were I to tender you my resignation?"

"My lord, I would accept it with the utmost gratitude, and wish you godspeed back to Stowe."

The white wrath crept further over Temple's cheek bones. "My dear young cousin, I felicitate you. You have so great a wealth of talent at your disposal, and you yourself possess such vast political maturity. Naturally you do not think twice before dispensing with my poor services. However, it may be the King will view the possibility of my resignation with less complacency."

He stalked to the door. Presently came the sounds of the Temple carriage growling away out of Downing Street. Pitt remained by the fire until the expected summons came from Buckingham House, then set out up the Mall. George and his Queen were at tea, Charlotte swathed in fichus, wraps and shawls, for she felt the English cold cruelly. Everywhere was the homely clutter of a Buckingham House tea —the teapot in its cosy, the brass toasting-fork to enable George to toast his own muffins as he preferred to do, the butter from cows that had grazed on the sweet grass of Windsor Great Park. Pitt was not told to take a chair. George liked to keep his Ministers standing, thus cutting them down to size. At that point the homeliness stopped.

George turned a disturbed face towards Pitt. "What's this, Mr. Pitt—eh. what? A note just handed in from your cousin —talks of resigning—what's gone amiss with him?"

Pitt enlightened him. The King gave a mutter of anger, prodding a muffin towards the glow as if it were Temple's flesh and the fire the roastings of hell. "These damned Grenvilles! Not," George added hastily, "that I mean any imputation to your mother. A very excellent woman, Lady Chatham. But the male issue at Stowe—if a neighbour has a waterfall, they must have a cascade; if a man boasts a Grecian pillar, they must have the whole Athenian temple; others have earldoms, they can't rest until they get their hands on the strawberry leaves."

He sat pondering, turning the toasting-fork about in his hands. "Well, then, Mr. Pitt," he said at length. "I do not approve. But your difficulties are already very great. If it is the necessary condition for keeping your cousin at the cabinet table I will make this creation."

He watched the obstinacy settle in his Minister's face with some perturbation. "For my part, sir," Pitt said, "I think Lord Temple would be quite as well occupied upon his estates as at the cabinet table."

"Eh, what?" the King asked uneasily. "Not told him so, have you?"

"I indicated as much, sir."

"Oh!" George said. He gave the toasting-fork another thoughtful twirl, then braced his shoulders. "Indeed it is always pleasant to say 'no' to blackmail. If you think you can do without him, Mr. Pitt—very well, all will be as you wish."

After Pitt had gone he broke into a chuckle. "So much for Lord Gawky, Charlotte m'dear. Told to go back to Stowe and bury himself in his own mausoleum, eh, what?" His gloom returned. "Well, young Pitt is entirely on his own now," he said. "There's no man now to take any of the weight. And if he trembles—even for a moment—we're sunk."

VI

TEMPLE'S RESIGNATION was nonetheless a reeling blow to the little Mincepie Administration. Pitt found no sleep at all during this, his first night in Downing Street, the great house hanging silent about him, the snow hissing on the panes and the draught howling under the door and stirring the bed curtains and covers. By three, when the cold and his own tossings had driven all hope of sleep away, he dressed, took a candle and found his way to the library. The night porter, going his rounds, and seeing the light under the door, tapped and looked in. "Is all well, sir?" he asked.

The taper he carried flickered against his gnarled alert face. It stirred Pitt's memory. "It is Simon, is it not?"

"So you recollect then, do you, sir? You were but a little lad of seven or so when I last admitted you into this house and you admired my porter's chair in the hall."

"You've been here a good while, Simon?"

"I remember your dad, sir," the old man said simply. "And your uncle too. The house was well with the first. So long as Lord Chatham was in the great fourposter yonder or walking along these corridors on his stick the house never shook nor trembled an inch." He saw Pitt's look of disbelief at what his words implied and went on, "You're young and don't credit the tales of the house shaking. But with respect, sir, you'd credit them more if you'd been here the last ten years. Mortal bad it's been—the fireplaces shifting out, the drawers moving open, the pictures jerking themselves awry. The kitchen maids have all been clinging together, saying it was the spirit of old George Downing himself, him having lived among Americans and maybe liking the war out there pretty ill. Half right, they were—the house had a dread of York-town long before there was ever a gun on the banks of the Chesapeake. But yet they weren't more than half right. It will happen again if things are like to go bad. The house always shakes when there's danger, and the wrong man is lodged under its roof."

"Well, Simon," Pitt said. "I but hope it don't shake like a jelly tonight."

"It'll need time to sum you up, sir," the old man answered with perfect gravity, and went out.

Morning brought an early caller—the Pitt children's tutor during their youthful days at Hayes Place, the Reverend Edward Wilson. Wilson's shrewd glance took in that his one-time pupil had passed a poor night. He said at length, in his old goodhumoured, tutorial tone, "Come, William, this won't do. You were sleeping well enough at Hayes, your mother tells me, and the situation has bettered since. It was a marvellous acquisition when your cousin Temple consented to serve."

"Cousin Temple has thrown the seals on to the cabinet table and gone back to Stowe."

Wilson gave a startled, somewhat unclerical mutter. When the entire story had been given him he had little in the way of consolation to offer. At the end of their conversation he remarked, "Perhaps I can render you some little assistance, William. You will need a secretary. Shall I find you one?"

"Yes, but not a paragon of neatness in a black coat, setting straight the papers on my desk every time I turn my head. You always dubbed me your untidiest pupil."

"Hm," Wilson said. "Yes, with regard to your papers, you were." He sat in thought. "There's young Joseph Smith," he said at length. "He was up at Cambridge at about the same time as you were—Caius College, so I doubt, with the walls of Pembroke about you, you would come upon him. At the moment he is engaged by the Treasury as a junior clerk."

"He has a Cambridge degree and could obtain nothing above a junior clerk's desk at the Treasury?"

"Not a degree. Smith did not graduate. To say the truth, William, I question whether he will do. But he is a good son to his mother and a good brother to his sisters. If you desire, I will send him along."

Smith came for an interview the same evening, presenting himself before Pitt with a sort of hostile defiance. He was twenty-six, a couple of years older than the Prime Minister, his shoes polished but worn down, with one of the brass buckles bent, his coat showing a Pulteney-like threadbareness. He had few qualifications; no degree, no experience, no credentials, no languages except a smattering of French, and in all his actions possessed of a sullen maladroitness that placed everything on mantelpiece, desk and table in the direst peril. He had seemingly little use for Downing Street. After they had talked a while he remarked as if he were challenging Pitt, "I have read Rousseau. For the most part I consider him a great fool, but I incline towards him in one respect. I dislike every form of government, as Rousseau does. To my mind power is the worst of commodities."

"Then doubtless you would prefer to remain at your Treasury desk?"

"Oh, I want to come," Smith answered thinly. "I have a widowed mother and sisters. An increase in emoluments would be welcome, even if it were only for eighteen days." As Pitt looked at him he added, "They are offering twenty to one in the coffee houses against it lasting longer for you, sir, as indeed you must be aware."

He made a clumsy movement as he spoke, his elbow catching the sandcastor on the desk beside him and upending it. But his very rawness and awkwardness, his angry defences, made an appeal to the Minister, feeling his own situation similar. "Well, Smith," Pitt said, "if you can bear with this place of penance, you had better come."

A faint, half-surprised flush spread across Smith's face, though it did not blot out the hostility. "Do you want me then? I am not afraid of work, sir. I shall give of my best."

His best did not seem to amount to much. He carried a plain resentment with himself for being in Downing Street at all, and a deeper resentment with his employer, edged with a strange personal antipathy that had been on him even before he had first set foot in a room with Pitt. It added to his natural disposition for overturning any object within reach. The servants were constantly running after him with damp cloths to wipe spilled ink from the desks or tea stains from the napery. He occasioned agony to Burfield who greatly loved Number 10 and thought it deserved better than Smith.

Burfield indeed mourned the going of Portland. "I prefer the dukes, Mrs. Burfield," the steward was saying to his wife in the hallway as Pitt came down on the day Parliament was due to reassemble. "A duke in Number 10 gives me uncommon satisfaction, I own to it."

Both Burfields addressed one another with stately formality, giving the impression they did so even with the four-poster's curtains drawn about them. His wife replied in the same fashion. "Well, indeed, Mr. Burfield, there's been so many changes here just recent it begins to look like one of those games of move-all the children play at Christmas."

"I could add 'with children to play it too seemingly'," Burfield answered darkly. "But it is not my place, Mrs. Burfield, to make malapert observations about the Minister."

He did not see Pitt but came to him later. He asked how many grooms Pitt required to attend upon him when he rode in the park and was told none.

"His Grace of Portland never rode in St. James's Park with less than three grooms, sir," Burfield said gently. It was not meant as an officious remark. Burfield was but trying to bring Pitt up in the way Prime Ministers should go. "You might be thrown."

"If I am, Burfield, it's but a short step back."

Burfield went out with a shake of his head. With the horse brought round from the stables Pitt took his way into St. James's Park. There was scarcely anyone afoot yet, only two dairymaids and a cowherd driving the cows in to their wintry grazing in the park. The herd's soft, plaintive lowing filled the city with stolen countrified echoes. Towards Buckingham House the Mall stretched emptily away, but presently a chair came swaying out from Stable Yard with a manservant walking beside it. From inside a voice commanded the bearers to set it down. As Pitt dismounted, Susan Weddell leant from the little framed window, the blue eyes bright as stars. "Good day, sir. How is it with you?"

"Well enough. And you, ma'am?"

She laughed breathlessly. "Oh, vastly well, marvellous well. I am to be wed in a month. I'll not give you his name.

It will mean nothing at all to you, nor does it, I fear, to any-one else. He is a gentleman of Devonshire. Scarce a head turns when he comes into the room. But I find myself quite giddy with happiness."

Pitt answered her with a plain sincerity, "I am very glad, ma'am. May nothing disturb your Devonshire idyll."

She recognised the goodwill behind the words and smiled. "I think we both wish each other well, though as to your situation, sir, yours is scarce an idyll and will be less of one this evening, I am afraid."

"Come along, little madam," the manservant advised, stepping restively forward. "I was charged to bring you direct to my Lady Spencer's for breakfast, not to stand by while you engage in conversation with some young gentleman riding in the park."

"Oh, fie, John, it's the Minister. Yes, it is—I am not stuff-ing you."

Her glance took on a greater gravity, going beyond Pitt to the grey block of the Admiralty across the park, the clock tower of the Horse Guards and the roofs of Downing Street set about in their winter trees. "You perceive I was right about you," she said. "For I was always assured you would command the gaze of England one day. For my part I hope when the roses are out again in the garden of Number 10 it will be you who are there to look out on them."

As the chair was borne on its way, her young voice called back to him, "Don't have Downing Street do to you as it did to my Uncle Charles Rockingham."

VII

Parliament reassembled at half past two the same afternoon. The weather, this January of 1784, had turned suddenly as bleak and buffeting as the session promised to be, the stoves all stoked and kindled, and Pearson or Jessel plying the bellows to the lobby fire.

"That's thin material for our coming all-night stint, Pulteney," Sheridan remarked as Pulteney entered the lobby in his customary worn coat. "On such an occasion could not the Bath estates rise to a better piece of broadcloth for you?"

Pulteney flushed. He could bear anything save an allusion that he was dependent on his wife's fortune. But he answered no more than mildly, "Why, Sherry, is this a wager you'll have me out of countenance before the session is a day old?"

"Cold?" roared Sir John Honeywood. "Yes—'tis perishing. My chamber pot was frozen in the bedroom this morning—I say my chamber pot was frozen." He fixed a riveted gaze down the lobby. "Upon my word, look at Fox."

Fox was coming up the vestibule steps, his appearance causing a considerable stir. Westminster indulged its old quirks of custom. Only the shire members were permitted to come spurred into the chamber, and only the King's Ministers appeared in full dress. In part this was out of deference to the House and in part a means of identification. Strangers in the lobby knew the county members by their boots and spurs; the Ministers by their swords and lace. Pitt, alone of the House, as the sole Minister and only occupant of the Treasury Bench, should have come down this day in formal attire. But Fox had taken to himself a similar privilege. He was dressed as he had been all last session when he had held the Secretary of State seals under the Coalition. All was ministerial about him—his hair powdered white instead of its customary blue, his dress sword against his great thigh, his shirt carrying its full falls of lace. As it was borne upon his followers what he was doing the shouts of laughter went up on all sides.

"Good God, Charles," Fitzpatrick said. "You and William, alone in your formal coats—you will look like Castor and

Pollux, the heavenly twins, facing each other across the floor of the House."

"To misquote the Bard, I hope Master Billy yearns not himself if men his garments wear," Sheridan remarked in a solemn voice. "Though for my part I think he might."

"I considered we might as well play this session out under the mask of Thalia, the comic muse," Fox answered with a laugh.

He saw the faint cast of anger in Pulteney's face and crossed over to him, both of them drawing a little to one side for private speech.

"You do not approve my attire, Pulteney?" Fox asked.

"I think it is a personal affront you could well have spared him."

"He has no mandate save from the King and his own ambition. If he arrogates himself Minister, why, so can any man."

Pulteney fastened his level glance upon him. "Charles, be warned. The Pitts were good endurers. They could lie to their arms in the ditch for an unconscionable time where the fire was hottest."

Fox returned his look. "Were I to exert myself I could have him on his knees in the House in a week. But I think it more efficacious for us to prolong this lesson. The House loves to teach over-ambitious and over-arrogant young men in the small hours of dark January mornings when they are cold and stiff and chastened. It is less comfortable than the library at Hayes but it imparts a greater wisdom."

He went back to his followers. The lobby now was almost rocking with mirth, the reporters grinning, the attendants grinning also, the foreign ambassadors restrained but curious. Pitt's friends drew together in a thin, furious and helpless group.

"Half the world's looking on," Pepper Arden muttered. "I'll cut through Westminster Hall and try to warn Billy."

But it was too late for it. Pitt was coming up the vestibule steps, Wilberforce walking with him. The sounds of the hilarity in the lobby warned him there was something here for his discomfort. But he had no expectancy of seeing Fox in full dress. This was a mock that the House in all its history had never before visited on a Minister. For a space his stride faltered—Wilberforce, at his side, feeling the check rather than seeing it, then he pulled himself together and came on.

"No need to forswear the contents of your gin cupboard yet, Pearson," John Courteney remarked to the head door-keeper. "You really are seeing two of them."

"Very comic, that, Mr. Courteney," Pearson said sourly. "You must have your supper table in a roar, you must, sir, with your wit."

Fox had turned towards the chamber. At the same time Simon Vorontzov, the newly-arrived Russian ambassador— Russia having just re-established diplomatic relations after the war—came in from the Long Gallery. Vorontzov's great-coat was tossed carelessly over his orders, which he knew proclaimed him. He had presented his credentials to the King only the previous levée day when Pitt had not been present. Finding himself face to face with Fox, he bowed, saying in good English, tinged by a slight French accent, "Sir, I shall be waiting upon you officially in the course of the week. But since we have walked clean into one another now perhaps we may be permitted to speak."

"The gentleman you require is yonder by the vestibule clock, Excellency," Fox answered amusedly.

"That's Mr. Pitt, sir," Barnwell, the Gallery attendant, broke in, trying to be helpful. "The younger one, what's thinner."

Vorontzov's face changed. He began to fear he had committed some grave English solecism and he turned his glance queryingly towards the French ambassador who answered with an ironic Gallic shrug. Pitt came forward.

"I am sorry, sir," Vorontzov said, recovering himself. "I was told only you, as Minister, would be formally attired.

Have I then been misinformed as to your customs?"

"No, Your Excellency has been told correctly."

"But this other gentleman—"

"Mr. Fox."

Vorontzov looked at him sharply. He realised now all was at the expense of the Minister and his glance held a hint of compassion. They exchanged a few diplomatic courtesies, Vorontzov excusing himself as soon as he could, and being handed over to the care of Barnwell.

With the lobby beginning to empty now Pitt's friends came about him. "My faith, Billy," Dudley Ryder said in a raging voice, "can't we do something about Fox—have the Chair call him to order?"

"He's not out of order because he wears his lace. It's a matter of form only."

"Move against it, then," Pepper Arden suggested savagely. "That this House views with disfavour the assumption by non-Ministers of the style and manner of dress customarily pertaining only to Ministers—something after those words. I'll put the motion."

"If you think you would carry it in this Commons, Pepper, you're a vast optimist," Pitt remarked. He added, half to himself, "I must be almost as raw as they dub me. I thought Charles would be content straightly to be my enemy and leave the jibings to Sheridan."

Distantly doors were beginning to open and shut down the Speaker's corridor, the first shouts of "Hats off, Strangers", apprising them of the Speaker's approach. Governor Johnstone came up the vestibule steps. He clapped a hand on Pitt's shoulder and silently went on through the double doors.

"I wish you good fortune, sir," Pulteney said.

"Good luck," Wilberforce said, while Eliot pressed his friend's arm. "When I said I would one day see you the first man in the land I meant in very fact."

"Good luck, Billy, my boy," Pepper Arden echoed. "Remember those proud tales I am to tell my grandchildren."

So, with his friends' encouragements in his ears, Pitt walked on into the House, to the hour of ordeal. The Galleries were as yet empty, the Government back benches almost so, with a figure here and there like a very thin audience at a bad play. Almost all those present seemed to be crowded into Opposition—the two great factions of England now ranged together, the men who followed North and the men who followed Fox, the inheritors of what had once been Tory and what had once been Whig, trailing about them still the splendour of their fierce traditions, their long-learnt skills of debate. Formidable apart, they made a terrible unity.

Since the rest of Pitt's tiny cabinet were in the Lords, the Treasury Bench had not a second occupant. Pitt turned aside to sit there alone. The shouts heralding the Speaker brought the House to its feet. Speaker Cornwall came in with the worn air of a schoolmaster who scented that the unruly elements in his class were gaining the ascendant. But the gusts of tradition and authority he brought with him—his clerks, chaplain and mace-bearer—imposed a calm. The House fell to prayer with as much gravity as its Reformation ancestors had done, when the wainscoting on the walls had been newly bright, and the prayers, spoken for the first time in the English tongue, had seemed strange and bold. Except during the Lord's Prayer, when they turned towards the walls, they remained as they had risen in their places. Pitt and Fox stood facing each other with only the famed two sword-lengths between them. They did not look at one another but kept their heads bowed.

The prayers done, Cornwall mounted to his place. The public were admitted into the Gallery and the trampling, gasping, grunting and shuffling overhead had the sound of a large army attempting to squeeze into a very small redoubt. With the King's message to deliver—always done at once—Pitt rose. The House permitted him half a dozen words, then howled him down. He tried again and once more they broke into uproar, drowning utterly and gleefully all he said.

He gave way to them and sat down. Into the ensuing quiet the Opposition flung all their individual and matchless quality—the erudition of Burke, the wit of Sheridan, the experience of North, the diamond brilliance of Fox. And with the division bells ringing and in mounting clamour and ferocity, the motions of censure began to be slammed through against the Mincepie Administration.

Dundas reached the Palace of Westminster after midnight. He had been in two minds whether to come, doubting if he would take much enjoyment in the night's spectacle. But he had succumbed at length, driving in from Wimbledon over icy roads to find the roofs of Westminster silvered with icy hoar.

"'Tis a frost hard as iron already, Jessel," he said to the doorkeeper as he came through the lobby. "Who's up now?"

"Mr. Fox, sir. And he's hot enough."

Inside Fox was on his feet, his great bulk outlined against the pools of candlelight, his splendid and scorching invective filling the little chamber—"a boy, without knowledge of the world, without even the common decencies, following the headlong course of his own ambition. Why, sir, he is already a plague to the country he leads and he will not be suffered to lead it much longer."

Pitt was unmoving on the Treasury Bench. Dundas thought he had never seen so masklike a countenance. He squeezed into a place on the crowded benches. George Sutton, his neighbour, remarked to him, "I thought you had decided to keep to your bed tonight like a wise man."

"The House affords me more warmth than does my empty bed."

It was in fact very cold. But all was so noisy, so bitter and so one-sided the atmosphere was one of sweaty heat. After Fox, Conway caught the Speaker's eye, rising up like an avenging devil in his British Army scarlet from among the sombre buffs and browns of the Opposition. Pitt heard himself arraigned again as a boy, this time a sulky one, sitting in sullen silence on the Treasury Bench, and then, in an attack grown so violent and personal that it stilled the House, as a backstairs creeper to office, his honour cast aside, his actions tainted.

The House, which before had given him no hearing, now swung on the opposite tack, and chorused, "Answer, answer." The exhaustion of the small hours was on them, the ebb of the river tugging against the walls outside, the ebb of the night tugging against the spirits. Pitt, silenced for so long by sheer volume of noise, seemed to have lost tongue. He sat still. The House roared again, "Answer, answer."

"In faith, he had better answer," George Sutton muttered. "The Mincepie Administration's dead in a night if he does not."

Pitt came to his feet. He seemed to have judged how little space the House would give him and he fell on Conway in three biting sentences. "The honourable and gallant member makes charges of corruption. Let him prove them. As to my honour, I am the best judge of that."

It was the voice of Chatham, imperious and dominant, without explanation or excuse. But no more spurt of triumph was to be the Prime Minister's that night. The windows, which had gone from light to a velvet winter black, paled again to dawn. At half past seven in the morning the House rose. For seventeen hours, from half past two the previous afternoon, and with five divisions carried against him, Pitt had had to answer for his sins in taking office.

Dundas came stiffly out into the lobby to join Pulteney. Pulteney had a wiry strength but he was fifty now and the marks of the sleepless night lay on his face. They walked together down the vestibule steps and into Westminster Hall.

"The spectacle yonder took me back to my boyhood," Dundas remarked presently. "My father had a young terrier he made much o' at Arniston. One sultry day his hounds set upon it from jealousy. The terrier fought the whole pack, wi' its back to the stable door. I ran in to seize one o' the big brutes by the tail to try to haul it off—until the factor's wife pulled me aside, asking if I wanted my limbs torn awa' too. Yet there were times tonight when almost I had the same urge to intervene."

"Then go in again, Dundas," Pulteney said. "Seize one of the big brutes by the tail and try to haul him off as you did at Arniston."

"Och, what use would it be? The terrier was still a mangled thing lying in its own blood by the stable door, for all the teeth-marks in my arm. The incident would but repeat itsel'."

VIII

BACK AT Wimbledon, Dundas, after a few hours' sleep, took horse to ride briefly on the Common. It was very cold, Rushmere Pond brittling already to splinters of ice. But after the foul air of the House and its fouler humour all was as fresh and invigorating as standing braced in the shrouds of a three-decker. A handsome curricle came sweeping up Wimbledon Hill, Lady Jean Hope inside, and her brother, Hopetoun, keeping pace as outrider. The little cavalcade reined, Lady Jean leaning out to ask Dundas to ride back with them to take tea.

Dundas declined, saying, "I've just breakfasted."

"Breakfasted, sir?" Lady Jean said. "It's half past three in the afternoon."

"He was from his bed all last night, Jean," Hopetoun said. "They all were." He had witnessed part of the debate and made reference to it, turning to Dundas. "So young Billy goes back to it all again in another couple of hours. He must, in truth, feel like a schoolboy waiting in the corridor for his headmaster's birch."

"He attracts me as no' North nor Rockingham nor Shelburne ever did. I'm gi'ing my voice to him."

They both sat regarding him, Hopetoun's brows lifting. "Most would be hard put to call the little Mincepie Administration the winning side, Dundas," he remarked at length in a dry voice.

"There'll no' be a winning side for any o' us unless he continues in Downing Street. It is wi' him as it was wi' his father. Whether he'll save us, I ken no', but he's the only one who can."

Lady Jean opened her mouth to make faint protest but Hopetoun cut across her with a burst of laughter. "Come, Jean, there's no arguing here. And to think I called you auldfarrant, Dundas. You toss up your bonnet for Billy Pitt as recklessly as any wild Duniewassal declaring for a chieftain with nothing to offer him save a losing bloody battle in the heather."

He signalled the coachman. As the horses went forward he called over his shoulder, "Ride over to visit us the instant you are back at Melville."

It rang as a friendly farewell. But Lady Jean continued to look back, her face wistful in its framing hood, as though all prospect of a Hope-Dundas wedding was being crunched to powder like the grains of frost under her curricle's wheels.

IX

DUNDAS SOUGHT out Pitt the same afternoon, coming upon him in the Smoking Room. At this early hour Westminster was empty and the upper corridor deserted. Dundas caught sight of the Minister through the half-open door. In that unguarded moment he looked much as the schoolboy Hopetoun had likened him to, waiting dejectedly in the corridor for the headmaster's birch. Then the floorboards creaked under Dundas's tread, and the contained Grenville expression was clapped back.

Dundas went dourly in. He had already sent a note to Downing Street and knew Pitt to be apprised of his intentions. But he expected no great welcome. It seemed to him he would be regarded as no more than a second Temple—Scotch Harry, despairing of ingratiating himself with the winning side, and therefore with his hand out here for some picking. It was much to his astonishment when he was greeted almost as Wilberforce or Eliot might have been.

With the night thrusting in from the river and the bare trees they sat and talked easily, as if they had long been colleagues. Dundas still questioned whether this young and inexperienced man altogether realised on what a knife-edge he was balanced. He broached the matter with a direct question. "You ken what you are risking?"

"Impeachment? Committal to the Tower? Removal from His Majesty's councils as an enemy of my country?" He added wryly, "Yes, I learnt enough constitutional history in the library at Hayes to know that Ministers out of favour with the House and holding on without a majority are greatly liable to be cuffed about the head with such penalties."

"Och, forgive me. There's been jibes enough wi' regard to your inexperience, God knows. But how do you assess the risk?"

"On my word, I don't know. But at least these things are for statesmen, not for a silly schoolboy who ought to have a stirrup strap on his backside which is Conway's prescription for my sins, and not for an indecent boy, a plague to the country he leads, who ought to be made a great public fool of in the pillory every night of the week, which is Charles Fox's prescription for them. If it came to impeachment or committal in preference to the indignities—my faith, it would give me a deal of sour satisfaction even in the Tower, knowing I had driven them to it."

"Aye, 'tis no' a juvenile's punishment," Dundas remarked

but he derived little comfort from the thought.

The old palace was beginning to awaken to its evening activity—the tramp of the reporters' feet sounding on the stairs and the clink of crockery from Bellamy's. They rose to go, Dundas voicing his initial misgiving. "Is it no' in your thoughts—as it'll be in the thoughts o' the rest—that I'll present my tally like Temple?"

"Viscount Canongate? The First Duke of Galashiels?" He mocked Dundas with a sort of affectionate gratitude. "Harry Dundas, who has a great compulsion to come to the aid of the underdog, and can't always resist it."

This was the Pitt of Wilberforce's table or of Goosetree's Club, among his chosen friends. Dundas was beginning to recognise here a strange aversion to the wiles of politics, so that, in public and before strangers, this grace was kept behind bolts and bars in case it should win votes or followers, or be thought of as attempting to. "I read you at Lincoln's Inn much otherwise to the manner o' man you really are," he said at length.

"I knew you had small liking for me that night."

"You presented an awfu' cold face."

"Forgive me. Until I am assured of a man—especially one whose business is politics—I am apt to cast up all manner of defences as assiduously as the engineers fortifying Gibraltar."

"Why, I find that strange," Dundas said. "Since it implies that at some point you imagine yoursel' vulnerable, and I canna' conceive what the point might be. You ha'e a brilliant intellect. Most would gi'e their right arm to ha'e a mind such as yours."

He was answered in so low a tone he barely caught it. "It might be they would make a poor bargain."

X

JOINED BY Wilberforce and Eliot, Pitt went down towards the

chamber. The lobby fire had been generously stoked, Edward Colman, the Serjeant-at-Arms, warming himself in front of it. Colman had been away sick and with his duties undertaken by his deputy did not realise how stormily the session had opened. "Now, Mr. Pitt," he remarked cheerfully at sight of them. "You've been annoying the gentlemen opposite, I hear. If you're not careful, sir, I'll be taking you in custody to the Tower, and it's a great pity you are not a knight for then my fee would be five pounds for it. As it is, since you are but a burgess, I can only claim three pounds, six and eight from the Office—and that will not reach far these days." He turned away chuckling.

"Ought we to jest on it?" Eliot muttered. 'Tower' and 'impeachment' were terrible words to the Eliot family, their past haunted by the shadow of Sir John Eliot, dying in bouts of bloody spittings in the damp chill of the Tower, while outside King and Parliament had sharpened broadswords and primed their pistols.

"They lodge you better today than they did your martyred parliamentary ancestor, Edward," Pitt answered. It sounded an airy dismissal of the threat but in fact the thought of the Tower daunted him less than the thought of public humiliation at the hands of Fox.

The Speaker was just behind them. As they went through the doors Jessel pushed a letter into the Minister's hand, remarking, "Brought in by special messenger but two minutes gone, sir—marked 'urgent'."

Pitt thrust the letter into his pocket. While prayers were in progress he could do nothing about it. But later, with the House listening to counsel for the Nisbit divorce petition—which did not especially concern Ministers—he drew it out. About to tear off its wafer seal he felt a warning prick of his parliamentary blood, as if a gust of expectancy had blown upon him from the Opposition benches. He looked up. A section of them were all agog, Hare already half on his feet, his mouth open.

There was not much experienced aid at hand for the
Minister to look to. Dundas, having had enough of divorce
petitions, had not come down and Pulteney was also absent.
Pitt leant back and muttered to Wilberforce on the bench
behind him, "Will, what's amiss?"

"Is somewhat?"

"Yes, they are going to call me to order and I'm damned if
I know why."

During his short parliamentary life he had seen many men
read letters. But he heeded his instinct and returned the note
to his pocket. Across on the Opposition benches Hare sub-
sided back with every aspect of disappointment.

Pitt left his place and after a few moments Eliot and
Wilberforce followed him. He had the letter open in his
hands as they came into the lobby, passing it to them in
silence. It was no more than an invitation from Hare asking
the Minister to dinner at his house in St. James's Street—
which he shared with Fox—on Wednesday week.

"One smells a mouse at least," Wilberforce remarked.

"So I think." Pitt turned towards the Long Gallery. "While
the House decides whether or not the Nisbits are still joined
together in holy matrimony we have time to look into the
library."

The Commons' library was almost deserted. Behind his
table, Rossiter, the librarian assistant, peered at them over
his glasses, his high stock collar elongating his neck, and his
cardboard over-cuffs, that he wore to protect his bands, giving
his wrists the same appearance of being stretched on the rack.
"Contrary to the rules, sir," he answered when queried.
"Reading letters in the House is disorderly conduct, though
you all forget that it is these days, do you not, and the
Speaker would wink at it unless he were called upon. That
especial standing order was carried on the 29th of March
1677. You will find it in Volume II of *Parliamentary Pro-
ceedings*. There's another reference in *Grey's Debates*,
Volume IV, page 331."

Pitt complimented him on his powers of memory, remarking, "You do excellent well to recall even the number of the page."

"Oh, I can't take credit there, sir," Rossiter said. "The fact is all you gentlemen seem to have become very nice in your conduct all of a sudden. I had Mr. Payne, Mr. Hare and Lord John Townshend in here just yesterday checking on that very point of order—that among others. They wanted those rules the House inclines now not to observe—"

Some light broke upon him. He smoothed a duster over the cover of *Grey's Debates* to the accompaniment of an embarrassed humming, then slapped down the cloth and spoke again. "There is another thing most of you forget now, Mr. Pitt. If you are speaking from the Treasury Bench you must have one foot within the floor of the House, and you tend to move back when you are tired, sir. Don't stand with both feet on the baize carpeting. Mr. Payne or Mr. Hare would be up upon the instant and there are so many foreigners and reporters and such in the Gallery these nights. You would feel it, I dare say, if the Speaker had to call you to order on a matter of procedure."

"I'm exceedingly obliged to you, Mr. Rossiter."

"Not at all, sir. But a word in your ear."

Outside in the corridor Pitt gave an exclamation of grim amusement. "So they wanted to find somewhat we had not touched on in the library at Hayes. They succeeded too. I'll decline Hare's invitation through Pearson and suggest that any future messages between us should be verbal."

He went back into the chamber to lay his own East India Bill before the House, not, during the length of a three-hour speech, using notes, since to have done so would have brought half the Opposition to their feet, riving the air with cries of "Mr. Speaker, he is reading his speech". Wilberforce, watching him, judged him undisturbed by the earlier incident. The Hares, the Jack Townshends and the Paynes might spring their traps, but he trusted to his stars and to himself he had defences enough against them. It was Fox, still contemptuously coming in in the full dress of a Minister, who knew much more assuredly where the armour gaped.

XI

WITH THE debate done Sheridan drew Fox and North into the Speaker's room. Sheridan's expression had lost its piquancy. In the privacy of the handsome room and with the door shut upon them he rounded on Fox. "My faith, Charles, how did you rate that? Three hours without a note, a heading or a falter. And it was a statesmanlike measure—a vast deal better than yours and Edmund Burke's, though I don't say so beyond these four walls."

"What strategy do you then advocate, Sherry?"

"Get him off the Treasury Bench. Impeach him, if you must."

"I think you do not favour that course, Charles," North remarked in his placid voice. "No more do I. Impeachment would arouse sympathy for him. Even now he makes a brave fight of it and the public in the Gallery can see it. Indeed, my good Sheridan, I wish you had the stage-management of this, our nightly performance, for, were it Drury Lane, doubtless you could alter the emphasis somewhat."

"If I had the stage-management of it, I would have him in Edward Colman's custody tomorrow and clapped into the Tower."

"Good God, you would please Master Billy if you did," Fox said with a laugh. "Treated in so adult a fashion—borne off to the Tower to tread in the steps of martyrs and heroes. You would elevate him to the stature of a statesman in the space of an afternoon."

"His situation is exceedingly desperate," North said gently. "For he must hold what little he has. The small core of men about him—Pulteney and Wilberforce, Johnstone, Bankes and Steele, Dundas too, after his fashion and at this hour—'tis an abused word in some circles these days, but they are patriots, not party men. If they become convinced that to keep him where he is is to the land's hurt, they would go from him. They might weep for it in private, but they would go. And when we see it so in the division lists we will know it is the finish and so will our young gentleman opposite."

He nodded and went out through the door into the Speaker's corridor. "Come, Sherry," Fox said, as Sheridan remained by the window looking towards the river and the greyly lightening trees. "The session's but four days old. Master Billy will present a very different aspect on the Treasury Bench by the middle of February. Indeed we must contrive to keep this present Parliament in being so that he may not escape from that stool of correction save on the necessary terms."

"You desire to teach him a lesson, Charles. But what if, in the end, it proves to be but the same lesson his damned father tried to teach him at Hayes? What if, by Easter, we have made a Minister of him—and a good one?" He looked round at Fox. "I still say get him out. But I own to it there are better methods than impeaching him. Withhold the Supplies. Not a ship could sail or a grenadier affix his bayonet without they are passed through."

"We would be great fools to do that. It would be to throw him out on a technicality. He could point to it afterwards in extenuation rather than to his own shortcomings." He turned towards the door, the candles in the wall sconces outlining his bulk in dominating shadow. "There is but one way here," he said. "He must be shown as unfitted to rule, publicly, in front of the House, in front of the reporters in the Gallery and the public sat there with them, in front of himself, so that not even his vast Pitt conceit can gainsay it afterwards. One night when he has been rendered sufficiently tongue-tied and foolish under the candles, when, as North says, even the men he has start to quit him, he will crawl in and resign. And that must be the manner of his going, by resignation, by his own admission that he cannot sustain this office he snatched at. And all is moving towards that end precisely as I would wish."

He clapped Sheridan on the shoulder and went out after North into the Speaker's corridor.

XII

INTEREST IN the contest had grown huge. From ten in the morning the Gallery was filled, the public sitting there most patiently, with only empty green benches or a lone cleaner to look down on, until four or five in the evening. Turned out for prayers they would file back to reclaim their places, continuing round the clock while below them the battle raged on the floor of the chamber.

Pitt knew now the strategy that was being mounted against him—the Opposition trying to ensure he could only quit office by one of three rough roads, resignation, impeachment or dismissal by the King. For hour after chill hour, with Dundas now on the bench behind him, he struggled to prop up the little reeling Mincepie Administration. The House still visited on him great gusting shifts of mood, rounding on him after spells of tumult, with shouts of "Answer, answer", then falling utterly silent awaiting his voice. In these quiescences there was always a rustle of expectancy in the Gallery, the reporters reaching for the notebooks they were not in fact supposed to bring in. These were the moments when his friends most trembled for him, and so, behind a stony Pittite mask, did he, hearing the ominous tiny flutter in the Gallery and knowing the reporters expected the end. The rustle of notebooks, of quills and clinking silver pencils began to have a sound as foreboding and ghoulish as the ring of a spade outside the window of a desperately sick man, or the hammering of the scaffold hard by the cell of the condemned felon. Speaker Cornwall, chained to the Chair, as surely as the Minister was chained to the Treasury Bench, had taken to kindling his energies with draughts of porter. An arm brandishing a tankard would thrust itself through Solomon's Porch, a hoarse voice muttering, "If you please, sir, the Speaker's porter." The House could have challenged the action but never did. Its wrath was reserved for Pitt.

On the 23rd he went up to the Smoking Room, intent on snatching some quiet before facing the din and tempest of the House. Reporters too were allowed to use this—the First Committee Room—making up, on the wide table and under the bright candles, the notes they could be challenged for taking down in the Gallery. One of them followed in after the Minister, the little white dog that constantly lurked at his heels sidling in alongside, though it would have occasioned the Serjeant-at-Arms no pleasure to have seen it here.

He gave Pitt a sharp glance, then touched on the situation —Fox, the night previously, having promised passage to the Supplies and the resolutions that Parliament ought not to be dissolved tossed broadcast on to the journals. "Well, sir, the pattern emerges—all loopholes secured against you. It is to be *à l'outrance* between yourself and Fox." He began to fill up his pocket phial from one of the great inkwells on the table. "And—that you might get your guard up against it—they mean to throw out your East India Bill at its Second Reading."

"I thought it likely, but I am obliged for being forewarned." He added, "I have seen you about in the lobby but I never learnt your name."

"O'Halloran," the other said, with a brief, workmanlike bow. "*The Morning Chronicle*, an Opposition newspaper, as, of course, you are well aware—founded fifteen years ago out of Lord Rockingham's affluence and now gone, as by the laws of testacy, to Charles James Fox, whose speeches I report with every mark of approval."

"Possibly that accords with your own views."

"Why, God bless you, sir," O'Halloran answered airily, "I have no views. 'Tis but my paper has views." His look became graver. "But I lie to you in that, for my time in the Gallery has given me one view, or bred in me one passion, if you should term it so—the balance of the constitution, resting squarely on its three stays, King, Parliament and the *vox populi*, each with about equal power and ready to assert it, so that if one of the three grows over-arrogant and over-dominant, the other two will combine against it—Parliament and people against the King; the King and his people against Parliament; Parliament and King against the worst excesses of the people, and the Gordon Riots weren't pretty, on my faith. Take yourself. The constitution will give verdict on you presently either by impeachment or the country pronouncing on you or—as we in the Gallery hold it will be—by Fox making an end of you in debate."

"You are persuaded it will be that, O'Halloran?"

"It must be, must it not, sir?" O'Halloran said with a straight look at him. "One night when you are especially fatigued or less than wholly in health, when the Opposition seems to have more men in it and your own side less, you will come to your beat point. And 'tis but fair to warn you we of the Rockingham press earn our daily crusts by our readiness to set it all down in bold print for London to rattle round in conversation along with the rattle of its morning teacups."

Outside the window the roofs of the city lay scaled in their frost under the moon. Pitt looked towards them, remarking with a small inflection of bitterness, *"Report, say they, and we will report it. All my familiars watched for my halting."*

"That's exceedingly apt," O'Halloran commented admiringly. "From the Book of Jeremiah, is it not? Contrary to what the *vox populi* thinks of Fleet Street, we do, on occasion, go to St. Bride's of a Sunday and hear the Scriptures." He clipped his bottle of ink into his button-hole and called the dog over to him. "And—that you might get your guard up against this too—your time of crisis will be the next forty-eight hours. Fox means to tighten the screw."

XIII

Fox TIGHTENED the screw in fierce turns—carrying an address to the King to dismiss his Minister and adjourning the next morning at seven for a bare five hours. While many of the weary members did not bother to go home, sleeping about the Smoking Room and committee rooms and fingering the prickling of chins that had that dawn gone unshaven, Pitt had to draft the King's reply and to wait upon him with it, nor would any Minister have dreamt of attending his sovereign unwashed and unshaven and in clothes that had seen the night out in the House. His resultant loss of sleep presented a grim threat to the Mincepie Administration.

With the Minister not yet back from Buckingham House, Wilberforce and Eliot waited in the lobby. It was only noon, the House already at prayer for its early sitting, and the public—not admitted until this was done—overspilling down the steps into Westminster Hall. At one side the ladies had begun their brisk hard climb up the housekeeper's stairs to the Ventilator Room; at the other, the long, wholly masculine Gallery queue snaked about the clock under the marshalling of Barnwell.

O'Halloran stood with his two fellow Irishmen, Mark Supple and Peter Finnegan. They and the rest of the reporters were ranged about their most notable colleague, 'Memory' Woodfall, who, with his gold-headed cane, gold snuff box and splendid queue ribbon, could have been—and sometimes was—mistaken for a prince of the blood. O'Halloran's little white dog still lurked at his heels.

Though it seemed docile it sometimes lived up to its name
—Fury—and had twice run amok, spreading tumult
throughout the lobby.

"You keep that dorg controlled, O'Halloran," Barnwell
said with a baleful eye upon it. "Creature straight out of
hell, that dorg is. And if you try to smuggle him into the
Gallery, like you did last week, it's h'out for the pair o' you."

"You're a hard man, Joshua Barnwell, so you are,"
O'Halloran answered blithely, then addressed the dog,
"Down, sir—wait." The little creature crouched at once by
the hearth with every aspect of obedience.

Pitt came up the vestibule steps at that moment, joining
Wilberforce and Eliot. With prayers all but finished it was
hardly worthwhile entering the chamber and they made
their way through the press towards the secluded dimness of
the Long Gallery. O'Halloran's glance had gone to Pitt, idly
at first, but now returning upon him fixedly. In the stillness
—the Lobby hushed for the worship going on beyond the
closed doors—the Irishman's soft voice spoke, reaching their
ears, "Clip another phial of ink in your pocket, Mark. They'll
have the boyo tonight."

Pitt stepped into the empty Clerk's Room. He had looked
contained coming through the lobby but the clawings of
defeat that O'Halloran had sensed upon him were there. He
said suddenly, "If I could but tell what the country is thinking—the shires under the frost, the cities and the villages,
the hamlets, Old Sarum with its one farmhouse. She waits,
I suppose, to see how quickly I am brought down and I but
know it will be a most damned public finish when it comes
about." He turned to the window. "I have had enough, I
think. Better to go in and tell them I resign rather than have
Fox make a tongue-tied end of me at two in the morning,
with the reporters settling their notebooks on their knees
and the Gallery gaping down on us—for I doubt I can marshal
six words together tonight."

At this moment he seemingly indeed found Westminster

what it had once been—Thorney Island, the one-time acreage of swamp and fever that the old Saxon chroniclers had never referred to except as *in loco terribili*, the terrible place. Wilberforce and Eliot could bring no help to this issue. They waited while he contested it.

From the lobby came the sound of the doors of the House being flung back, announcing prayers were at an end. The traditional shout carried down upon them, "Speaker's in the chair." Pitt stood unmoving. Again, more insistently, like cocks tossing to and fro one another's dawn crowing, the attendants' voices echoed along the stony corridor, "Speaker's in the chair."

There was an outbreak of talk and laughter from the Long Gallery. Fox, late into the House like many others this noon, went by with Hare, Fitzpatrick and Sheridan. The open door afforded a clear sight of him as he passed, amusedly confident, still in the full dress of a Minister which he had worn every night without variance. Pitt lifted his head. He said softly, not for Fox's ears but for his own,

"But to have me resign is what Fox wants, and this time—this time—Charles, my fine friend, you are not going to get it."

He turned back towards the lobby. "Young Billy's late for his pasting this afternoon," Sutton was saying, as they regained it. "He had better be here soon."

"He's here now," Pitt answered from behind.

"Oh, there you are," Sutton gave his ironic grin. "I began to think you had quit."

He moved away from them. Pitt glanced through the doors to the crowded benches of the House, then back to Wilberforce and Eliot. "Well, let's get in," he said in a low voice. "And if I can endure beyond two of the clock tomorrow morning, my word on it, I believe I can get through anything."

He did endure beyond two of the clock but it was an exceedingly rough night, the watching Gallery seeing him as if he were in the centre of dashing tides, deluged and sometimes all but submerged by them, but each succeeding wave spending itself against him and receding. The more he held on and fought them, looking capable of state and office, the nearer they drew to impeaching him. By midnight, with Lord Surrey spluttering out menaces of committal and punishment, they were only inches away from it, half the Opposition beginning to bay at their own front bench, "Move—move—Tower—Tower."

Edward Colman, in the Serjeant-at-Arms' little partially curtained recess behind the Bar of the House, turned deadly white—Eliot equally so. But Pitt himself was by now in such revolt against the jibing merriment at his youth that to have the House visit upon him its highest censure gave him in that hot moment almost a satisfaction. Fox caught his look, seeing again the little boy in the long grasses at Kingsgate who had always desired to be treated adultly. He was determined it should be his own parliamentary prowess and not the Tower walls that would decide the issue here. He turned his black brows grimly on his followers. Most of them had read Pitt's expression for themselves. They knew that to render him inept and fumbling under the eyes of the Gallery was the better way. The baying broke off, and the quarry, escaping that check for the night, had to fight the hounds over the old rough ground of his youth and incompetence.

"William makes a mighty fight for his parliamentary life," Sutton said as he came out through the doors with Pulteney. "I thought he would be breakfasting in the Tower this morning. He did not look as if it would exercise him much if he did."

"Good," Pulteney commented briefly. "They threaten vastly more and laugh vastly less."

As Pitt and Eliot came out together, Edward Colman followed. "It was almost as if I had wished that upon you, Mr.

Pitt," he said in a low shaken voice. "And, my word on it, sir, I never did."

"God with us, that was awful," Eliot muttered. He was as upset as Colman. At the foot of the stairs leading up to the greatcoat room, Pitt turned to him. "Come, Ned, walk with me down to the river."

"You've been from your bed forty-eight hours. I should have thought you could scarce wait to regain it."

"The fresh air will do us good. My lungs are full of candle smoke and Opposition invective."

Eliot guessed he had something to say in private. They collected their coats, going down to traverse the dank musty passageway—its stones still smelling of the Plantagenets—that led out into Cotton Garden. Cotton House had long been demolished, its fine library packed off to the British Museum, its site occupied now by the modern house of the Clerk to the Commons. But its old garden, of riverside lawns, willows and hornbeams, lay at the feet of Parliament like a robe. On this misty winter's morning there was not a gardener in sight and scarcely a craft out on the river to stir at her moorings.

"I wish your troubles were fewer," Eliot said as they checked at Parliament Stairs.

"My troubles can wait. What of yours?" When Eliot looked at him questioningly he went on, "You love my sister and she loves you—yet all is at a standstill between you."

"You say your sister loves me," Eliot said after a hesitation. "I wish to God I could be sure of that. I approached her at Christmas. She would not give me an answer. She wanted me to tell my father first—to see if he approved the match."

"Does he?" It was grimly asked.

"No," Eliot answered uncomfortably. "He's set against it —quite opposed."

The tide sighed and sang at their feet. Eliot began to fear the words had given affront—as though his family held their heads higher even than the great Grenvilles and the great

Stanhopes who had been glad to ally themselves by marriage with the Pitts. "It is only because your sister is dowry-less. That is the only objection."

"It is not because she is dowry-less. It is because she is a Pitt. The Pitts were Cornish once, as the Eliots are. Your father knows the nature of the malady that struck at mine—at my family."

"Lord Chatham suffered breakdown for a time, like many another man, we know that," Eliot said blankly. "What of it? He came back to public life. He lived to be over seventy." A thin discernment broke upon them. "What do you mean, your family? There were others?"

"Yes, there were others."

Eliot turned to stare at him. The grey of the river lay ageingly on Pitt's face. He did not look now the young man against whose youth all the mirth of the news-sheets and all the wrath of the Opposition were directed. It was as if they both stood here reaching back into the long past, when the Armada had stood in towards the Lizard, and the Eliots had built their modest manors and the Pitts ploughed their fields and gone to quiet graves in humble churchyards, unremarked, except perhaps for this, that could only be the taint of madness. Even now it lay still unnamed between them.

"I don't believe it," Eliot muttered. "Not you. Not the Pitts. You've been hearkening to some old countrywoman weaving imaginary horrors at her hearthstone at Boconnoc." But the Pitts were not ones to start at shadows. Their ghosts were real. As the tide lapped on, murmuring through the silence, he thrust out a halting query. "Your brother—betrothed to Mary Townshend?"

Pitt's answer was scarcely above a mutter. "Townshend was my father's close colleague—he knows. And John is an honourable man. He would no more have the Townshends step blindly here than she would have you."

"Does she want me?"

"Yes."

"And I want her," Eliot said fiercely. "I have no care what has come upon your house in the past. There is no one save her in this world for me—as this was once holy ground, I swear it, and I swear that, if she will have me, nothing will hinder me from taking her to wife."

The grey fatigue vanished from Pitt's face. "For sure she will have you. You'll get an answer when you ask a second time, I'll warrant—and the right one. I had high hopes even at Cambridge you would one day stand my brother-in-law."

From the Speaker's Garden on their left, across the low walls that enclosed Mr. Hatsell's garden between, came a cheerful outbreak of noise. Speaker Cornwall's children, muffled against the cold, had burst from the Speaker's House, awakening the echoes about the Speaker's lawns and well-dug winter flowerbeds. Pitt looked towards them, then spoke suddenly as if he were driven to make this one comment and would not touch on the subject again. "All will be well for you, Ned. Your children will be as whole and happy as the Speaker's yonder."

"As will yours be."

"Yes, as will mine be. But you have stolen a march on me here, since you have already met the one to hold your heart and I have yet to do so." All his optimism had returned. "My word on it, your father will give his blessing on this match eventually."

With Eliot having turned back to Old Palace Yard, Pitt came on alone round the corner of the cloisters. Ahead O'Halloran's little white dog scampered gleefully among the riverside trees, plainly savouring fresh air and freedom. O'Halloran himself emerged from the great doors of Westminster Hall, with a cracking yawn, to cast a sleepless blood-shot eye at Pitt. "You, sir? Up to the point of midnight last night I was persuaded we, your familiars, would see your halting—you had a beat sort of feel to you when you came through the lobby. Beyond that point we were all in expect-

ancy of seeing you committed to the Tower. Still you out-
rode the storm." He thrust his notebook into his untidy
pocket. "By the way, there is support for you from one
quarter—one of the most damned important quarters of all—
the City of London. The city fathers met last night. They like
to observe a man making a good fight of it. They have voted
you a golden casket. You are to be made a city freeman."

He whistled the dog to heel and went on. It was a most
precious crumb of comfort that the city had tossed to Pitt.
He looked down river, seeing the Tower, where he might
have lodged this day, and the city's domes and pinnacles,
muted to a smoky charcoal in their mantle of morning mist,
and felt his fatigue much less.

XIV

SMITH, BACK at Downing Street, brooded in the secretary's
room, prickly, resentful and sullen. He and Pitt, in a sense,
mirrored one another's situation—both wrestling with a task
that was new to them, both burdened by a native awkwardness and rawness. But they were beginning to try each other
exceedingly. When, after a few hours of dead sleep, Pitt
went down to the library, both the steward and the secretary were there, Burfield inspecting the shelves for dust and
the corners for fluff, and Smith maladroitly carrying an over-
full cup of coffee towards the doorway of the secretary's
room.

"Have a care for the carpet, Mr. Smith, if you please,"
Burfield said sharply, turning a wincing glance upon him.
"This is an exceedingly expensive Wilton carpet, especially
woven on their looms, and was given to Lord Bute by the
Duke of Cumberland."

"In consideration for some political job or other, I suppose,"
Smith answered on a half sneer.

He followed Pitt into the Minister's study. Later, with the morning's work almost completed, Pitt made an effort to break through the shell of antipathy that always seemed to encase Smith when they were in the same room together. "I am told you were in college residence at Caius. You must have been up at Cambridge at about the same time as myself."

Smith gave him a hostile look. "I had no great use for the place, sir. Those were three damnable wasted years, on my word." He went on as though driven by some personal daemon to seize upon an opportunity for unpleasantness. "Incidently, you fell asleep in your clothes across your bed last night—or rather this morning. Your servant, Ralph Holmes, sought my aid since he could not get your boots and greatcoat off alone. I took your watch from your pocket and set it on the side table. You did not stir. It was like ministering to a dead man. However, doubtless you would be glad to find it there when you got up and know I had not appropriated it."

"God with us, Smith, why should I think you had appropriated my watch?"

"Why, possibly you have no vast expectations of honesty, sir, surrounded as you are by all the jobbings of politics. I don't intend offence. It is merely that there are certain professions in which no man can be virtuous. Plato wrote that, did he not?"

"No."

"No?" Smith repeated, staring.

"It was Aristotle."

"I don't question your superior knowledge, of course, sir," Smith said, with a faint angry flush. "Plato or Aristotle, it scarce matters. It but means no politician can be upon the square and for myself I have yet to recollect one who was."

Pitt regarded him across the desk with narrowed eyes. "My father was in this house too, Smith. As to myself you are altogether welcome to think what you like. But if you have any observations to make regarding corrupt politicians that you would relate to him I hold it wiser for you not to make them to me."

The dangerous calm intimidated Smith. He turned to a sullen retreat. "I mean nothing against Lord Chatham. Everyone holds he was an honest man. I am sorry, sir. I was but speaking generally."

Behind him, at the door, as if the words had evoked a ghostly visitant, a servant announced, "My Lord Chatham."

It was John Chatham's scarlet coat that loomed on the threshold. Pitt rose to meet his brother with an astonished pleasure. "John."

"I was in town," the other answered somewhat awkwardly. "I thought I would call in to see how you were getting on."

Since their curt parting at Hayes they had not met. They looked at one another with a re-dawning, hesitant friendliness, Pitt introducing his secretary, then bringing his brother alone into the library. With the chairs pulled up to the fire he asked what had brought the other to town.

"The business of purchasing a town house for Mary and myself after we are wed. It scarce requires the Chancellor of the Exchequer to tell me I can't afford it. I have been to a money-lender—to three money-lenders, if you would know."

When no criticism came their talk grew easier, turning to the coming ceremony on the 28th of the month when Pitt would receive the city's freedom at the Grocers' Hall. John remarked, after a hesitancy, "Shall I come with you?"

This unexpected offer was received with much gratitude. "Why, God bless you for it. I'd be glad beyond measure if you would."

"Well then, let it be in my carriage. You can drive back with me afterwards to view my new acquisition in Berkeley Square." But he had still not lost his anger nor his certainty that his younger brother had committed folly. As he rose to go he gave a bitter glance about the handsome room. "That you are gaining a golden casket don't mean much. Wilkes and the city fathers are but cheering you on, as they would any over-matched contender in the boxing booths on Hampstead Heath who showed spirit but who is certain to be hurled on his back on the turf at the finish. I was right when I said you would make a great public fool of yourself one day."

To his next caller, his one-time tutor, Mr. Wilson, Pitt spoke of this parting brush. "Many men would resent seeing their younger brother lodged in Downing Street, I own. But John never seemed to take it ill before when I succeeded."

"Oh, my dear William," Mr. Wilson replied, "it is not when you succeed that your brother resents it. It is when you appear to fail."

XV

ON THE afternoon of the 28th Pitt awaited his brother. Punctuality was not one of John Chatham's qualities. With the clock already standing seven minutes beyond the time set for the arrival of the Chatham carriage, Pitt looked from his despatch boxes across to his secretary. "You can use the evening as you will, Smith. After the Grocers' Hall I am going on with my brother to Berkeley Square."

"I know that, sir," Smith answered. "All London appears to know it, I think." All the week he had seemingly had something constantly on the tip of his tongue. He came near now to saying it. "By the way—"

"Yes?"

"Oh, nothing of any consequence, sir," Smith said, plunging back to the sneer that was generally his only variant from sullen dislike. "You are going to be late, are you not? Nothing exceeds the splendour of a city banquet, I am told. In truth, it's as well to be a Minister."

"Ministers have their hair-shirts. Consider Lord North's defective eyesight, Lord Rockingham's mortal bout of influenza and the fact that in a moment of mental aberration I acquired you as a secretary."

Smith gave him an angry look. Pitt laid down his quill. "Smith, you are exceedingly at odds with me. On the other hand I think it somewhat hard if nothing remains to you except a junior clerkship in one of the departments. The battle's too hot about me for changes now but once it is resolved one way or the other, would you have me cast about to see if I can secure a private position for you?"

"You would speak for me, sir?" Smith asked in a surprised voice.

"As to your honesty, yes. Possibly for your diligence too, if you gained employ with someone you could stand the sight of."

"I should be glad of your good offices there, sir," Smith answered in more mollified fashion. "I sought about for a private secretaryship for a considerable time when I came down from Cambridge, though without securing anything."

Across the room the door opened admitting John Chatham. "My apologies, William. Are you ready?"

"Only my greatcoat to don." It lay across a chair back. Pitt rose to pull it on. As he stood fastening the capes, he asked, "John, do any of your army friends require a secretary?"

"That, doubtless, depends on the qualifications. What's offered—an M.A.—a B.A.?"

"My faith, are even the Army insisting upon a University degree these days? To be sure, it's not necessary." In an ill moment for himself, Pitt added to his secretary, "Still, Smith, it was a pity you came down from Cambridge without graduating. A degree would have opened many more doors to you."

The hostility flamed back into Smith's face like a torch. "The Joseph Smith's don't graduate by privilege, sir. That belongs to the William Pitts."

John Chatham turned a high stare towards him. "Oh, God with us," Pitt exclaimed, driven from patience. "Can't you open your mouth without you sour the atmosphere as if you breathed fumes of vinegar into it?"

"I'm sorry, sir," Smith answered on an acid rush of words. "However, doubtless, you'll find the atmosphere after the Grocers' Hall much less chill. There'll be a warm reception awaiting you in the streets of London, I'll warrant."

He stood aside to let them pass. But the look he gave Pitt held a sort of half-sarcastic, half-challenging promise of levelled scores, as if he said, "But wait a little."

The carriage, standing in front of the door, already contained an occupant—Lord Stanhope, the brother-in-law of the Pitts, who had wed their now dead sister, Lady Hester Pitt. Stanhope did most things casually, casually deciding to attend at the Grocers' Hall this day, as he had casually remarried within five months of Hester Pitt's death. So brief and apparently indifferent a mourning had greatly scandalised the country folk all round Chevening. They had been affronted by the sight of the great house alive with lights and dancing and guests, before, as it seemed, the first wife was barely cold in her tomb. But the Pitts knew their brother-in-law—his eccentricity, his brilliant mind bent avidly towards the sciences but not much moved by the humanities, his bafflement at being left with three tiny daughters to bring up. They made allowances for Stanhope that the solid Kentish yeomanry on and about his estates did not.

"Good day to you, Charles," Pitt said, clambering in over his legs. "How are Louisa and the children?"

Stanhope started out of some scientific reverie. "The children? Oh, a perfect pestilence—forever under one's feet when one is engaged upon an experiment. Hester takes after your side of the family—a little tigress when she is roused. I strongly advise you both—don't burden yourselves with children."

It had been the bearing of Stanhope's children with so little respite between that had cost Hester Pitt her life. Her brothers gave him a mutually grim look but they made their customary allowances for Stanhope and restrained any comment.

"You have a surly dog for a secretary, William," John Chatham said, as the carriage turned into Whitehall.

"Surly as a thunder-cloud. He has a great loathing of me."

"Your politics, doubtless," Stanhope remarked. "He may be a fervent Whig with three ringing huzzas for the Great Rebellion and Dunning's motion—or he may be a fervent Tory toasting divine right and the King over the water."

"I doubt that. I think it is personal."

"Kick him out," his brother counselled him briefly.

"I'm too exercised to be breaking new secretaries in to the bit and bridle. Also I would wager Smith is an honest man."

Stanhope gave him a faint grin. "In addition to which he is groping his way, as you are, William. You have a fellow feeling for him." He touched casually on the fact that he had declined a cabinet position under his brother-in-law. "I could not risk my reputation as far as to take any of the seals of state under the Mincepie Administration. However, I give you my word, William, I'll be entirely predisposed to grant your next request. Hold me to it."

"I shall, Charles," Pitt said. "To the half of your kingdom."

They had come to their destination. Though it sounded mundane, the Grocers' Hall held all the ancient splendour of one of the city guilds, full of gold and silver plate that had been hidden in vaults and dusty attics from Cromwell; full, on this occasion, of the red robes of the Aldermen, the midnight black of the Recorder, the scarlet, ermine and gold of the Lord Mayor, the purple of the Worshipful Companies of Grocers, of Girdlers, of Chandlers, of Shoemakers. The crowd about the doors gave Pitt a good greeting. But how far this was London cheering on the underdog and how far genuine support was hard to tell.

With the ceremony over, the early winter dark lay on the

city. The carriage took its way back down the Strand and into the Mall, turning right towards St. James's Street. The Tudor turrets of St. James's Palace rose here crenellated against the sky; and ahead, on both sides of the street, and as if of another world, clustered the great clubs of London— Brooks's, White's and Boodle's, the Cocoa-Tree, Almack's and the Thatched House Tavern, hiding behind plain straight façades their fine gaming-rooms and scented rear-gardens.

As a rule this—the modern end of St. James's—had a sufficiency of lights, as befitted a street which turned night into day and dropped drowsily into bed when the cocks crew. But now it was plunged into a singular darkness. Everywhere, in a welter of glass and destruction, the oil lamps and the candle lanterns outside the doors had been smashed, as though by brick or boot or stick, and the street lurked ahead, silent and dark, as if stalking a prey.

Stanhope had taken out a notebook and little silver pencil. For most of the journey he had been engaged in calculations, moving decimal points and working out equations. He looked up, remarking sharply, "Where are we? My faith, 'tis a poor sort of reception to have every window darkened."

The words brought back to both Pitts the echo of Smith's voice talking in acid fashion of warm receptions. John gave a startled exclamation, "God with us, William."

"What is it?" Stanhope asked with a quick look at them.

"After the Grocers' Hall feast, the reckoning, as I think, Charles," Pitt answered. "I am sorry to have occasioned your presence at it."

Stanhope methodically closed his notebook, setting it in his waistcoat pocket and placing the little pencil beside it. The carriage was too far now down the dark street for there to be purpose in retreat. For a space the lighted squares of White's windows flung slabs of brightness across them like a benison. Then they slid from the last gleaming patch of comfort into a well of blackness. At one side of them rose the high dark wall of Brooks's; at the other, Catherine Wheel Alley snaked, unlit and deviously, towards the Cockpit. It was no surprise when the coachman's voice roared out, "Whoa there, my beauties," and the carriage jerked to a halt, quiveringly, like a ship receiving a broadside full in her timbers.

The door was tugged open from outside. In front of a dim filigree of clubs and sticks and heads a man stood, bearing a shrouded bull's-eye lantern, its pinprick of light striking upwards on to his muffled face. The lantern was raised higher. For the moment its bearer did not notice Stanhope sitting with his back to the coachman. But he scanned the two Pitts, his eyes, above the masking muffler, amused and baleful. The prick of light crept on, searching out the elder brother's scarlet regimentals and braided epaulettes.

"Ah, the head of the family," the lantern-bearer said sardonically. "Climb down, soldier boy, and run away. It's your younger brother we want, not you."

The voice was cultured. It seemed to both Pitts that it was familiar—an enemy's voice. But they had been so long surrounded by the voices of enemies that they could not be sure. John Chatham did not move.

The accoster spoke again with a greater impatience. "Run, God damn your eyes. Your kind ran fast enough at Yorktown." He swung on Pitt. "And you, Master Billy, out. We have business with you."

Stanhope moved suddenly, seizing the door and slamming it shut. Stanhope was vague sometimes but he acted swiftly in this, holding the door secure on the inside before any boot or club could jam between. At the slam the coachman made an effort to whip up the horses. But there were too many hands grasping the bridles and his own arms and legs. The carriage quivered back into immobility again.

A breathless respite lay on the three beleaguered men in the carriage. All, for the moment, was quiet about them— the tiny still eye in the swirl of the hurricane. But the noise began presently, as if the street had started to snarl in its throat—the peculiar, trampling, swelling noise of the mob lusting for violence that no man who had lived through the Gordon Riots could mistake. A club butted its weight savagely against the carriage door. It proved to be the fore-runner of a hail of blows, a devil's tattoo, ringing against the cringing steelwork.

"Well, William," Stanhope remarked dryly, using the blasphemous grace of the gundecks, "for what you are about to receive may the Lord make you thankful."

In the dim carriage there were very little means of defence. Only John Chatham, in his army scarlet, with his colonel's accoutrements, wore his officer's sword. Pitt and Stanhope sat unarmed. Stanhope's light walking cane lay beside him on the carriage seat. He made no move towards it and Pitt took it up.

"Resisting, William?" Stanhope asked, turning at one illogical jump into the grand seigneur of Chevening. "Don't you think it stooping somewhat low to exchange blows with the London rabble as if you were in the prize booths?"

"Charles, you belong to every reform association be-tween here and East Kent. Is that the manner of your com-ment?"

"Take the cane, William, by all means," Stanhope said with a thin smile, "though I scarce think it will avail you much."

The glass from the windows showered in upon them, bit-ing and stinging as if it were a cloud of tiny insects. There was a faint rasp in the carriage. John Chatham had drawn his sword and the lantern light from outside leapt upon it, dart-ing up the blade like some fiery will-o'-the-wisp. He said, in a husky voice, "Stanhope, sit back and give me sword room."

With a final splintering, the caving, creaking door burst open, by ill chance on Pitt's side, where the onslaught had been greatest. John saw his brother at once under the sticks and clubs of his assailants. He leant across him, parrying as best he might the blows that were aimed at his brother's body. Above the stark outline of heads and clubs the shrouding of the lantern had been ripped off and the light sprang out, running wildly up the sword blade and spitting against the silver head of the cane which was all Pitt could ply in his own defence.

The resistance in the carriage was hot but it could not last. Pitt was hauled out into the street. Hard by loomed Catherine Wheel Alley, its bollards gaping like blackened teeth in a wide mouth. Once he was dragged into its dark throat, sealed off from help and with the beating beginning in earnest, his situation would be desperate indeed. His accosters knew it and exerted every effort to impel him there, and he, realising it too, did battle with them as fiercely as he had had to engage the Opposition nightly in the Commons.

Behind him his brother and the coachman were both struggling uselessly to reach him. But the coachman, finding himself neglected a little in the heat of the affray, tore himself free from the hands that held him, lashing about him with his whip and shouting despairingly, "Help, sirs, help —would you see murder done?"

There were some sounds of answer—the most welcome to ears that had begun to despair of any such comfort. Brooks's Club, under whose dark wall the uproar had taken place, remained implacably deaf and indifferent. But higher up the street doors were opening. Another lantern came tossing above the heaving press of bodies. A voice called out sharply, "Why, a whole troop of you scurvy scoundrels and you set upon one carriage."

It was the voice of Bob Macreth, the owner of White's Club. He had assistance with him, the men at his back carrying hastily snatched sticks or pokers or the occasional sword. "My brother," John gasped to them. "Over yonder—"

"Oh, my faith," Macreth said. "Is it young Pitt? Don't let them get him into the alleyway, for God's sake. Mullins—"

Tom Mullins, the porter at White's, who had once worked the prize rings, came forward, doing great execution, the others following. Pitt had need of aid now, brought to his knees by the black bollards of the alleyway, the kicks and clubs about him. But his assailants had to turn from him to engage or escape. All about the sounds of battle still proceeded, Mullins's great fists working untiringly. But the attackers were everywhere in flight. Hands helped Pitt to his feet. The wrecked, broken-backed carriage still stood with its shattered doors, the frightened horses whinnying between the shafts. In the light of the lanterns the Pitts blinked upon each other and upon their rescuers.

"My thanks indeed, Walker," Pitt said, as the coachman limped up in his torn capes. "How goes it with you?"

"Much as it goes with you, I daresay, sir," the coachman answered with a faint grin. "Bruised and beat—sore tomorrow. But thankful on my word it's no worse. I thought you were done for, I own to it."

They turned towards White's, crammed with jostling members and staring waiters. Macreth had his hand under Pitt's arm but he remembered in time it was a Pitt he was assisting and tactfully withdrew it. Pitt walked up the steps unaided. Macreth brought them to one of the pleasant back parlours. His cousin, Chambers, who ran the club for him and who went by the nickname of Cherubim, was already there, marshalling two waiters, their arms laden with towels and carrying jugs of steaming water.

"You ought to bathe your faces, gentlemen," the Cherubim said and gestured the waiters to set down the utensils.

Macreth had left them but he returned now, balancing a tray of wine on the fingers of one hand with a deftness that marked his one-time trade. In the days when White's had been Arthur's Coffee House he had worked here as a waiter and billiard's marker. Now he owned the club, dining with duchesses and speaking in the House of Commons, as member for Castle Rising, in a voice that still held its native

Cockney intonation. His own rise had given him a cynical belief that a man ought to die rich. Since the Pitts rarely achieved this end, Macreth had held aloof, watching the struggles of the Mincepie Administration from Opposition.

He had a plain concern for them this night, however, pouring the wine and pressing it upon them. Stanhope went to the wall mirror and began to adjust his stock. The battle had largely passed him by. Against the battered and bedraggled Pitts he looked spruce and unmarked.

"That was a far cry from all the plaudits of the Grocers' Hall, was it not?" he said. "What occasioned so marked a change of temper?"

"Time we enquired," Macreth remarked. He went to the door and flung it open. On a chair in the corner of the hall the Pitts' coachman was seated at a jug of ale, and, barred from escape by Mullins with his reddened face and fists, a bare half-dozen captives stood huddled together. It was a thin haul out of the numbers that had swarmed about the carriage. Plainly, in the dark and confusion the bulk of the attackers had got away.

Macreth ran his eye over them. "Covent Garden chairmen, by my oath," he said softly. "Ripe for any rough house, are you not, my bully-boys?"

He picked up one of the knotted clubs that lay on the carpet, examined its gnarled and bulbous head, then began to slap it against his boot in a steady threatening tattoo. The captives watched him with a growing unease. Macreth brought the club down with a final thwack of wood against leather and stood glaring at them.

One of them spoke up with a thin returning defiance. "It weren't all on one side. They fought, those two. If the British Army had fought like that in America, the war would still be on."

"Battle, was it?" Macreth asked. "It sounded like it. And what did you intend—to smash their skulls?"

"No, nothing like that, so help me," another broke in in a

scared voice. "We was to lay him on his back three weeks—
the young one, not the soldier. It was just a drubbing."

"You're a clever fellow if you know where a drubbing ends
and murder begins, with gin on your breath from the dram
shops and a toy like this," Macreth remarked. He launched
out upon them in an aggressive Cockney snarl, "Well, my
bullies, how much—how many little gold boys came clinking
into your palms for this night's work?"

"Three," the first spokesman answered. "Three guineas
a-piece. And don't ask us who paid us neither. There were
some fine flash cully boys in on it and they paid us at the
side door of Brooks's yonder, but we don't know who they
was. May my bloody eyes drop out if that ain't God's honest
truth. Ask him who his enemies are. They get them when
they rise like what he has."

"Then you knew it was the Minister?"

"Yes, we knew that," the man said sullenly. "They come
young these days. That one ain't been licked off clean by his
mother yet."

Mullins raised a ham-like fist and his charges lapsed into
silence. Macreth turned to enquire of Pitt if they should send
to Mr. Justice Whittacker, across the street, and prefer
charges. Pitt shook his head, saying, "The big fry swam out
of the net."

"So I think," Macreth answered briskly. "Stand over them
for a while, Mullins. I'll quiz them again later before we
kick 'em out."

He and Stanhope withdrew out of the room. The Pitts were
left alone to repair themselves as best they might. Through
the mounting steam they looked upon one another, finding
their sudden fierce display of brotherhood strange after the
weeks of standing at odds.

"John," Pitt said hesitantly, "my word on it, I am grateful
to you beyond measure."

"Don't start wringing my hand and thanking me," his
brother answered curtly.

"God with us, but I must. I owe you much. They gave you the chance to quit me."

"Yes, damn their eyes—'Run, soldier boy, you ran fast enough at Yorktown.' " He tossed his scarlet regimentals over a chair back with distaste. "Even in the streets of London it's reckoned a craven's colour now."

His brother took up the coat and the candlelight spilled down the folds burnishing the cloth to a bright blood red. "The election will come," he said. "When we have all lain to our arms long enough in the ditch, it will come. Fox already has his colours—his Foxite blue; and since I'll be obliged to hit on a colour too, let it be this, your army scarlet."

"Few would hold it lucky now."

"It stood me in marvellous good stead out there among the clubs this night."

Stanhope put his high-domed scientist's forehead round the door, surveying the litter of towels, of steaming basins and discarded coats. "Somewhat restored to health and beauty?" he enquired. "They have got the horses from the shafts and calmed them. But the carriage has certainly completed its last mile."

A carriage was a costly item. The Pitts exchanged a dismayed glance. "Oh, we'll be driven back to our various destinations, depend upon it," Stanhope said, misinterpreting the look. "Every member of White's seems desirous of lending us carriages, coats, cloaks and horses. You'll be to the House, William?"

There was a silence, almost a momentary faltering. Stanhope, noting it, continued, "I scarce think you have much alternative if you want your Ministry to survive. And I own to it, I would take it somewhat ill were the Rockingham press to comment—as they would—that you were chased up St. James's Street and out of office. You are, after all, my brother-in-law."

"God save us, Stanhope," John Chatham said with a snarl of fury. "He feels as if he has just gone ten rounds with Dan

Mendoza. So do I. You had a ringside seat and I hope, in truth, you enjoyed the bout. Yet now you say he has to endure another six or seven hours in the House because he is your brother-in-law."

"Indeed you both remind me of my daughter, Hester," Stanhope conceded gracefully. "Nonetheless, that was the object, to keep William off the Treasury Bench—to lay him on his back for three weeks. For my part I think three weeks was altogether over-emphatic. Three nights would achieve the same result—possibly one."

"All's well, Charles," Pitt said. "I'll but change my coat at Downing Street and then go on to the House."

His brother gave him an anxious look but said nothing. They were brought outside, their sympathisers gathering round them again. The dark street lay quiet now, full of a shipwrecked stillness of debris and stranded flotsam. Yet it smelt of violence, as for weeks after the Gordon Riots, all London had smelt of violence. Once again King Mob had passed this way and his imprint and odour and the torn and trampled trail that marked his passage were all about them.

XVI

BACK IN Downing Street only the fire burnt in the Minister's bedroom and a single candle, dimly, on a side table. Ralph came in, much upset, his countryman's brown face, with its gentle old man's lineaments, working. "The great scoundrels," he said, using the expression many times. "The great scoundrels." He took the torn coat from the chair back where Pitt had tossed it, then let it fall to the floor as a thing of no further use. "That's beyond repair—not the cleverest tailor in New Bond Street could do ought for that. Well then, sir, even when you were but a little lad back at Hayes or Burton you would never have us fuss you or tend you when things went ill for you. I'll but fetch you another coat, as you're just going to bid me, for none of us'll be able to argue you out of going down to the House of Commons, I know that."

"You're the best of servants, Ralph," Pitt said. "You altogether counter-balance the fact that I seem to have acquired a secretary who vastly enjoys throwing me to the lions."

There was a knock. As if he had divined there had been mention of his name Smith appeared in the doorway, ringed in the brightness of the full cluster of candles he held. His expression spoke for him. What he judged the night's work to have been accorded him an acid pleasure. He was prepared to accept even his own dismissal as the price of his foreknowledge and silence concerning what St. James's Street had had in store for his employer on his journey back to Berkeley Square.

"So you are back, sir," he said. "They tell me you have had an eventful return from the Grocers' Hall."

His foot nudged the coat lying on the floor. He bent to pick it up and the candlelight fell on the torn back and the rents in the sleeves. Smith stared at it, then thrust forward the candlebranch so that the light spilled up, glancing from the white and yellow bed curtains on to Pitt's face.

Smith uttered a startled exclamation. "Oh, God with us, you can't have had a blow, can you? Your cheek—and your lace, torn like that—"

"Aye, sir, aye," Ralph said. "Your lace has gone the same way as your coat. Oh, the great scoundrels, if they had got you into the alleyway, why, what of her poor ladyship at Hayes—her first-born gone already and her youngest? How would we have broke it to her if it had been you as well?"

Smith turned on him in fierce argument. "It was nothing of that sort. He's been jostled—used somewhat rough perhaps—but nothing more."

"Don't talk so plain ridiculous, Mr. Smith," Ralph answered sharply. "If you can't see what it's been from that coat in your hands or by looking at Mr. Pitt, go downstairs and talk with Robert Walker, the coachman. He'll tell you it were a fight for Mr. William's life at the finish."

With more light kindled he went out into the dressing room. Pitt turned to strip off his bedraggled lace, the tapes, fastened under his stock at the back, ravelled now. He worked at the knots with no visible tremor, Smith still staring at him from behind the brilliance of the candles he carried.

The silence lay on them. Smith cleared his throat. "Sir— I never thought—I never believed—"

Pitt looked round at him. "I want none of your explanations now, Smith. Later—when I choose—we'll talk on it. Now but get out."

"Out of Number 10, do you mean, sir?" Smith asked in a subdued voice.

"Out of my bedroom. If my hands begin to shake on these knots I have no care if Ralph sees me, but I'm damned if I want you standing there to witness it."

Smith answered on a muted "Yes", laid the coat on the bed and went out.

XVII

In the buzzing lobby, the same evening, Macreth beckoned Eliot, Wilberforce, Arden and Dudley Ryder over to him. "Ah, gentlemen, you that call yourselves 'the old firm'— young Billy's especial intimates—a word with you." He drew them aside to the vestibule clock. "Brooks has owned to it, in talk with me, that there were comings-and-goings to his side door all the week. He thought it were but some sort of wager—a race of chairmen across London. He knows otherwise now."

"Could you learn nothing as to the originators, Macreth?" Eliot said.

"Well, certain there were some fine flash cully boys among them as we were told," Macreth replied. "Lord Chatham saw Hare out there in the mob—and being as damned active as his name. Stanhope saw John Crewe. One of my waiters thinks he recognised Fitzpatrick. I'd go on oath Jack Payne cut off round the nearest corner when we came up with the lanterns. It's but our separate words against theirs, but—yes, they were there." He eyed them sardonically. "Hare, Crewe, Fitzpatrick and Payne—all Opposition gentlemen, all of Fox's close circle, swimming about in the elevated society of Devonshire House and Carlton House, all ready to stand at his elbow at the faro tables and advance him hard cash when he loses. There's a monstrous great rattle of tongues going on about it already, believe me."

"And Fox himself?" Pepper Arden asked grimly. "Had he any part in it?"

"He's rendered damned uneasy in case it is thought he had," Macreth answered. "About an hour ago he produced an alibi for himself." He plunged a hand into his pocket and brought out a slip of paper. "Mr. Fox has averred to Mr. Grose as follows, 'I was in bed with Mrs. Armistead at the time and the good lady is willing to go on oath to testify as much.'"

"Early in the evening to be exercised between the sheets, I would think," Dudley Ryder remarked.

Macreth raised a brow at him. "Not for Fox. Nor, on my soul, for Mrs. Armistead. Against that, the good lady, as he calls her, has a sound sense of money. She's made a mint out of the world's oldest profession in general and drives to the races in her own carriage and with her own servants because of His Grace of Dorset and My Lord Derby in particular. Some will ungallantly hold she would say she were in bed with the Archbishop of Canterbury, if there were a purse of guineas in it—say it or be it." He regarded the paper with a Cockney irony. "This don't amount to anything. A little blowing on these coals and it won't help Fox if every bawd in Soho Square rushes forward, Bible in hand, to swear on oath she were in bed with him at the time. Your boy need not say a word in accusation. If he but resigns from Brooks's it will point the finger sufficiently."

"He'll do nothing to suggest Fox were implicated," Wilberforce said.

"Well, put it to him," Macreth remarked. "Here he is now. And I hope, by God, no man's fool enough to enquire how he does."

Pitt had just come into the vestibule. There was an icy and forbidding hardihood to him—a marked distaste for public pother, for solicitude, for being asked how he did or how he was, above all for any political gain that might come to him from the night's roughness. His friends took the hint and did not launch themselves upon him, while even his enemies, for once let him have his way and for the most part kept tactfully back.

The one exception was Sir Horace Mann, lurking behind the vestibule clock. As Pitt came abreast he pounced forward to enquire, "My dear boy, are you all right?"

Pitt had no love for Mann who was the gossip-sheet of the House. Nor did any man endear himself to the Minister by addressing him as 'my dear boy'. He answered icily, "Yes."

Mann seized his arm the better to secure him to the spot. "Indeed I scarce think you can be. A shocking occurrence— who was behind it, do you suppose?"

"As to that you have as much knowledge as I have," Pitt answered, and detached himself from the detaining grip.

"I meant it civilly, good God," Mann remarked in an offended tone, moving off up the lobby to a group of the Opposition. "Mannerless, the young men, these days, entirely so."

Macreth regarded the scene with a wry grin. "Your young man might have gained a vote there. Lord love us, they left a lot out of the curriculum at Hayes, did they not?" As Pitt came up, he said, "All's well, sir. No one here is going to ask you how you do."

"Macreth holds you ought to resign from Brooks's," Ryder said. "It would be sufficient to put Fox in a deucedly bad box if you did."

"God with us, Macreth," Pitt spoke in an astonished voice. "You can't think Fox had any part in it?"

"Why, I don't know, sir," Macreth answered cheerfully. "I don't know what you gentlemen born get up to when you begin to take the hide off one another. There's no proof either way—nor will be. But you can rake him broadside over this. Considering your case since Christmas I would have thought you'd be eager to apply the match."

"You can scarce want to continue rubbing shoulders with Hare, Crewe and Fitzpatrick in Brooks's public rooms after this damned occurrence," Pepper Arden remarked.

"I doubt either I or my brother will cross Brooks's threshold again. But we'll remain as members. If we resign it will be as you say, Macreth—every coffee house in the city will tattle that we hold Fox responsible. And he would not have done that manner of thing to me." He amended it to "to any man". But the tatters of old friendship, even the scent of the Kingsgate grasses blew across them down the crowded lobby.

Dudley Ryder began a protesting, "But—"

"Oh, have done, Dudley. Fox was not a party to it."

"Well, if you want to go on paying your four guineas subscription to safeguard Fox's fair fame, that's up to you, sir," Macreth remarked. "For my part if my enemies dealt me a fistful of aces—as yours have you this night—I played 'em. I would still have chalk on my fingers marking a hundred up at Arthur's Coffee House otherwise."

With the Minister's thanks rendered to him for his great assistance outside Brooks's he left them. Pitt leant against the newel post of the stairs leading up to the greatcoat room, beset at last by the aftermath of the night's violence, its sweat

and stench, blows and danger. "I am going to say it, in faith,"
Pepper Arden said. "How do you feel, in actual fact?"

"Oh, my good Pepper, in actual fact I feel as if I had been
under a carter's wain."

A group of six of the Opposition came down the stairs. Pitt
straightened at once. The Opposition men looked subdued
and uncomfortable. Mansfield stopped. "A damned scurvy
business. We are sorry."

"Thank you."

Dempster began in awkward fashion, "I hope you do not
think that we—that any of we six—"

Pitt answered instantly, "No, certainly not."

"I am glad of that," Dempster said. "None of us would
stoop so low." He added, "Can't speak for all."

He and his companions went on towards the chamber.
"Out of our precious trio, Hare, at least, seems to be staying
away," Eliot said. "My faith, Billy, it is going to be awkward
when you meet."

"So I think. What do I say if I come upon him on the
committee room stairs—'You know you were there and I
know you were there but it's a fine night and I'll continue to
address you as the honourable gentleman opposite because
the Speaker will have my ears if I don't'?"

"Damn the Hare," Dudley Ryder said. "You had the Fox
at a cheek and you whistled all the dogs off. You're too
deucedly forgiving."

"Not I," Pitt answered. His face had hardened in the
candlelight, set in all the ironcast Grenville implacability.
"There's no forgiveness where there's no injury. There was
none done to me by Fox this night. But there have been
other nights and matters I mind more than a blow or two
about the face and body. If the majorities are ever mine
and he is sat there with the benches empty about him, he
had best remember it's a long tally I owe him from Christmas
until now."

For this moment he sounded the vengeful schoolboy set on

repaying old scores. "I always held you were a bigger man than that," Wilberforce remarked.

Pitt gave him an acid look. "Hearken to our old morality yonder."

With the House moving the reading of the orders of the day, Fox came to his place in a visible anger. His position was difficult. He shared a town house with Hare in St. James's Street. They were constantly at the tables together. He had had time now to consider his over-hasty alibi which, by morning, would split London almost equally between merriment and distaste. Any other man save a Pitt he would have used easily this night and there were those on the benches about him who would have been content to allow the Minister to gain his bed and his rest. But Fox made no concession here. And Pitt, with a Chatham-like fury at any suggestion of pity, asking no quarter and getting none, turned his bruised face away from the eyes of his enemies, and continued the evening in almost similar fashion to the way in which, earlier in St. James's Street, he had begun it.

XVIII

FOUR NIGHTS later, Macreth crossed the floor of the House, joining Sutton on the Government benches. "Damned if I quite know why I am here," he remarked as he sat down.

"Nor I," Sutton said wryly. "I never voted before for any man who did not stand squire to me for at least one good dinner a week in the Speaker's dining room. But last night I went in the divisions with Billy Pitt. Did he hasten up to press upon me his thanks and an appointment from the civil lists? Nothing of that manner. He walked straight past me in the lobby afterwards. But I am still ready to be counted with him."

Sheridan had watched the little trickle of men going over

to the Mincepie Administration with a mounting anxiety. Coming through Westminster Hall the next evening with Fox he launched out upon the subject. "Charles, we are not achieving our end. If he would but take out his handkerchief and mop his brow sometimes—if his voice would tremble sometimes—if he himself would tremble sometimes—my word on it, I begin to feel like Don Cordova besieging Gibraltar—floating batteries, mortar fire, twenty-six pounders, all manner of shot hurled across and at the end one cannot discern even a dent in the rock."

"What, more urgings to impeach him?"

"The hour has passed for impeaching him. You could have taken the House with you on that in January but not now. For God's sake, do what I urged upon you at the first—stop the Supplies."

"I never favoured that method."

"We have no choice but to favour it. There are men going to him nightly, and he gives them nothing for it—not even a few kind words. He is doing what I feared. He is turning the ship into the winds and tides and holding her there."

They had come to the stairs leading up into the vestibule, the stone lions on the balustrade couched upon their shields. Fox set a hand about one of the stony throats. "A week, Sherry. Give me but one more week."

"This running fight has gone on from Christmas until March. What makes you think one more week will occasion you success?"

"Because, Sherry, you rogue," Fox said, with a return to lightness, "now he is tired."

The faces opposite in the House bore token to this. For the older men, for Pulteney and Governor Johnstone, the endless nights were beginning to cause real physical distress. But the Pulteney-Johnstones sat grimly and uncomplainingly on. Dundas—whose hardy Scottish frame rarely showed much in the way of fatigue—looked now as he had done when he had tramped out the nights on Wimbledon Common with his divorce upon him. Wilberforce's small figure sat hunched and seemingly shrunken. On the Treasury Bench Pitt felt the pressures stronger than ever. This was in fact the last wave of battle coming upon him—sustained and ferocious because it was the last. But he was too weary to realise it. Even Dundas—far more experienced in judging the shifts of the House—did not, in the grip of his own fatigue, realise it either. To them the pelting storm had not abated; the wind still shrieked in their faces.

On 6th March, at two in the morning, Pitt left the House to snatch a hasty coffee at Bellamy's. He dared not be absent long. With the double doors closed behind him he went at a charging run through both lobbies and up the committee room stairs. Even this exertion worked no magic. When Dundas followed within the space of five minutes, he found him standing propped against the eating-house mantelpiece, struggling against sleep, the coffee in his cup black as the night outside.

"You'll ha'e to come back to the chamber," Dundas said. "Fox has just gi'en notice he intends to move to postpone the Supplies."

Pitt, jerked fully alert again, set aside his cup with an exclamation of dismay. "Oh, my faith, Harry, he said back in January the Supplies would be voted through."

"Aye, you're too fatigued to grasp the implication," Dundas said slowly. "I was mysel' for a space. The initial strategy was to break you down in the House, to exhibit you as the schoolboy unfit to govern. By moving to stop the Supplies they acknowledge Fox canna' do it. He himsel' acknowledges he canna' do it. You ha'e bettered him."

"I—bettered Charles?" It was close on an astonished gasp. "They all thought I could not."

"But you ha'e." Dundas took a pace or two across the floor and repeated, "But you ha'e."

They blinked at each other almost owlishly in the candlelight, the tang of the coffee in their nostrils, scarcely able to credit that the tug of the tide was slackening for them and might even be on the point of turning. "They'll doubtless succeed in postponing the Supplies, Harry," Pitt said at length. "But not perhaps now in blocking them outright."

"So I think. In twa' days Fox intends another motion o' censure against you. He's slammed through plenty o' those, God knows, and by huge majorities. But this time—this time —we'll see."

Two evenings later, with the Supplies postponed but not blocked, Fox moved again angrily for Pitt's dismissal. With the public bundled out of the Galleries, Speaker Cornwall put the question and, assailed by the answering chorus, pronounced his verdict. "The Ayes have it."

He was instantly challenged by Eliot, "The Noes have it."

"The Ayes will go forth," Cornwall said, using the ancient parliamentary phraseology.

From doorkeeper Pearson came a gin-laden bawl of "Division." The clerk turned about the two-minute sandglass on the clerk's table. The 'Ayes' moved out into the lobby with Fox. The 'Noes' sat solidly on in their places bunched about Pitt.

"I had a faro bank arranged for tonight, time permitting," James Hare—telling in the House for the Opposition—said in a sour voice as he joined Eliot at the Bar. "Damn your eyes and limbs, boy, you had no hesitancy about dividing and wasting the time of the House."

"You can see for yourself that on this occasion it is going to be close."

They began to move along the benches counting heads. With the same business completed at the doors, the tellers compared their tallies, then advanced towards the Speaker, making their three ceremonial bows. The House hung upon them silently. But once again, as in all the long nights from Christmas up to March, the two Opposition tellers took their stance at the Speaker's right, the Government tellers again in the ancient place of defeat on the left hand.

"We're downed again," Pitt said, not able to keep the disappointment from his voice.

"Wait," Dundas muttered into his ear from the bench behind.

The Speaker gave the numbers. Fox, in truth, had triumphed again. But only by one vote. As men's minds went back to the snows of January, to the division bells clanging every two or three hours to ring the Mincepie Administration to reeling defeats and vast humiliations, it was almost impossible to credit. Amid the mounting tide of excitement and noise on the floor of the House Pitt slewed round in his place to face Dundas.

"That's enough, Harry—enough of the pelting storm. Now we dissolve."

XIX

PITT WENT the next morning to Buckingham House. The days when he had been kept standing in the King's presence were long over. One glance at his face, with the marks of the endless all-night sittings upon it, and George was prepared to hurl him into any chair in the room.

The request for dissolution was made. Charlotte leant towards her husband, saying in kindly, well-intentioned fashion, "Why, my love, now it is altogether over for Mr. Pitt, we ought to despatch him to Weymouth where he can get the sea breezes and languish in bed until noon every day for a month."

"Well, well, m'dear," George answered awkwardly. "We must hope it is not altogether over for Mr. Pitt."

The Queen bit her lip. "Oh dear, I did not mean—"

Presently she left them. George cleared his throat. He had never found it easy to thank Chatham. Nor did he find it easy to thank the son, looking upon him with a face unlike

Chatham's, yet who, nevertheless, moulded himself fiercely on his father. But George knew quite well the enormity of the battle that had been fought. He made up his mind to it, saying suddenly, with a graciousness and a kingliness, "What, what, Mr. Pitt, I give you my most grateful thanks. Whatever the outcome at the polls—and I know that Mr. Fox is confident—it occasions me much pride to have witnessed your skill and courage in facing the Coalition all these past weeks."

His Minister looked upon him with a painful, flushed embarrassment. Such thanks over-set Pitt's concept of the ingrate King, who had rarely spared a word on Chatham, even for continents toppled and enemy fleets dismembered. He could do no more than answer on a hot, inarticulate mumble. George regarded him shrewdly, remarking as the silence grew, "What, what, Mr. Pitt, we can do no more now but to wait for the votes to be cast. And, indeed, waiting is what I have been doing all my life. You Whigs disallow it sometimes. But it is one of the bitter aspects of kingship that it should always be the other man who fights the battle —the man in the red coat in the forests of Saratoga or the entrenchments of Yorktown, the man on the gundeck, the man on the floor of the House of Commons. The harder part is to sit watching the trees in the Mall. One day you will learn it yourself."

The King had a reserve in some ways the equal of Pitt's. He had never spoken of what lay so close to his heart before. Pitt looked at him in puzzlement, and George, regretting instantly this display of feeling to so young a man, began to talk of his grain crops and his turnips, the familiar 'what, what's', and 'eh, what's', scattered broadcast to mask the emotion that lay behind the determined cheerfulness and the incessant talk.

XX

BACK IN Downing Street, in the secretary's study, Smith was at his desk, his sullenness transformed these days into a muted diligence. "Come through, Smith," Pitt said, as he entered from the library.

"Sir," Smith answered in the subdued almost submissive fashion that had lain on him ever since the night of St. James's Street.

Inside the Minister's study they drew out the chairs at either side of the desk, facing each other across the litter of papers, inkwells and seals. Pitt gave his secretary a thoughtful appraisal. "You have been here longer than the eighteen days we originally contracted for?"

"It is fifty-eight," Smith answered with a faint bitter smile. "I have marked them off on the calendar. And indeed you are going to broach the matter, are you not—the affray in St. James's Street? I knew there was going to be trouble that night, as you are, of course, aware. I had been in St. James's Street—in King's Coffee House—about a sennight previously. I overheard some conversation—three men sat in the table box alongside mine—not ill-dressed and not ill-spoken either. Something was said to the effect, 'Outside Brooks's would be best, but damned if he ever goes there now.' One of the others said, 'He does on the 28th when he goes to his brother's house from the Grocers' Hall,' and then there was a remark about a few guineas not being over-payment if it conveyed to Master Billy he was not required in Downing Street. I knew they had something in store for you. Once or twice I came near to warning you, but I—but I neglected to." He drew in a hard breath. "That then is how it was."

"I had already in a manner guessed how it was," Pitt said grimly. "I would know why it was."

Smith gave a hesitant answer. "I have never loved the man in power. I told you so when I came."

"No, that was not your motive. You had a great personal antipathy to me before you even came in through yonder door, and I scarce understand why, for if we had ever met before I should have recalled it."

"Yes, you would have recalled it," Smith repeated. "You have that manner of retentive memory." He looked at Pitt directly. "It's true we had never met before. But I had seen you on one or two occasions when we were up at Cambridge. You would not guess there to be a connection since England pushes up Smiths like heads of barley, but Dr. Smith, the Master of Caius, is my uncle."

He got up and went to the mantelpiece, scrutinising its china pieces and ornaments. "Upon the death of my father, my uncle agreed to enter me as a fellow commoner on the Caius board and to pay my fees for three years. He considered I would then graduate B.A. or M.A. and be able to make my own way. Cambridge has much to commend her, I own, but she's not the place to reside on one's uncle's charity. In those circumstances one is neither fish, fowl, nor good red herring."

"But there were many sizars there on grants. They were, without question, brilliant scholars."

"That was much of the trouble. There were many there on grants and bursaries, in more straitened circumstances than myself. But they were all brilliant—all sure of their degrees. I did not shine, especially in the classics. This is where it first touches upon you, sir—in the classics. Once I so exasperated old Truscott on some point of translation in Thucydides that he roared out before the rest, 'Save my patience, Smith, and use whatever brain the Almighty—with what I cannot but feel was ill-considered liberality— bestowed on you. I have a little boy in Pembroke Hall— and, upon my soul, I mean little, he's but fourteen—who could render that passage without taking pause for breath.'

I knew he meant you, sir. There was no one else who was fourteen at Pembroke."

Pitt sat silent. Smith continued, still with a seeming absorption in the mantelshelf's pretty toys. "I began to sit up half the night working on Thucydides. I remember thinking, 'On my faith, this is beyond me. But it is not beyond Master Fortunate William Pitt. Master Fortunate William Pitt could, doubtless, do it with one arm bound behind him.' Then I had my first sight of you, sir. You remember how a couple or so of the wilder sparks would ride for a wager hell for leather round one of the college closes, with their hats pulled over their faces so that the porters could not recognise them, and losing off sporting guns. It infringed about three of the college regulations and endangered other folk. But it was done that afternoon, when you were mounted just outside the gates of Pembroke. What with the noise of the guns banging off and the yells and hoofbeats, your horse bolted—do you recall?"

He glanced round. Pitt conceded so with a nod. Smith went on, "I thought you would be carried clean out of the town. But you managed to rein in not much beyond the end of Tennis Court Road. Someone remarked that your mother —that Lady Chatham had been the best equestrian in England in her day. Riding is another thing I would like to do well, but which I do exceeding ill. I thought, 'So, in addition to translating Thucydides, Master Fortunate William Pitt also rides; observe him, when the time comes, taking his degree.' As it happened we would have sat together, though you were the younger and had lost a deal through sickness. You were sick again when the time came. There was some relief you could not compete—it let someone else in. Not I, of course. I still think I might have achieved it had I had another twelve months of study. But my uncle was of the contrary opinion. He thought it but a waste of fees. I came down—without a degree—and could find nothing more elevated than a junior clerk's desk at the Treasury."

"And I graduated by privilege, as you reminded me."

"Had you sat, we all knew you would have sailed through like a frigate under full canvas. That was not what irked me. All would have been well if you'd been Lord Chatham's son and a buffoon. But in that you were Lord Chatham's son and brilliant—my faith, I resented it. I thought, 'By God, his father gives him his brains; his mother gives him her horsemanship; Lowther gives him a pocket borough; and the King gives him England. But this last is too prickly a gift. This will burn his fingers.' When you offered me the position as your private secretary, I could in a manner have tossed the offer back at you. But the money was too great an inducement. I pocketed my Cambridge resentments and came," He added on another long breath, "As to St. James's Street, there is just one small mitigating factor. I thought there would be a deal of mud and humiliation flying round for you—but no more. When I realised the truth I had three damned awful nights lying there considering how I would have felt myself a murderer had they clubbed you to death in the alleyway."

"So St. James's Street was my coin for Thucydides," Pitt remarked. Suddenly he broke into a smile. "You're an honest man, Joe. You could have denied it entire and left me but my inward convictions to feed upon."

Smith looked at him, startled by the use of his Christian name for the first time in this quiet room. "Do you want me to get out?"

"There's not the least necessity for that. But I am to Cambridge now. If it is an ill wind that blows for me up the Cam I'll have neither the need for a secretary nor the means for one."

"Cambridge? You mean that, now the election is upon us, you intend to contest the University? Ought you not to stick to Appleby? You would be safe there." It struck him some of his old sneering nuances could be read into the words. He added uncomfortably, "I did not mean it quite after that manner, sir. But Cambridge is an Opposition seat and well held by them. It will be a most bruising battle."

"Worth all manner of bruises if we can achieve her." He picked up his quill again. "But if I do not, Joe, and have to forgo your services, we'll find something better for you than a junior clerk's desk at the Treasury, my word on it."

Smith mumbled astonished thanks. He half turned towards the door, then broke out on a rush of words, "Aside from Thucydides, aside from the Cambridge resentments, aside from St. James's Street, I can't, in truth, have given you much satisfaction. When I came here in January I must have been the rawest secretary ever to set foot in Downing Street."

Pitt regarded him across the desk. "And I was the rawest Minister. We combined excellent well together."

XXI

THEIR LEAVE-TAKING came next day, Pitt about to set out first for Hayes, then ultimately for Cambridge. He had already stood for the University in the Election of 1780 when he had been too young for so lofty a seat of learning to take seriously. The University had placed him bottom of the poll.

"You think there are other boroughs, Joe?" Pitt said with a glance at his secretary's set face.

Smith smiled faintly. "But you do not, sir. For you it must be Cambridge or nothing. In a measure I understand. I've looked down in sunshine from the Gogmagog Hills too. But if you are to fall in love with a place, parliamentarily speaking, it might be better to do so with one that is certain to return you."

"Yes, doubtless you are right." He drew one of the books out of the lower shelf and set it on the table. "These in the brown bindings are the few volumes I brought with me from Hayes. If I can't improve on my last Cambridge showing would you pack them for me and despatch them round to my brother's house in Berkeley Square?"

"To be sure, sir." Smith checked and broke into uncertain query. "There is a tradition that a Minister quitting office can take something from the house, is there not—a keepsake? Would you indicate what you want, so that if—if it should go ill for you at Cambridge, I could have it boxed and sent by carrier to your brother's along with the books."

"Oh, God with us, no. We'll wait until the house owes me something."

"For my part I think it owes you something already," Smith said. He hesitated, then came across and put out his hand. "Good luck, sir. I hope, in truth, there's a fair wind to blow for you up the Cam. I hope there's a fair wind to blow for you everywhere—up the Thames, the Humber and the Trent, across the shire fields and the borough boundaries. I hope it is victory."

Yet, though they parted speaking of victory—Pitt turning to the door without a backward glance at the great room—Smith knew he must question whether he would set foot in it again or whether, within a couple of weeks, some other man would stand here on the rich red carpeting, among the gold-leaf lettering and burnished bindings, and look out towards the spring green of the park.

BOOK III

1784

The Downing Street House

"A vast, awkward house, the best summer residence in London." PITT.

I

ENGLAND HAD to pronounce on the Mincepie Administration now, whether or no it had been a silly schoolboy flippancy. The battleground was about to become the boroughs, sprawled and netted in a charming hotch-potch over the face of the island, their boundaries limned by Saxon earthworks or medieval cornfields or proud Tudor townships. All of them had a differing franchise so that, like women, they had to be wooed by unlike arts. Those they returned dubbed them in slang parliamentary phraseology according to their natures—the rotten boroughs, from which, over the years, the population had ebbed leaving behind a handful of voters; the pocket boroughs, not to be despised, since these were the means whereby the young men and the poor men gained Parliament—often the best men of all, whom Westminster taught quickly and roughly, as she had taught both Pitts and both Foxes; the cheerful potwalloper boroughs, where a man could vote if he had no more than his own hearth to cook upon; the venal boroughs, which were what their name implied, grimed over by a thick film of corruption, none knew how to alter or dispel, and where the fists and the guineas flew; the burgage boroughs; the corporation boroughs; the two stately University seats, Oxford and Cambridge, proud, independent and utterly incorrupt; the great shire seats, incorrupt too, with the blood of Magna Carta in their veins.

As the hustings began to raise their wooden ribs the contestants converged upon them—Dundas to cloudy Edinburgh, the castle and the rock; Wilberforce, engaging for Yorkshire, to Hull, where the square-sailed luggers breasted the brown Humber and the tides lapped his garden stairs; Fox to rowdy Westminster, with its battling chairmen and bully-boys and canvassing duchesses; North to Banbury, clustered about its medieval cross; Pulteney to the serene spires of Shrewsbury.

Eliot's ultimate destination was Cornwall. But he took his way first to Hayes Place to stand alone with Harriet where they had once stood over the Christmas logs. Already she wore her brother's colours, the scarlet ribbon slotted through her lace cap of fashion and trailing from it like strands of summer pimpernel. Eliot touched the dangling silk, saying, "May I beg a length of your ribbon for luck?"

She took the scissors from the workbox, snipping off a few inches and knotting them about the brass button of his coat, where his lace brushed. "There, Sir Knight. Ride into Cornwall and do battle."

He set his hand about hers, holding it to his coat. "My dearest, will you take my token in exchange for this—a betrothal ring?"

"But your father is still firmly opposed."

"Once he sees us wed, and you turn your fair Pitt face upon him he will be as much at your feet as the rest of us."

She looked at him with quick startling distaste. "My Pitt face?"

He answered her gently, "I know there have been demons to lurk in the dark for you. But if you can risk the rotted Eliot lungs, I'll risk whatever family ills the Pitts think were theirs in the past."

"We do not know if they are in the past."

"They are," Eliot said fiercely. "God with us, they are. My sweet, don't think of it—don't talk of it."

She spoke with a faint return to humour. "I'll at least pledge myself to the latter."

She was pressed close to him now, her cheek against the falling lace on his breast. He knew he had won her. He held her fast, muttering into her ear, "If I but lie one night with you beside me as my wife I'll have obtained all that I want from life."

With the stern preoccupied gaze of Governor Pitt bent upon them from his portrait on the wall, his great-granddaughter stirred at length in Eliot's arms. "Thank you for all, my love—for bearing with me when I must have seemed Lady Disdain, and for standing so staunch by my brother in the House."

"As to the first, I love you. You were ever the only one for me. And as to the second, for England, so is your brother—the only one for us now—the only one for survival."

"Why bless you, Mr. Eliot," she said, stepping away from him and smiling, "I hope they agree with you in the shires."

After Eliot had left, narrowing the miles between himself and distant Cornwall, Pitt prepared to take his own journey. He and John walked together round the corner of the house where they had not walked since the crisp snow and lowering winter sky had wrapped Hayes in a grey gloom. The antagonism the elder brother had shown at that time had gone now. But he made an abrupt reference to it, remarking, "The day you took the seals I could have clouted you from here to Portsmouth."

"But when they begin to do it in St. James's Street you stand by me better than a detachment of Guards." He added, "John, I'm sorry for much."

"What—that you took my birthright? I would not have Downing Street were it given me on a plate. 'Tis too much the epitome of all hard work." He walked on for a little in silence. "You think I resented it, that you were the desired second son. On my honour, I did not. But I had my share of the Grenville pride—pride in the British Army, and all there went down in a welter of mud and blood at Yorktown. And pride in the Pitt name, and I thought all there were going down in a welter of bad jokes at Westminster. That was why I were so damnably wild. But there were sufficient abusing you or mocking at you. I should not have joined in their damned chorus."

He put out his hand. Pitt took it. "I owe you many thanks, John—and for more than St. James's Street."

They came round to the front of the house. The carriage stood there, the horses fresh between the shafts, the baggage being loaded upon it. Lady Chatham, Harriet and Mrs. Sparry were all on the steps. Harriet ran down to clasp her younger brother by the arm, her old dog, Muff, following rheumatically at her skirts.

"Goodbye, my dear son," Lady Chatham said in a steady voice. "My prayers are all for your good."

He looked at her, reading something more behind the words, then put his arms about her. For a moment she embraced him as if she would in no circumstances let him go, then stepped back unchanged of face. The carriage rattled off to be hidden by the trees and scrub of the Common, stained now by the green of spring. With Mrs. Sparry following her, Lady Chatham went back into the house. Her glance went to the workbox on the table spilling its scarlet ribbon. "Well, Mrs. Pam," she said with a sigh. "It all begins again."

"Yes, I'm afraid so, my lady," Mrs. Sparry answered. "I remember his lordship—not his lordship then, but only Mr. Pitt—hobbling about this room on his stick, waiting for the results, and the news eeking through by dribs and drabs, and all the rat-tat-tatting and coming and going. But indeed I think it is worse for the women—the wives and the mothers. They have to sit by, trying to put on such brave faces, and all the while their hearts are bursting." She added hesitantly, "If he should be beat, will it be altogether the end for William?"

"If it is a heavy defeat—yes."

"Oh, dear me," Mrs. Sparry said. "It brings back so much —the night he was born, and all the doctors telling us he would not live above twenty-four hours, and his lordship walking about this room, saying, 'He must live, this is William Pitt.' It seems so little time ago. It seems no more than the day before yesterday."

"That is the hard part, Mrs. Pam," Lady Chatham answered. "It was in truth no more than the day before yesterday."

II

WITH THE flat lands dappled in sunlight and shadow, Pitt jolted towards Cambridge. He had been joined in the carriage at Saffron Waldon by his co-candidate, Euston. Euston was a cheerful young man, an undergraduate when Pitt had been so and one of the twenty-five founder members of Goosetree's Club in Pall Mall. He was quite as inexperienced in election matters as the Prime Minister. But they consorted easily together as old friends, and in Euston's company there was never a hint of the Pitt reserve.

Euston had already been in Cambridge a week, engaged in canvass. "Still the same regulations frowning down at one from the college boards," he remarked. "'No one *in statu pupillari* to keep a horse without the consent of parents or guardians and the head of his college—guns and sporting dogs forbidden—dice forbidden—no one to ride out of Cambridge without leave of his tutor, nor to be out after 11 p.m. nor to go to a coffee house, tennis court or cricket ground between 9 and 12 a.m.' It seems a vast number of years since it all applied to us."

"It is only four but I own it seems nearer a hundred."

The carriage set them down at the Blue Boar in Trumpington Street. They were glad to stretch their legs after the journey, observing the familiar scenes. The little town was much as it had always been, full of students in their black gowns and caps which they would raise only to the Vice-Chancellor or the Proctors; the sturdy farmers on horseback with their wives riding pillion behind them, in a fashion London considered antediluvian; hard-bitten men coming in from a night's otter-hunting in the fens, their clothing scented by water-rush and befouled by blood; the so-called 'loungers' who seemingly spent their lives almost entirely on Newmarket racecourse, their ivory toothpicks dangling at their coat-tails. Pitt and Euston reached the Backs. The daffodils here were just beginning to pour in a golden torrent down into the Cam; the little bridges fashioned in stone or lattice-work, filmy as lace; and behind them, the two great queens of the University, the mighty twin consorts, Trinity and St. John's, with their fair flinty shoulders raised against the wide fen sky.

"Oh, Fitzroy," Pitt said. "I'm glad to be back and out of the dust of politics."

"But you are not out of it, are you?" Euston remarked. "Our friends have much warned me about you, Billy-boy. They tell me you are no hand at canvassing—a good Minister, they think—but a god-damn awful canvasser."

At this hour the college bedmakers were crossing the courts and closes, swinging the huge tea-kettles they hired out to undergraduates and fellows. As one with a benign glazed face, brown as a walnut, passed near by, a side door was hurled open. A young don appeared to shout wrathfully after her, "Sal, you old cormorant, Sal, you human dromedary, you've been at my madeira again."

"I took no more but what you can afford, Mr. Sheepshanks," the bedmaker answered, continuing placidly on her way.

Sheepshanks addressed Pitt and Euston with some excitement. "Did you hear that? What she thinks I can afford and what I know I can afford are as apart as the poles. It don't matter where I hid it—down a riding boot, in the chamber pot, behind the books—she still finds it. Bullock swears she drinks the spirits he pickles his specimens in. He accosted her on it once and she said it had cured her hacking cough—" He checked, then added, "Oh, 'tis you two. It's going to be a damned tight, hard-fought contest this time. By the way, I think the V.C. has his blue-coats out looking for you."

Pitt and Euston turned back towards Emmanuel College. Coming towards them near the gates were two of the Vice-Chancellor's servants in their light blue Cambridge livery. Both ceremoniously raised their cocked hats, the spokesman delivering the message formally. "Lord Euston, my lord— Mr. Pitt, sir—Mr. Vice-Chancellor presents his compliments and pray be so good as to attend upon him as soon as convenient to yourselves."

Inside Emmanuel College Lodge they were greeted by Dr. Richard Farmer, the Vice-Chancellor of the University and Master of Emmanuel. Farmer's eyes held their customary twinkle, his orange felt carpet slippers exceedingly shabby and bespattered liberally with darnings of crimson wool.

"Good, good," he remarked, giving his hand to Pitt. "Just in time for tea, though the two ladies are not here yet." He spoke over his shoulder as if to insist on the touching of points before the tourney or the rough handclasp at the start of the prize bout. "Mr. Mansfield and Lord John, be so good as to step over here a moment."

The two sitting members for Cambridge University, James Mansfield and Lord John Townshend, came from out of the parlour to renew the acquaintance of their rivals. Before the Coalition these two had sat on opposite sides. But if there were any unease in their political marriage now they did not show it. They were intent on defending the comfortable majorities whereby, four years ago, the University had despatched them to Westminster.

Mansfield was over forty, and had been one of the Government's law officers in the days of North's premiership. His colleague, Lord John Townshend—he was no relation to his namesake, Tommy—was much younger and a personal friend of Fox. Everything about Townshend was modish. He knew the latest play, the latest novel, the latest epigram, the latest way to let fall his lace or embroider his coats. The fashion-conscious section of the House doted on him. It was rumoured that Beau Nash in the Assembly Rooms at Bath had once asked who his tailor was. But the languid elegance deceived, and behind it lay much skill and bite. Townshend knew that if he brought Pitt down all was over, no matter how the votes fell elsewhere, and his personal devotion to Fox brought a hint of spleen and feeling into the pretty black-panelled hallway.

There were others gathered for tea in Farmer's parlour, all, at this moment, male. Cambridge still, in a measure, clung to the celibacy of her old monastic past, and only the Heads of Colleges were permitted to marry without resigning their appointments. Farmer's two close colleagues, Wilcox and Crisp, were both present, as was Dr. Robert Glynn, seated somewhat apart on the window seat. Glynn's degree was in medicine. He had tended Pitt during the serious illness which had come upon him during his first University term, and he rose as his ex-patient came in. They greeted each other with pleasure. With the room turning to private conversation Pitt joined him on the window seat. "We are awaiting tea for Mrs. Barker," Glynn said, lifting a greying eyebrow at him. "She has been telling us all for the last sennight how vastly desirous she is of meeting you."

"She never cast me a glance when I stood for the University last time."

"There is a difference between being mere W. Pitt, with no prospect save the lowly place at the bottom of the poll, and First Lord of the Treasury," Glynn remarked. There was a step outside and a rustle of vast skirts. "Put a brave face on it, William. The fact that you have seen the inside of Number 10 will draw that woman like a pin to a magnet."

Mrs. Barker, the wife of Dr. Barker of Christ's, came in attended by her daughter of her first marriage, Lydia Bellenger. Both were hooped and plumed. At sight of the candidates Mrs. Barker flung wide her arms, exclaiming, "Our four gladiators, Mr. Vice-Chancellor—our four gladiators."

"We do not throw them to the lions until Saturday, ma'am," Farmer answered goodhumouredly. "Come, you know them. But to make all strictly formal—ma'am, Miss Bellenger, may I present, in no order save that of the alphabet, Lord Euston, Mr. Mansfield, Mr. Pitt and Lord John Townshend."

Mrs. Barker bestowed a most profound bow on Pitt, her manner contrasting greatly with what it had been in the days of the 1780 election when she had been accustomed to pass him glassily by on the towpath.

"And how are you, Miss Bellenger?" Townshend said, bowing modishly over her daughter's hand. "If I may say so, eyes to out-sparkle the fountain in St. Catherine's Court."

"La, Lord John," Lydia answered. "La."

"Indeed, Lord John, I am glad you discern as much," Mrs. Barker said firmly. "Of course Miss Lydia looks vastly well in that gown." She turned to Pitt. "Between ourselves, sir, *entre nous*, the Prince of Wales remarked upon her when she wore it at Newmarket races. He enquired of his equerry as to the identity of the divine creature in the green velvet."

"Did he so, ma'am?"

The Prime Minister, bored, did not always hide it. Hearing the indifference in his voice Mrs. Barker's expression set somewhat and Townshend regarded them both with a faint sarcastic satisfaction.

"Well now, gentlemen," Farmer remarked, seating himself. "How fares London? The only time I regret Cambridge is when I conceive myself missing Mrs. Siddons as Lady Mac-Beth, or *The Dream* which they can make so pretty on that great stage at the Lane, with its floats and fairies and gauzy backcloths."

"Miss Lydia," Mrs. Barker said, "is engaged upon a novel."

Glynn, from his place on the window seat, sighed gently as if at some private recollection. From across the room an elderly don spoke up in a fretful tone. "Yes, yes, but this is mere afternoon tea chit-chat. What I want to know about is policy. If we are to be represented by a pack of younglings I want to know if any one of them has any policy."

"Miss Lydia is going to give a public reading of the first few chapters at Christ's College Lodge on Thursday evening," her mother continued. "Dr. Barker and I will be dispensing madeira beforehand. I trust all here will attend. Mr. Pitt, I know you are returning to London. But only for a night, I understand. You will be back in time."

The room fell deadly silent about her. She went on temptingly, "I, too, will be rendering a few musical items."

Lydia piped up, "What are you going to sing, mama?"

"Lord, child, I scarce know yet. I prefer the old songs."

"You should include at least one that is topical, ma'am," Townshend said, then muttered into Lydia's ear.

"La, yes, Lord John, *The Baby and the Nurse*," Lydia exclaimed on a peal of laughter. "''Tis vastly funny, they say. Pray do sing it for us now."

"Now come, Miss Bellenger, this is not a college sing-song," Farmer said promptly. "Let me wait upon you for more tea."

From across the room the elderly don spoke again, still fretfully, "What of the National Debt? The National Debt plagues my dreams. Even to dwell on our necessity to pay the interest on it serves me more ill at nights than the buttery loading my plate with slabs of Cheddar cheese and pickled cucumber. Well enough to have a youngling at the Exchequer, I daresay, but has he any policy whereby we can reduce the National Debt? Answer me that."

"I doubt he even knows what the National Debt is, unless instructed on it by his father or having had the cabinet ex-

plain it carefully to him at one of their meetings," Townshend said on a carrying murmur.

Mrs. Barker cut across them all. "I shall certainly include
some of the items I sang at Madingley during the Commence-
ment Week Fair three years ago. Sir John Cotton was good
enough on that occasion to liken my voice to Mrs. Sheridan's
when she sang professionally at Drury Lane and Lady
Cotton professed herself quite enchanted by my range and
tone. Indeed, sir, I believe you were there yourself that
time."

She paused, willing the compliment, but Pitt merely
assented to the fact that he had been present. Almost they
seemed to have embarked upon some stubborn English
game, the one grimly determined on extracting praise and
fair speeches, the other equally set on making no ploy of
gallantry. Farmer was regarding both with a deepening
twinkle in his eyes. Mrs. Barker, not yet defeated, rose, bringing the room to its feet with her, and announced, "Mr. Vice-
Chancellor, I am altogether too warm sat here by your great
fire. I shall join Dr. Glynn and Mr. Pitt on the window seat."

She installed herself there. For the remainder of the
occasion, while the tea was splashed out and the good
Cambridge country fare handed round, Pitt was told in much
detail how greatly Sir Thomas Hatton had admired Lydia in
her rouched yellow, or Mrs. Barker herself in plum-coloured
velvet, how they had concertedly knocked the Pembertons
all of a heap by their country dancing at one of the Bury
balls, how their singing, watercolouring, authorship and em-
broidery were the delight and rage of Cambridge. He
listened to all with a plain boredom. By the time the Vice-
Chancellor's tea party had come to its close all present could
see that from Mrs. Barker's direction the wind had shifted
a point or two towards the Coalition.

Farmer, having despatched his guests, came back to Wilcox
and Crisp who still sat on. Glynn also remained. He had
taken a medical book from his pocket, his grey-powdered

head bent over the pages in the failing light.

Presently Wilcox rose with a chuckle and helped himself to a neglected slice of ginger cake. "This titanic struggle diverts me greatly. Will Madame B. secure her compliment or will young Billy Pitt not pay it? Of course the good lady pays herself so many doubtless he thinks one more is not necessary."

"But it is," Crisp answered softly. "God with us, if the boy still has as much to learn as a Minister as he has as a canvasser he is not the man for us."

"It is his sickliness as a freshman that troubles me most. What say you, Glynn? Is he strong enough for Downing Street?"

Glynn lifted his grey-powdered head. "In purpose or in health?"

"You know my meaning."

"If the voting goes against him here on Saturday he will not set foot in Downing Street again."

"True," Wilcox said. "If Cambridge throws him out, as she did before, he has lost the whole game. Bearing in mind it will be a damned near thing he had best unbend a little to Madame B. or anyone else who might blow a vote in his direction." He crumbled the ginger cake suddenly into angry fragments on his plate. "For my part I think it does not matter who gets back to Downing Street now, for it is too late. My mind is full of your Shakespeare, Dick—of dying Gaunt mourning his other Eden. The floods of debt and conquest and degeneracy wash in, and the royal throne of kings drowns and is lost in them."

Farmer drew on the pipe he had just kindled. "It is a splendid speech but I have never heard it rendered well on the stage."

"Nor I," Wilcox answered. "It is never given its right huge despair. It will be now—mark it, it will be now, if that is of any consolation to us."

III

Mrs. Barker, in the college court, took a cold leave of Pitt and no leave at all of Mansfield.

"Madame B. and Barker between them can exert influence through Christ's College Lodge," Euston muttered, watching Townshend handing the ladies into the Barker barouche. "Sometime, doubtless, you ought to tell the woman you can well believe Prinny pronounced Lydia all the nines at the Newmarket races."

"I'm damned if he ever did," Pitt answered.

"I'm damned too if he ever did. But Jack Townshend is saying as much to her at this moment, depend upon it."

Mansfield came over to them. During the Gordon Riots he and Pitt had manned the barricades together at Lincoln's Inn, Mansfield too having had chambers there. Their greeting held a somewhat awkward enemy's regard each for the other.

"From that quarter I am getting the sort of treatment you got last time," Mansfield said, with a dry nod at the departing Barker barouche. "With two sprigs of the nobility—Euston here, and the son of the Lord Viscount Townshend—to say nothing of a First Lord of the Treasury, Madame B. wastes no civilities on a common or garden lawyer. Besides, I am wed, thank God, and of no use to Lydia. You three, with your family seats or your tenures of commodious town residences in Downing Street, are all marked men."

Townshend joined them. The verbal buffet he had landed on Pitt in the Vice-Chancellor's parlour had been taken much more quiescently than would have been the case at Westminster. In gentle Cambridge and with the aftermath of his three months in the House still upon him, Pitt for these few hours had quit the battle. Townshend's look said so plainly, "Have we tamed you, my boy?" that a prickly anger settled on Euston's face.

*   *   *

It was midnight, that same evening, when Pitt and Euston escaped from the combination room of King's College, from donnish probings and curling tobacco smoke. There was no speechifying nor addressing an audience at Cambridge. The candidates went by invitation to the combination rooms— once the parlour or 'parlez' rooms, where the monks had met strangers and disputed with them—there to be what the University termed 'quizzed'. In the mellow old rooms, beamed in black oak, it seemed an urbane process, milder by far than the hustings. But, this night as always, the questions had been hard, plying and unremitting. Dr. Smith, Smith's uncle, followed them out into the close, attended by a servant with a lantern for his walk back to Caius in the starlight. The tenuous light fell on the scholar's stoop of shoulder and on the clever, narrow face that betrayed no kinship with Smith.

Euston, in order to allow them to talk alone, had walked on. Pitt lingered to say, "I have to commend your nephew to you, Doctor."

Dr. Smith gave him a dry glance. "I am told you have him in your employ. My respectful condolences. I can think of no worse predicament than to be sat in Downing Street, vastly terrified for England, and with Joseph in the secretary's room."

"I am not vastly terrified for England. England will stand till the day of judgment. The Joe Smiths will help to ensure that she does."

"For my part I always thought the boy a perfect harbinger of disaster," Dr. Smith remarked with a lift of brow. "Still, I own I never thought Joseph would see the inside of Downing Street in any capacity whatever."

He nodded and went on his way. Pitt followed after Euston. It was fresh and reviving here, the fens at this spot lapping to the very feet of Cambridge to catch in their black marshy skirts the glint of the stars; on the Trumpington side of the river, the osier bed filling the night with a hissing

sibilance. Dr. Smith's bull's-eye lantern had now gone from
sight in the direction of Caius but a second pinprick of light
twinkled round the wall of Pemberton's garden, groping over
bush and bullrush and osiers towards Pitt. A hoarse East
Anglian voice muttered to him, in goodnatured advice, "You
run for it, sir. Doctor's just behind."

Another figure loomed up round the wall. A voice said
gently but with firmness, "Come, come, your name and
college, sir. It is much after eleven o'clock. Let me look at
you—Giles, the lantern."

"Told you to run for it, I did," the servant muttered.

The light was elevated. It glanced on Pitt's face and on the
face of his accoster, Dr. Hallifax. Hallifax looked hard at
him, then said quickly, with an old man's courtly apologising
grace, "Why, pray forgive me. You are not now *in statu
pupillari*, I think—though, unless I mistake it, you were
up to a short time ago."

Euston came out of the shadow of the trees and joined
them. Hallifax gave him an absent nod, then scanned Pitt
again. "Indeed I know your face—not your name—names
increasingly elude me—but your face. You are the one who
penned a quite outstanding paper on Newton's *Principia*. Tell
me now, what are you doing with yourself these days? Not
idling about London, I trust, like so many of today's young
men?"

"Not idling, Doctor," Pitt answered. "Since Christmas I
seem to have been pretty much occupied."

"Good—apply yourself," Hallifax said in a kindly fashion.
"You will rise in the world, I am persuaded. I have the most
inordinate hopes of you, my boy."

He and his servant and lantern dwindled away into the
dark. "Dear old Hallifax would mistake almost anyone as
being still *in statu pupillari*," Euston remarked in a soothing
voice.

"Honest Giles-of-the-lantern thought so too. I must," Pitt
said bitterly, "be the first First Lord of the Treasury to be

mistaken for an undergraduate out from college bounds after eleven and told to run for it."

"Well, as a First Lord of the Treasury you're not altogether in the customary mould," Euston answered, and broke into a chuckle. Pitt presently echoed it, and the sighing of the osier bed at their feet was, for much of their way back to Emmanuel, punctuated by the sounds of their amusement.

IV

ON TUESDAY, Pitt returned to London, journeying back again to Cambridge the day following. It was a long, wearisome, jolting journey—some eight hours in the summer when the going underfoot was hard and firm; ten, with the mud of winter still on the roads. But if he had gone instantly over to Christ's College Lodge on getting in he would have caught the last sixty minutes of Mrs. Barker's select madeira party there. He put in no appearance. It was eleven, just on the hour for bed, when he and Euston met in the buttery of Emmanuel. Pitt, with the stainings of travel on him, looked done up. Euston looked no less.

"What an evening," he said. "Madeira—one small glass— seed cake, Madame B. singing *Britons Awake*, accompanying herself at the harpsicord. Crisp nodded off. For my part I felt like old Boreas on the Treasury Bench—not asleep, but only wishing to God I were."

"What of Granta's Fanny Burney?" Pitt asked. "Did she read her novel?"

"Did she not," groaned Euston. "Five chapters of *Lavinia —or The Entrance into Fashionable Society of a Young Woman of Quality*. Jack Townshend vowed she had only to complete it and he would bear it off to Crowders, the booksellers in Paternoster Row. He's entirely safe. She will never do it." He gathered together a plate of college brawn and a cup of coffee and flung himself into one of the buttery chairs. "I but hope they don't find out what time you got in."

But Mrs. Barker was determined on discovering no less and the next day descended on a group in Mr. Delaport's Coffee Gardens, hard by Emmanuel. It was Thursday, the occasion of the first open-air concert of the season in the coffee gardens, and the thin, pretty notes of flute and fiddle blew about under the scented trees. In the still sharp spring air the audience looked chilled but was sitting on with hardihood.

"I am trying to establish what hour Mr. Pitt returned last night," Mrs. Barker remarked. "I asked Williams, the Vice-Chancellor's groom, when the horses were brought in but he said he did not look at the clock—an unlikely thing, to be sure, since the rogue never takes his eyes off it as a rule. The Vice-Chancellor also says he did not happen to look at the clock either. There has been such a deal of not looking at clocks one begins to think it deliberate. Can anyone here tell me when our *premier homme* got in?"

"Nine, I am told on good authority, ma'am," Townshend answered.

"As I positively suspected. He could certainly have come over to us for an hour to allow Miss Lydia to read out the first five chapters of her novel again, and I would willingly have re-rendered my musical items. But plainly the whole thing was altogether beneath him."

"Fatigued, perhaps, ma'am," a tall, thin don sitting with them remarked. "'Tis a devilish journey after the spring rains. He has had twenty hours of travel in two days."

"Nonsense," Mrs. Barker said. "No one is ever fatigued at his age. I am the last woman in the world, I hope, to talk ill behind anyone's back, but I begin to think all this noise and fame and notoriety has made him entirely swollen in the head."

One of the dons, vainly trying to attend upon the music, made quelling noises.

"Pray don't shush at me, Dr. Yates," Mrs. Barker said. "The idea of being governed by so rude and talentless a young man makes me quite *distrait*."

Thus, on the very eve of polling, the toasts in Christ's College Lodge became all 'Fox and North forever', and Mrs. Barker and Lydia progressed down Bene't Street or walked the Backs festooned in Coalition ribbons as blue as the spring skies that hung above Cambridge.

V

EIGHT O'CLOCK on polling Saturday brought Euston to Pitt's room. Outside there was spring sunshine, the daffodils starring all the college lawns, and the waterwhorl grass and English galingale—with whose ginger-tasting roots the monkish cooks had flavoured their dishes in the abbot's kitchens—thrusting greenly up about Emmanuel's garden stretch of water.

The college residents took breakfast in their rooms. Pitt and Euston ate together, the buttery sending up beef and brawn, the crisp wheaten loaves that Cambridge called 'Brown Georges', and the butter, which, by another quirk, was sold in the town by the yard, so that the college gyp who carried in the food asked, "Is six inches each enough, gentlemen?"

Euston had tossed his gown over a chair back. He was one of those privileged to wear a coloured gown, and its sour and sickly yellow was embellished here and there with jagged bombazeen tufts.

"That's a criminal-looking thing, Fitzroy," Pitt said, regarding it across the table.

"I bought it in the Dudderies for one and six. I own I always thought it were lucky to me."

On a sudden, from across the town, the University bell in

Great St. Mary's began its deep-throated, commanding peal. This was the peal that would ring for an hour, its chimes borne out over the fens and the flat lands as far as Ely and Cherry Hinton, to summon the Senate to the Senate House to vote the University's two burgesses into Parliament, as had been done since the days of the first Stuart King. It rang on vigorously. Pitt and Euston exchanged a glance, then rose and tugged on their Masters of Art gowns.

"Well, Fitzroy," Pitt said. "My thanks beyond measure for all your toil here. I scarce think I helped you much over the tea cups, but I would not gladly have had anyone else beside me these past few days."

Euston looked at him with a faint flush of pleasure. "Why, indeed since the Pitts pay no compliment they do not mean, I take that kindly. It's true I may have supplied the bows and the grins and the social small talk, but when it came to those fierce inquisitions we underwent in the combination rooms—no, it was you who rode out the tides for both of us there." He hesitated. "I am not so greatly exercised about myself. I shall be Duke of Grafton one day, I suppose, and doing my damnedest to avoid inviting Madame B. to Wakefield Lodge. But, God knows, after those monstrous rough three months alone facing the Coalition I hope you achieve it."

They quitted the room and went down the corridor. Through the half-open door of the Vice-Chancellor's dressing room there was a glimpse of Farmer's form recumbent under a towel. Above it, Bob Forster, the college barber, stood in his shirtsleeves, brandishing a razor.

"Not the wig, Bob?" Farmer's voice was saying plaintively. "A little hair powder will do, will it not?"

"Now, now, Doctor," Forster answered adamantly, "it's an occasion. Can't have you counting the votes in the Senate House looking as if you was carrying guts to a pig."

Farmer came out presently. He looked exceedingly handsome in his white breeches and stockings, his wig in place

and his Vice-Chancellor's scarlet robes over his arm, but also
as if his finery chafed him.

"What a penance formal attire is," he remarked. "I shall
be glad when the occasion—as Bob terms it—is over, though
doubtless not as glad as you will be." He groped for his pipe
and turned towards Pitt. "Taffy Williams, my good Welsh-
man, tells me you require two horses for yourself and your
groom saddled in readiness outside the Senate House to wait
upon the results. Once they are declared do you intend to
set out for London?"

"There'll be less haste in victory, Mr. Vice-Chancellor. But
I will have to post back to the city the instant the poll closes
if I am defeated."

"Yes, of course," Farmer assented. "It will be necessary for
you to render the seals immediately back into His Majesty's
hands in the event of the count going against you." He put
out his hand in a provisional leave-taking. "Very well,
sir. If it is victory I hope you will continue here as our guest
for at least the weekend. If it is defeat I wish you safe into
London tonight."

Pitt and Euston made their way outside. Beyond the walls
of Emmanuel a great converging movement was spilling
through the streets towards the Senate House—the regents
with white silk linings to their hoods, the non-regents with
black hoods, the doctors in their scarlet gowns, and here and
there one or two permitted, like Euston, by privilege, to
wear a coloured gown, so that among the black and the
scarlet there was a glint of apple green or grey or even rose-
pink against the flinty Cambridge stones.

At the top of Jesus Lane Sheepshanks, whom they had
not seen since the day of Pitt's first arrival in town, was
promenading moodily, his black gown flapping from his
shoulders. He gave them a morose nod and remarked, "I've
put a loop of string round its neck and hanged it up the
chimney."

Both looked at him uncomprehendingly.

"The madeira bottle," Sheepshanks said in not-too-patient explanation. "Sal Elvedge is going to reap a rich harvest, is she not, with all we in the Senate House? There'll not be a drop of gin, brandy or port left in the place, I'll warrant—Bullock's specimens all standing high and dry above their spirit levels, like rocks at low tide, and decomposing gently. I hope the voting's done by three. If it goes beyond 'tis all Pompey's pillar to a stick of sealing wax that damned woman will consider looking up the chimney."

The press bore them on towards the Senate House. On Senate Green there were barouches drawn up, isled in a crowd of noisy townsfolk. Though the town, as a borough, despatched its own separate representatives to Westminster, it bestowed much rowdy attention on the University's election. The spring morning was loud with shouted advice which the gown, pushing through, properly ignored. In the Barker barouche Mrs. Barker and Lydia were seated, their blue Coalition plumes nodding skywards.

"Barker entirely agrees with me," Mrs. Barker was announcing to her assembled court. "We can do no better than to return Government into the capable hands of dear Mr. Fox and dear Lord North."

The Senate House filled. It was cool here, the great building permanently chilled by its black and white marble floor, its wide galleries fashioned out of Norway Oak and its ceiling icicled and dimpled in stucco. The official processions began to come in—the two Proctors in their squared hoods, and, on their heels, the Vice-Chancellor's procession, the three Esquire Bedells walking first with their silver maces, followed by Farmer in his robes, attended by two blue-coated servants. In front of the raised voting table, at the east end, a Justice of the Peace waited, Bible in hand, ready to swear Farmer in as Returning Officer. His plain snuff-coloured coat and high riding boots marked him apart.

The oath taken, Farmer seated himself at the voting table, joined there by the two Proctors, the junior Doctor of

Divinity and the four scrutineers. Each scrutineer stood to safeguard the interests of his own man, as he would have done on the hustings. But in the calmness and incorruptibility of a University election their presence was superfluous. With the bell quiet and the noisy townsfolk shut out, the senior Esquire Bedell shouted in Latin, the language of the Senate, *"Ad scrutium pro electione duorum burgensium hujus academiae."*

The Senate voted in colleges—ancient Peterhouse, the royal foundation, her arms of four pales gules charged with golden crowns, first; and modern Magdalene last. Each man wrote out his own voting slip in the correct Latin format before carrying it up to the Vice-Chancellor. It was not a secret vote. The Registrary published the lists afterwards for any to consult. But some thought it a furtive method and would have preferred to declare themselves openly as was done on the hustings.

There was much coming and going, the candidates and those not immediately engaged in voting walking about or quitting the building. Townshend, watching Pitt, saw a glint of scarlet swinging from his waistcoat pocket. "He's carrying the Treasury seals to get them back into the King's hands tonight," he muttered to Mansfield. "That'll be a ride into the dark and obscurity, by God."

To them, as to their rivals, standing together just below the platform, it seemed that the Senate was tackling the business of voting all too sedately. "Look at old Wallop doddering yonder," Euston remarked sourly. "Two quills broke and three voting slips blown off the table already. They'll have us hanging by our thumbs until three or four o'clock, depend upon it."

"I am of your mind, Fitzroy," Pitt answered. "This must have been devised by some Regius Professor of Torture in the thirteenth century."

About noon he went out alone by the secluded side entrance. A cowherd, in his brown Anglian smock, his dog running at his heels, was droving his quiet cows the length of Trumpington Street, and in front of the stable yard of the Blue Boar, Taffy Williams, Farmer's groom, was walking two saddled horses up and down. These were the horses Pitt would take if the voting went against him. The gentle clip-clopping on the cobbles came to his ears as his own political requiem, so that, in that moment, he felt a pang for Appleby or the dozen or so safe seats the Treasury could have given him. Then the subdued hubbub of the voting Senate, the University's splendour and independence and grace came upon him, and he was young enough to feel joy in the battle for such a prize.

Euston joined him and they returned together inside. The University did not as a rule dine before three. But if the polling continued beyond that hour it would still go on without a break. The foundations were completed at length; the *commorans in Villas*—the men not in college residence—began to go up to the voting table. Farmer signalled one of the Bedells. The man went out. Within a few minutes the University bell broke out again, cleaving the Cambridgeshire air, to signify the poll was nearing its end. The Senate House started to fill, the regents and non-regents coming back from pacing the river walks. The University bell, after its ten-minute peal, fell silent once more. Farmer, with the quill in his fingers, remarked, "Then only myself remains."

He scribbled his choice on a spare voting slip and looked up. "The poll is closed."

Instantly the Esquire Bedells set up their shouts of *"Cessatum est a scrutino."* The great doors were swung shut, Farmer drawing his robes about him and mounting to the lofty eminence of the Vice-Chancellor's official chair.

Under the stare of the Senate the three Esquire Bedells came down from the voting table, their footfalls muffled on the eight carpeted steps from the platform, loud and echoing when they trod across the marble of the well of the floor. They bowed to each candidate in turn, their senior repeating the phrase, "Be pleased to approach the table, sir."

Mansfield and Townshend went first, as the two sitting candidates, Pitt and Euston, the two challengers, behind them. Above them Farmer sat benignly impassive in his robes. The faces of the four scrutineers—still ranged behind the voting table—had gone wooden. Honour did not permit them to betray anything of what they knew the results to be and each avoided looking at his own man in case he should inadvertently show elation or gloom. As the last candidate mounted the platform, the Junior Proctor instructed them, "Face the Senate."

They turned about, standing behind the Bar of the House, below them the ranks of red and black, and the flecks of colour. The Senior Proctor joined them. In his scarlet gown, his nose beaked like one of the Caesars, he might have been a Roman praetor delivering judgment in some ancient forum. The crowded Senate was now so unstirring he had no need to raise his voice. He read in normal tones from the paper in his hand, "For James Mansfield Esquire, one hundred and eighty-five votes cast. For Lord John Townshend, two hundred and eighty-one votes cast. For Lord Euston, three hundred and nine votes cast. For the Right Honourable William Pitt, three hundred and fifty-nine votes cast."

"Oh, my stars, we've done it," Euston said on a delighted gasp.

Beside him Townshend muttered a bleak and pungent, "God-damn."

"Felicitations, Pitt," Mansfield said, putting out his hand. "Euston."

"Felicitations," Townshend echoed, but without great warmth.

The Senate received the result with decorum, as it always did. But outside, the town—the news conveyed to it by one of the blue coats—fell at once to a considerable good-humoured uproar. Pitt made no move to court the plaudits of his admirers, slipping out of the side door, largely unseen by them. Only Sheepshanks, scudding past to the rescue of his madeira bottle, with an expression of anguished doubt, seemed more intent on quitting the scene.

"Done it then have you?" Taffy Williams remarked as the newly-elected burgess for Cambridge University came up. "Good for you is that then, sir. Not be wanting the horses after all, I take it."

Mansfield joined Pitt. They walked on together, their gowns slung over their arms. Behind them the pediments and pilasters of the Senate House rose serenely above the cropped green grass, the little dormers scalloped like shells encrusting a rock above the sea-green tides. "Well, that is that for me," Mansfield remarked with a backward glance upon it.

"You'll stand again?"

Mansfield gave a dry smile. "I think not. The trouble with you is that you make a man feel so confounded old. Jack Townshend will find another seat presently, I don't doubt —Fox will see to that. But you have observed the last of me at Westminster."

"I think that will be somewhat to Westminster's and the land's loss—if you will accept the testimonial of an enemy."

"An enemy?" Mansfield said, still with a faint irony. "Not entirely that. You and Jack Townshend perhaps. But for my part I wish you at least tolerable well and I think you do the same for me."

The Vice-Chancellor had walked back in formal procession to Emmanuel Lodge, but once there had donned his carpet slippers and gone out to breathe the air of his garden. Glynn joined him. They walked together in the spring sunshine, the one taking his medical book from his pocket, the other fingering his pipe.

"Well, Bob," Farmer said at length. "We're old friends, and if I ply you with questions you had rather not answer you have but to tell me to mind my own business. I could not forbear to notice your vote when you brought it up to me in the Senate House—a split vote, and, in truth, there were not many of them. You coupled Pitt with Mansfield."

Glynn nodded.

"I own I wondered what you have against Euston."

"I have nothing against Euston," Glynn answered quietly. "He is honest, hard-working and loyal. I count myself well served to be represented by him."

Farmer regarded him above the bowl of his pipe. Glynn went on, "Perhaps there in the Senate House I became mindful of my Hippocratic oath. Pitt was my patient once. I would gladly see him returned to Westminster. But to see him lodged again as premier, with his majority about him and a monstrous toil awaiting him—of that I have reservations."

"This then is the question you so neatly turned when Wilcox asked it the other evening. In your heart you do not think he has health enough for Downing Street?"

Before them lay the shining garden pool, starred about in the bright spring sunshine with its glinting daffodils. Glynn said slowly, as if he found it an ill day on which to pronounce a death sentence, "Pitt is still a long way from Downing Street. But, if he is returned there, I think that—in course of time—it will kill him."

VI

THE NEXT day, being Sunday, the candidates went to the University Church of Great St. Mary's to hear the Vice-Chancellor preach, the tired victors and the tired vanquished sitting together in the Proctors' Pew. After the service— with Euston having left for Wakefield Lodge—Pitt and Farmer took horses and rode up into the Gogmagog Hills. Below them stretched the wide fens—full of fledgelings, of pheasant, snipe and partridge—the town nestling in their dark marshy skirts, and, alongside it, the silver thread of the river, with its little spanning bridges, girdling the cool and cloistered courts of Clare. Buttressed and mullioned, crenellated and cantilevered, the college buildings lay among the green and black fens like stony stars; the jewel of them, King's College Chapel, tossing skywards the splendour of her medieval pinnacles in an ecstatic torrent of praise to the good hand of God.

Pitt, regarding his hard-won prize with a lover's fierce pride, remarked, "Almost I could spend the next seven years here rather than back at Westminster."

"Ah, you are succumbing to what I succumbed to years ago," Farmer answered cheerfully. "The peculiar Cambridge-shire sin that seeps up into us from the fens—sloth. I am told I have some small gift with the pen, yet in twenty years all I have published is one little mean volume on Shakespeare that stands on the top of the bookshelf in my study."

"One little mean volume! Nothing better on Shakespeare ever came off the presses."

"God bless my soul, a compliment," Farmer murmured, the twinkle leaping to his eyes. "*Quantum mutatus ab illo.* The election is over, in truth."

But in the rest of the country it was only just beginning. Pitt, on the morrow, set out for London and whatever news awaited him there.

VII

THE BRILLIANCE of the April day dulled by evening. Pitt arrived back at Downing Street in sluicing rain, the porter helping him off with a greatcoat that streamed rivulets on to the marble of the floor. Burfield came out to greet the returned traveller. It was fairly certain that Burfield's allegiance lay with the Coalition, whose victory would ensure

Portland's ducal presence again in Number 10. But he prof-
fered congratulations on the University election, remarking,
"It was a great gain, sir. I was told the result at the Coal
Hole—the hostelry in the Strand—the same evening."

"Felicitations, sir," Smith said, clattering down the stairs
with a welcoming delight. "I'll wager Cambridge looked uncommon fair from the Gogmagog Hills."

He and Pitt went up together, Smith lighting them with
the candle-branch. "There's not much to hand yet, sir," he
said. "A day's polling at a time, a report, at a time—when
the Post Office does not lose the mail bags, which it does
exceeding frequently. Mr. Rose thinks it will be a week or
even a sennight before we know how it has gone. Still, Cambridge has much cheered me."

"And you need cheering, Joe?" Pitt asked.

"Do I look so? Damn—that's a fine way to receive you
back when you've achieved the University against the odds.
It is only that I took in one of Fox's meetings at Covent
Garden yesterday and he is so monstrous confident. He told
the audience he was sure the Coalition would be returned.
The Prince of Wales has an equal confidence. They have the
victory celebrations already planned at Carlton House."

They had reached the withdrawing room. Dundas—returned from Edinburgh and lodged now at Number 10 to
be on hand for the results coming in—turned as they entered.
He gazed at Pitt's wet clothes. "Man, you're soaked to the
skin."

"I rode post from Braintree. I could not abide jolting
longer in that damned carriage."

He took off his coat and they saw his waistcoat patched in
damp too upon the shoulders and back. The Treasury seals,
which he had carried with him into Cambridge, swung from
his watch-chain like little red flowers. He unfastened them,
dropping them into a drawer of the table and turning the
key upon them.

Under the urgings of Dundas he went to change his wet

clothes. The kitchens sent them up soup and sandwiches and hot coffee. They ate for the most part silently, the house hanging still about them, not only the occupants but even the bricks and mortar breathing an expectancy, as if Number 10 stood about its hearthstones ruminating on what harvest the hustings would bring to it.

"By your leave, sir," Smith said, gulping down the last of his coffee. "I'll spend the night at Duke Street. I've done so on several occasions since the election got under way. Mr. Rose has a bed put by for me."

As was customarily done in all elections the results were expressed first to the Secretary of the Treasury. George Rose, in his Duke Street home, would receive any despatch on any borough's state of polling before sending it round to Pitt.

"It's raining cats and dogs, Joe," Pitt said with a glance at the watery cascades spilling unremittingly down the windows.

"But at Duke Street one learns the results but that little space sooner," Smith answered. "Besides 'tis well enough, sir. I'll take a hackney."

He set aside his cup. At the same instant Burfield's tread echoed in upon them from the corridor. Burfield never ran but he sounded close upon it now. The floorboards lurched under his punishing weight.

"Here's somewhat from George Rose now," Dundas said and snatched up the note Burfield proffered round the door. He ripped off Rose's seal and scanned the contents with a rising and visible delight. "My faith, your friend, Will Wilberforce, may be but Lilliputian in size but he's struck a giant's blow here. He's secured Yorkshire for you—no contest—results declared on canvas and a show o' hands only. The two Coalition men declined the poll."

"Oh, God with us, sir," Smith said with a joyous gasp. "That's a marvellous result."

Pitt took the note, his intense pleasure at Wilberforce's success blotting the fatigue from his face. "So Will is one of the shire men now—entitled to wear his spurs in the House, and entirely the right stuff for the shires. He will go his own way and damn me or anyone else who tries to stop him."

Burfield, having hovered on the threshold long enough to hear the news, retreated down the corridor, his going much more stately than his manner of arrival had been. Smith left them and they heard eventually the grind of his hackney on its way out of Downing Street.

"You ought to get yourself a-bed, Mr. William," Ralph remarked, tapping and looking in upon them. "They'll be reading the burial service over you, sir, and not the results if you don't."

Pitt answered he would come in a few minutes. When Ralph had gone he said to Dundas, "What of you?"

"I'll sit up."

"You'll have nought to do save wait and listen to the rain."

"Aye, wait and listen to the rain and question how it goes, and whichever way it does, maybe for mysel' it'll ha'e an ill side to it." Pitt looked at him queryingly. He went on, "I desire beyond measure you should achieve it. But if you do, will they no' but say o' me that yet again Scotch Harry had a nose for the winning side—that I scented victory across the heather when all that the rest o' them could scent were but resounding defeat."

"Does it much exercise you what some men might say?"

"Och, no. I ha'e the right manner o' skin for politics. But my fear is that one day you'll entertain that same thought yoursel'."

"You're a great fool then. I would as likely believe Wilberforce had pocketed the parish dues or Joe Smith walked off with the Downing Street plate as to think you abided the pelting storm with me those three months in the House only for the sake of a majority that might not exist." He got up and went to the side table where the wine stood. "You're tired, Hal," he said. "As tired as I am—and Edin-

burgh is many leagues beyond Cambridge. Take some wine.
We've not drunk together since Lincoln's Inn."

He handed Dundas a glass and tossed his own back.
Dundas watched, seeing the youthful lineaments of the figure
that stood in much contrast to the accomplishment of the
drinking. Pitt caught his look. "You found out I could drink
—that night at Lincoln's Inn?"

"I but wondered where you learnt it. I learnt in a damned
hard-bitten school among the Edinburgh lawyers in the dram
shops o' the Canongate. The drink was whisky there and
we plied it all night talking o'er our cases after the courts
had risen. But you—there's been blether enough, God wi' us,
about your sheltered upbringing—where did you learn it?"

Pitt answered with a wry, weary grin, "Where did I learn
anything?—taught by my old dad at a stool."

VIII

MORNING BROUGHT an unexpected caller in the person of
Temple, coming through the library with his baronial stride.
Once again he brought with him an air of owning the
house, the gardens, the great park beyond, even the city that
spilled about them in its rose-red brick. Smith, returned from
Duke Street, confronted him on the threshold of the study.

"Then you are the secretary," Temple said, with his high
stare. "I am told my cousin is still sleeping." It would have
been like Temple to say, "Go and wake him."

"Will you wait, my lord?" Smith asked, to forestall as
much.

"Did Mr. Pitt give orders he was not to be disturbed?"

"No, but I take it upon myself."

"And I stand upon it too," Dundas said, appearing from
the inner study. "Let him sleep, Temple. He's frashed
under."

"I observe my young cousin has two exceedingly efficient watchdogs to stand guard upon him," Temple remarked with a surprising grace.

Pitt, when he came down, regarded his visitor with some astonishment. But their greeting was more cordial than the manner of their January parting had been. Temple made reference to it, saying, "Well, William, it did not trouble you seemingly that I took your advice of January and retired to Stowe."

"Oh, but it did. I had a wretched ill night."

"I am glad my departure occasioned you that much discomfort at least," Temple said thinly. "To own the truth I never realised you had so much Grenville bite in you until that day. I begin to understand why my father's sister married where she did."

It was the nearest any Nugent-Grenville-Temple could come to proffering an olive branch. Pitt acknowledged it by saying, "I am glad you called upon me, cousin."

George Rose's note from Duke Street, containing the overnight results, lay on the table. Temple picked it up and stood scanning it. "The game, at this point, is to anyone. Rose told me yesterday he has hopes you may succeed in dividing the shire seats equally with Fox. However, from this I can scarce say Derbyshire looks over-healthy for you."

"No, we hardly seem to be prospering there."

The door was opened to another visitor—George Jackson, who had been contesting Penryn in the West Country and who, since he had reached London ahead of the posts, had brought Pitt the tally from there. He was travel-stained, and his jaded countenance spoke his news before he gave it.

"Only three votes kept Jack Smith out. Not a great many more in my case either, though it might equally well have been three thousand. I'm devilish sorry. I feel we have let you down."

"Rubbish. You could scarce have come nearer. My thanks for all your toil and effort."

"Well, there it is," Jackson remarked, adding after a pause, "Incidentally I came round here by way of Covent Garden hustings. Fox has a marvellous electioneering committee—all the men in identical dress, a uniform to tell true, buff breeches and blue coats—fleets of carriages waiting to whisk any Coalition supporter off to vote—handbills being plied about all over the place—the Duchess of Devonshire kissing any man within sight—any man who pronounces himself for Fox, that is, and, this being England, I suppose there are several to preen themselves, saying, 'Martha, I was kissed by a duchess today.' They were announcing Derbyshire when I was there." He checked. "You know about Derbyshire?"

"Only that we are trailing," Pitt answered.

"No, I'm afraid it has gone," Jackson said uncomfortably. "Poll closed there two days ago. It's damned disappointing."

"I hope this is not about to prove Black Wednesday for you, William," Temple remarked with a return to dryness. "Penryn and Derbyshire declared contrary in the space of two minutes. A few more results of a like nature and you had best see how the occhio de paone vases in the Cabinet Room will pack."

Derbyshire especially was of major consequence, for it was another of the great prized and proud shire seats—most hugely important, since, not only did they return good men, they, along with the open boroughs, most surely spoke the mind of England. Rose had had great hopes of it. His note from Duke Street, confirming the loss, was handed in on the heel of the words, even his handwriting lying across the paper in a dejected slant.

When the house was for a little empty of visitors Pitt and Dundas tugged on boots and capes and brought the horses directly from the stables into the park. It was dusk now, the birds going to roost among the darkling branches of the trees about the lake. But Fox's supporters in their neat cut-away blue coats, their ribbons pinned to hat or lapel, were still combing through the park and along the Mall. Pitt and Dundas were halted almost at once by the question, "Scot-and-lot men, gentlemen?"

"No' in this borough," Dundas answered curtly.

"A pity you are not," their waylayer said. "Had you been enfranchised here and for Fox I have a carriage in the Mall to take you to the poll. The Prince of Wales's grooms would have attended upon your horses until you got back."

"Why not carry them off to the hustings whether they are enfranchised here or not, my blue boy?" remarked a second bystander. He wore no colours but he was plainly a watchdog for the other side. "Theirs won't be the first bad votes you have passed off since you found out the Returning Officer is as blind as a bat and in a mighty great funk when it comes to arguing with you."

The Coalition man swung round upon him. "As to bad votes others besides ourselves are passing off a few of those. You Treasury nightingales will sing softer when the results come in. Have you heard Derbyshire has declared for Fox? The Prince is lighting his windows for it tonight."

Westminster always elected after this manner, in a rough maul, fought viciously by both sides—different from serene Cambridge,, from the goodnatured potwalloper boroughs and the great shire seats, the ribs of their hustings raised under the shadows of their ancient cathedrals and beneath the mullioned windows of their moot halls, different even from the City of London to the east, with the pride of her livery companies upon her, from Southwark across the river to the south, and royal Windsor to the west. But Westminster's restlessness and brilliance matched Fox's own. He had brought all his vast electioneering skill to this narrower battle as he had brought it to the broader battle for the whole country. Little Downing Street, nestling plumb in the heart of Fox's borough, felt the gusts of his confidence beating upon her as she might have felt a gale rattling her shutters in the night.

The dusk had deepened. As Pitt and Dundas rode back across the park the great windows of Carlton House began to leap one by one into light until the whole house stood blinking and beaming through the trees, in token of victory for Derbyshire. Nor was it yet the end of Black Wednesday. In the study Smith was standing reading a second note from George Rose with an expression of concentrated fury on his face.

"Something more gone a-miss, Joe?" Pitt asked.

"The damned weathercock, William Colhoun," Smith answered almost with a snarl. "You recall the fellow—he was elected as your supporter at Bedford. Now, but a single day after the returns are made, he announces he is going over to Fox. They are in a fine fury about it at Bedford. But what can they do? Since the sheriff says the election is legal they can't unseat him. For my part I hope the damned dog sees the inside of Newgate one day. I suppose he thinks Fox is carrying it."

There were others besides William Colhoun assured in the course of that twenty-four hours that Fox was carrying it. With the windows of Carlton House blazing out from across the park and the nightly procession of callers coming up, all glumly unconversational and dejected, only Pitt remained in the midst of the gloom as unchangingly cheerful as if he were host to a gay and greatly enjoyable supper party.

"God bless us, William," Tommy Townshend remarked, as his humour flashed out upon the company. "One would think today had been nothing but a tally of Yorkshires, and not a whole succession of Derbyshires, Penryns and William Colhouns."

IX

THE RESULTS crept in in dribs and drabs. The election crowds

—goodhumoured, except round Covent Garden hustings, where it was war—had begun to mill into the little cul-de-sac itself, annoying Pitt's private neighbours who could not get their chairs and carriages to their own front doors. Pitt, if he wanted to ride without escort, could only do so now early morning or late evening. When George Rose's first note for eighteen hours came round in the early dark of Saturday morning he was already horsed and out. With Smith having passed yet another night at Duke Street it fell to Dundas to read the scribbled message and to despatch a part of the household in search of Pitt. As the lanterns were borne out he watched from the window, seeing the pinpricks of light flickering like fireflies to probe the dark prospect of the park.

Pitt came in to be handed the note and to read what Dundas had already scanned. Rose had headed his message, *Duke Street. 3 a.m*, scrawling below it, *"More good news. We seem to be prospering everywhere. Joe Smith will bring you a full account when it is light."*

Timed an hour later, at four in the morning, came an exultant postscript. *"I am pretty well persuaded you can't be beat now—Pitt forever—huzza—huzza—huzza."*

They had become so used to the pitchings and tossing of fortune, the pummellings between defeat and victory, that they took the news almost dubiously. Pitt turned the note about in his hand. "What do you make of it, Harry?"

"'Tis hard to say. George Rose thinks you are there. No Secretary to the Treasury would write in that vein if he did no'. But we canna tell yet what the margin will be, and all hangs on that."

There was a tap on the door. The Burfields came in, followed by Ralph, all greatly agog. "Just to enquire, sir," Mrs. Burfield asked. "Is it certain?"

"We scarce know yet, Mrs. Burfield," Pitt answered. "They seem to think at Duke Street I am not to be beat now. But

whether that implies an adequate majority must wait on a
few more expresses." To the steward he said, "Is this ill news
for you, Burfield? I know you prefer the dukes."

"I own I did not vote for you, sir," Burfield conceded. "I
pay scot-and-lot on some small property east of Clapham
Common that enfranchises me for Southwark. I mean nothing personal, to be sure. It is merely that, to my certain
knowledge, we have never had a gentleman of your situation
—a second son, if I may express it so—lodged in Downing
Street before."

"An impoverished second son?"

"I had no intention whatever of using the term, sir," Burfield said with a deal of dignity. "It is true Mr. Pelham was
a second son but he had a considerable fortune. However, I
can but say we have found you exceedingly undemanding,
domestically speaking, these past weeks."

"Why, God bless my soul, sir, you've been no bother at
all," his wife added.

Pitt looked at them with amusement, then reached for
the glasses and decanter that stood at his elbow. "It's prema-
ture to cry victory yet. But I hope you three will take wine
with me and then carry up a couple of dozen bottles from
the cellars for the rest of the household. Here is yours, Ralph
—and your pardon it is not Somerset cider. Burfield, it is
not required for you and Mrs. Burfield to drink to my sure
success, or anything of that nature."

"We will drink to your very good health, sir."

Ralph spoke his own toast, "And I that the next few expresses will set it beyond doubt for you, sir."

With the servants gone Pitt and Dundas resumed their
seemingly endless waiting. "Well, the household are getting
their wine at least, Harry," Pitt said presently. "Even if my
majority amounts but to five, all of whom will instantly rush
over to Fox the first evening I don't bow low enough to them
in the lobby."

"Aye, will it be enough—your majority?" Dundas muttered. He took a stride or two about the carpet as if its pile were the rich sprung turf of Wimbledon. "Where's Joe Smith got to? 'Tis well light now. The sun is coming up over the park."

The knocker rattled below violently. A bare half minute later Smith burst in upon them, his greatcoat tossed haphazardly about his shoulders. He saw George Rose's note on the table and broke out exultantly, "That's outdated, sir— it's old news. We have had another six expresses into Duke Street since that was despatched to you. Conway's out at Bury St. Edmund's, Coke at Norfolk, Lord John Cavendish at York City—and he a Minister of the Crown under the Coalition. It's gone on all night—there we would be sitting, with a great litter of tea and coffee cups on the table, and Mrs. Rose dozing in her chair and Mr. Rose saying presently, 'Well, perhaps we ought to try to gain our beds for a space.' Then up we would go and I would have an arm out of my waistcoat when I would hear the express riding up out of the dark and sounding pretty sharp on the cobbles—and we would all be in the hall again. Five times it happened, and every time the news marvellous—the open boroughs falling to you like apples from a tree—Dover, Shrewsbury, Chester, Leominster, Worcester—"

The proud Domesday names, full of their ancient sonances for English ears, spilled out upon them in a mounting cock's crow of triumph. "God wi' us," Dundas said, with a catch of breath. "You're a wonderful laddie. You are going through them like a knife through butter."

"The shires, Joe?" Pitt said. "The shire seats?"

"Oh, in faith, you're sweeping those," Smith exulted. "Rose says you are entirely certain now of sixty of the shire seats of England."

But the news had leapt upon them too little heralded and almost too violently, as if the sky about the slow-mounting morning sun had been riven by an unexpected stab of forked lightning.

"Oh, my faith, Joe," Pitt said. "I am not sure but that you have knocked the breath clean out of me."

"I am rendered after that manner too," Smith answered in much more subdued a fashion. "It is going to be so huge a victory—and we were at the very feet of Fox's hustings here, and he was so damned sure. I began to be persuaded he were right."

"No," Dundas said slowly. "I own him brilliant. But he canna read the mind o' the land—what Shelburne called the pulse and the tides. He canna tell what folk think."

"And I," Pitt remarked in a stiller voice. "With the Hayes walls about me most of my life, is it yet to be hoped I can?" He splashed wine into the glasses. "We are like England— grown unused to victory. It pinches us and we hobble about in it as if it were a new shoe. Tomorrow, doubtless, we will find it fitting more comfortably."

He pushed the wine towards them. "To yoursel'," Dundas said, raising his glass. "To your guid success."

"To you, sir," Smith said. "To the next seven years."

Beyond the window lay the wide park with its splinters of aconite and pools of daffodils, its trees greenly fingered now in the shafts of sunlight. Pitt turned towards it. "Yonder is that which we should be toasting—the dwindled island."

X

WILBERFORCE, AFTER his hard campaign among the York-shire wapentakes, the bare moors and the ancient fossways, journeyed south, his voice reduced to a croak and suffering from a heavy cold. His way took him first to the Guildhall. The City of London poll was on the point of closing, the uproarious city crowd in full clamour all about. Pitt's sup-porters had gained the first three places, the fourth—Atkin-son—only failing by nine votes. Bellowed snatches from the

Returning Officer reached Wilberforce's ears, "By the powers that are vested in me—returned for the City of London—four burgesses—"

Wilberforce's neighbour, standing beside him, broke out laughing, then turned to comment, "Another three names to be inscribed in Fox's Book of Martyrs."

"This is something that has not reached us in Yorkshire."

"It's a pretty bad pun, I own. But the Coalition men are being dubbed Fox's Martyrs, after the title of the old book by the Quaker, George Foxe. So many of the poor fellows are losing their seats."

Wilberforce drove on westward to Downing Street. Here the crowd had overspilled the enclosed confines and washed out into Whitehall, blocking the way to the Eden carriage which had attempted to turn up to the Eden's home at Number 14. Sir Robert Eden and his wife—both elderly—were seated inside looking a little lost. The Watch, who should have gone to their help, had abandoned the task and was standing at the corner, regarding the heaving mass with a bleary, indifferent eye.

Wilberforce began to push through on foot. Another pedestrian engaged in the same struggle remarked in exasperation, "This is just the manner of crazed thing that we, as a nation, would do—select an official residence and put it in the narrowest cul-de-sac in London. It is on a par that we put a schoolboy into it for the next seven years—if he don't bankrupt us in seven weeks."

"You can rest assured he will achieve a deal better than that."

"Oh, in faith," the other groaned. "Not another to say 'Pitt forever'. That's all I have heard from Holborn to here."

Pitt came out of Number 10 the same moment. Wilberforce could see him bare-headed and unpowdered, the sun on the reddish-brown Grenville hair. He had had to come out several times already to the rescue of his neighbours, since the press of folk would move for no one else, the Watch, the porters and the chairmen all ignored. The crowd received him with a noisy warmth, mixed with half-amused astonishment that the husbandry of their country should be rendered into the hands of one whose youth startled them afresh every time they set eyes on him. He had almost to cajole them out of the way, saying, "Come, you'll let my neighbours through, will you not?"

Tom Raffles, the master gardener at Number 10, added his own Cockney voice. "Come along, sirs, out of the way. Can't keep these folk from their own firesides."

Wilberforce shouldered through until he was alongside the carriage shaft. The pleasure leapt into Pitt's face at sight of him. "You, Will. Give me aid here and then we'll achieve three minutes' talk between callers."

The Eden carriage was edged up to Number 14. "Thank goodness you are not elected Minister every day of the week, Mr. Pitt," Lady Eden said somewhat tartly. "It will be exceedingly pleasant to call our street doors our own again."

With the Edens having alighted, Wilberforce followed Pitt back into Number 10. The visitors' room, on the ground floor, stood untenanted, with its door open. "How have you been engaged since you were elected?" Wilberforce asked, as Pitt drew him inside.

"Principally in annoying the neighbours, I think. However, thrown out of here, I might succeed in getting employ as an ostler. The Burfields seem to be prepared to give me a character since they say I am not much bother about the house."

Despite his seeming light-heartedness—of a piece with that of their good days among the strawberry beds and the greening garden peas of Wimbledon—Wilberforce could see the fatigue upon him. "I think you are tired?"

Pitt answered more mutedly, "If you want to know, Will, fagged half into the ground—tired of the boroughs toppling down to me and the votes mounting up, tired to death even of the victory, when I thought once—if it could but happen

—there would be enough exultation in it to last me a life-time."

"There's a morrow of battle."

"Yes, my stars, there is." He regarded Wilberforce. "And you? You look as if your northern clime had used you pretty rough."

"There was a blizzard during the show of hands in Castle Yard at York. I lost my voice."

"But that was all you did lose." He swept his fatigue to one side and broke out with an exultant gaiety, "You're a marvel, are you not, you old sobriety. You had the hardest contest of us all and you rent the Coalition in pieces. I can't either thank you or congratulate you enough, but this I know—the shires will not regret you."

The knocker crashed demandingly. They heard the porter muttering as he went to answer it, "Must have walked near five mile back and forth over this floor today."

Wilberforce got up to go broaching one final matter. "I met with Mr. Vice-Chancellor Farmer at the posting-house at Huntingdon yesterday. He was riding back to take Lenten evensong at his church at Swavesey—the best of seasons there, he says, the springtime of the year, with the daffodils out from Holywell to Smithey Fen. He wondered what prayer a man might make for himself, coming to Downing Street, in the springtime of his life, with the daffodils out the length of St. James's Park but all else darkling about him."

"As in the Book of Common Prayer, I suppose—'give peace in our time, O Lord'." He added, as if seeking Wilberforce's seal upon it, "Do you approve?"

"For sure I do. Amen to it."

XI

EVERY POST washed up more wreckage of the Coalition like

successive tides piling up spars and beams upon the beaches. The jest was no longer 'The Baby and the Nurse', but 'Fox's Martyrs'. It was plain now that, when the final returns went in to the High Bailiff, at least a hundred and sixty Coalition men would have lost their seats.

On the Tuesday Lady Chatham journeyed up to London, bringing Mrs. Sparry with her. Behind them, set in the midst of its gorsey common, Hayes Place was littered with travelling chests and packing cases, the window curtains stripped down and the bed covers folded. The house was awaiting now the occupancy of John Chatham and his bride, Lady Chatham preparing to give up the Pitt family home to her elder son while she herself returned to Burton Pynsent in Somerset. With the carriage halted, Number 10 opened its doors to her. There were many ghosts to tug at her skirts as she walked across the marble of the floor. But her face was still and composed. Mrs. Sparry, wildly agog with excitement and triumph, rushed up the stairs to hug her one-time charge, exclaiming, "Oh, Mr. William, there's such a great noise everywhere that you've won. Just to know you is enough. I am become one of the most important women in all Kent."

"Why, Mrs. Pam," Pitt answered, submitting to his nurse's embrace, "you always were possessed of that status."

Later mother and son were left alone. In the quiet room with the candles about them they had nothing but frankness for each other. He asked at length, "Has it fallen out ill for you? I knew back at Hayes that a part of you desired me to lose."

"Did you see it then?" Lady Chatham said. "I was not too great a traitor. I wanted no vast defeat. But at this ill hour for the land, lying in my bed of an early morning, perhaps I half wished for a few boroughs to stand between you and this house."

"No, do not be afraid for me now. It was a rough, rending baptism of fire, but it's over. I think I will not again have to endure a like three months to those I had from Christmas to Easter facing Fox."

"Will you not, my son? It is what other men have sown and what you may have to harvest here that troubles me."

"And the manner of the harvest—ruin—bankruptcy—the end of us?"

She did not answer. "It will not come to that," he said. "I feared it myself once or twice those nights in the House, when I was chilled and tired to death and there did not seem to be a gleam for England anywhere—London dark and silent outside, the people silent in the Gallery. But the pulse was still beating. Harry Dundas felt it too. He will tell you the same. I used to watch the east window lightening behind the Speaker's head, and I knew the country would both survive and revive." They were both conscious of the past breathing all about them here. He added, "My father came to this house in a dark hour too."

"Your father came to find a losing war facing him from the desk yonder. You have found a lost one." She rose, going to the desk to turn about in her hands the silver ink-well that stood there. "It is nigh on seventeen years since I were last in this room. Your father's sickness was drawing upon him then. I do not know how many letters I penned here among these quills and sandcastors, how many times I affixed his seal for him. There were some who—out of compliment—called me 'the best man of business and politics' in the kingdom. But I would have laboured my heart out to have supported your father through that time."

"On my word," he said in a low intense voice, "you did support him. He could not have lived through it without you."

She answered quietly, "But the hard years have taken their toll. My health has failed me a little, but something other has failed me more—my will perhaps, as my country's will has failed her. And that is a hard thing for a Grenville to admit."

"Do no more now than play the countrywoman—walk the dogs across the heath at Burton or watch the village at cricket outside your windows. You've toiled enough for the rest of us."

"Indeed I think it must be that." She turned and faced him. "Write to me or come to me at Burton any hour of the day or night. If you desire my counsel on any matter I will give it. But I can give you no more and it is little enough." Her calm broke. She clasped him fiercely as she had once done when he had been a boy of eight at Hayes and Chatham had been tossing in his darkened room. "Oh, my dear son, it has been your father's madness—watching its onset, standing with a single candle outside his bedroom door, my breath held in case he should groan or rave. It has taken all my strength. I have none left now to help sustain you here as I sought to sustain him."

The door handle rattled. They stepped hastily away from each other—the Grenvilles with their hot hatred of display. But it was only Mrs. Sparry, anxious, now the daylight had ebbed, to start upon the journey back to Hayes. All three came outside. Downing Street, bathed in an evening drizzle, lay empty of sightseers. The scene was most strangely quiet, the spit of the rain on the oil lamp above the doorway of Number 10 hissing softly into the night, the harness chiming melodiously like little bells as the horses pawed or shifted. With the two women settled and the coachman about to climb upon the box Pitt leant forward to ask of his mother, "You will come here and stay with me sometimes?"

"It is for you to come to me now, my son."

The light from the porter's lantern glanced on her chestnut hair, showing it greyly streaked now under her hood where once it had been as untouched as his. They both knew that however many years of life were left her she would never set foot in London again. The queen had abdicated. The proud and able Grenville woman, who had upborne her husband through his black hours, had walked out of

Downing Street, across its cool chequered floor and under its hissing oil lamp, for the last time. Hereafter she would not quit Burton Pynsent even for a night; and their meetings would never be other than with the quiet heath stretching beyond the windows and the butter churns, fresh with the smell of milk, standing about the dairy.

He bent to kiss her cheek, then shut the carriage door on them. The carriage rattled out into Whitehall. It was presently borne on Mrs. Sparry that Lady Chatham, beside her in the dark, was silently weeping.

"Don't cry, my lady," Mrs. Sparry said helplessly. "Please don't cry."

"Oh, Mrs. Pam," Lady Chatham said in a stifled voice. "It is such a cruel house. It eats men alive."

Short Selected Bibliography

THE MORE detailed studies of Pitt seem to me the more rewarding. In this category come *The Younger Pitt, The Years of Acclaim* by John Ehrman (1969), *William Pitt and the National Revival* by J. Holland Rose (1911) and the first volume of Earl Stanhope's *Pitt* (1861). J. Holland Rose, Lord Rosebery (himself a Prime Minister), Sir Charles Petrie and John Wesley Derry have all written shorter studies.

For Fox see *Charles James Fox* by John Wesley Derry (1972); for Dundas, *The Life of Henry Dundas* by Cyril Matheson (1933); for Wilberforce, his own *Private Papers*, edited by A. M. Wilberforce (1897); for George the Third, John Clarke's short pictural study (1972); for Cambridge and the University, *Cambridge Social Life in the 18th Century* by Christopher Wordsworth, and H. Gunning's *Reminiscences* (1874).

The atmosphere of Westminster and the day-to-day life of the Palace have to be gleaned from all kinds of likely and unlikely sources. For procedure one turns to Pitt's contemporary, John Hatsell; for the lay-out of the Old Palace, a venerable book, Smith's *Antiquities of Westminster* (1810); for an eyewitness account (the sometimes inaccurate) Wraxall, writing in his old age; for biographical details and the boroughs, the three invaluable volumes edited by Sir Lewis Namier and John Brooke, *The House of Commons 1754–1790* (1964).

Finally what of the formative years of the two protagonists? E. Tangye Lean's *The Napoleonists* (1972) contains a useful sketch of Fox's boyhood and the influences that helped to mould him. Sir Tresham Lever's very well-documented *The House of Pitt* (1947) gives plenty of evidence of the malady that repeatedly struck at the Pitts but does not relate its stresses specifically to William. None of the historians (all concentrating on the public face) has in fact seen the Younger Pitt against the background of these stresses or examined his boyhood and the man he became in the light—or shadow—of them.

This book, for the period of the early years, attempts to do so.